SWING INTO MURDER

VANESSA M. KNIGHT

Swing Into Murder

Copyright © 2023 by Vanessa M. Knight

Published by Inked Publishing

Cover Art © 2023 by Christine Cover Design

Edited by Megan Kelly & Nancy Canu

The characters and events portrayed in this book are fictitious. Any similarity to real persons, living or dead, or events, is coincidental and not intended by the author.

ISBN: 978-1-7344206-6-1

To Jen AS for being my ride or die. I couldn't have gotten through the past few years without you. And this book would not have happened without your support and encouragement.

CHAPTER
ONE

"HARPER, the cops are here for you."

For me? Harper Lange spun on her espadrilles toward the door of her second-grade classroom. Sure enough, a police officer stood in the doorway. Not a usual thing for Il Vincitore Academy in Lake Las Vegas.

She didn't need this again. It had been almost a year. A year without police station coffee and fluorescent lights. All things she could live the rest of her life without.

"Someone is here to see you." Vice Principal Steve Clemmons spoke a bit louder this time, even though he stood next to her desk. Close enough to hear a whisper. Close enough that she could see bits of salad in his teeth. "I'll take over the class so you can talk to them." Them? She turned her head and saw a second cop standing behind the first. Multiple cops was worse than just one.

They weren't like potato chips.

Instead of saying all that, she just nodded. "Thanks."

Clemmons turned his neck to block the officer's view of his face. "Is it about the hit and run?"

She had no idea. How would she? Harper tried to shrug, but her shoulders were locked. Random visits from cops always ended badly. "I haven't talked to them."

"Right. Right." The Clemmons backed up to a normal distance.

"Ms. Lange has a boyfriend." The words came out in a singsong only a room full of mostly eight-year-olds could pull off. A chorus of kissing sounds came from her usually adorable, well-behaved students.

Today, not so much.

"All right. That's enough." Harper tried to keep a lilt in her voice. Something that said she was in on the joke. But she wasn't feeling the humor. Not now. She turned to her supposed boyfriend in the doorway. Brown hair, light brown skin, and deep brown eyes. He had a thin scar along the side of his face and a frown that verged on a scowl. A badge hung on the belt loop of his jeans. Another cop stood behind him, far enough back for the kids not to notice.

The frowny officer's lips quirked up at the edges. Switching back to a frown, he almost seemed to fight back his amusement. She fought the bile churning in her gut as she stared at the officer.

"Class, settle down." Clemmons rested a hand on Harper's arm. "Are you okay?"

No, she was not okay. She was so far from okay she'd need a passport to get back. "I'm fine. I'm just trying to decide what to have you work on with the class." She needed a second. Maybe a few. Harper took a deep breath and pretended to look over her desk before handing her replacement this week's spelling words. She ran a hand along the brunette hair at her nape. Her bun holding tight. No tendrils hanging. "We need to get ready for the quiz on Friday."

"My office is open if you want privacy." Clemmons thumbed through the papers in his hands.

She turned to the class. "You will be on your best behavior. Right?"

The class might have nodded, but the giggles told her they were not going to be on their best behavior. Not that it mattered. She had bigger problems.

The soles of her espadrilles swished against the floor as she walked to the doorway. Even her feet didn't want to do this. She hadn't dealt with cops and interrogations in almost a year.

A year of moving on from Brad and all she'd lost, gone in one minute. She led the very tall men to the administrative hall and into the vice principal's office. They towered over her. Which was unusual, because at five foot, nine inches she was quite often the tallest in the room. To be fair she worked with children, so her height comparison might be a little skewed.

She went around the wooden desk and pulled out the chair. One cop stood behind the visitors chairs, while the scowly one leaned against a bookcase near the door.

"Ms. Specter, I'm Detective Cabrero." The scowl didn't leave his face. "And this is Detective Lucas."

"Lange. I'm back to my maiden name. Please sit."

Harper sat down and waved at the pleather chairs on the other side of the desk. It had hurt to lose her husband's name—although it had been her choice. It hurt to lose anything associated with him. For a while, honestly everything hurt. "Do you know something about my husband's accident?"

Detective Lucas sat in the left-hand chair. He was a nice-looking guy, in a dad-with-a-minivan kind of way, complete with receding hairline and a belt trying to escape the paunch in his middle.

"We don't have anything new, Ms. Lange." Detective Cabrero angled away from the bookcase and sat in the remaining chair. "We've reopened the case because we have another incident in front of DeVout."

DeVout. The house that was home to the secret club where she'd last seen her husband, Brad. The club took everything away from her. "An incident?"

"Do you know Madeline Williams?" Detective Cabrero placed a leg over his knee and leaned back. He looked so comfortable, which made Harper nervous. Comfortable cops usually meant higher stakes for her.

Harper hadn't talked to Madeline in weeks, which was sad since they'd been best friends. "I do."

"When was the last time you saw her?"

"Saw her? About a year ago." When Harper's husband ran a hand down Madeline's naked back. "Is she okay?" She'd been a great friend and strong shoulder when Harper needed to cry. And she was one hell of a kisser too.

Detective Cabrero leaned forward, his eyes felt like xrays reading her every move. "Madeline was killed last night."

Killed? The word slammed into her chest and sucked the air from her lungs. Madeline gone. No. Harper had spent a year getting over the loss of her husband—and some would say she still hadn't gotten over him. Hell, she'd say that.

"I'm sorry for your loss." With a whoosh, Detective Cabrero pulled a tissue out of a box at the corner of Steve's desk. He held it out to Harper.

"Thanks." Why did he think she needed a tissue? She blinked, and wavy lines distorted the room. Okay. Maybe that was why. She took the tissue and dabbed at her eyes. "What happened?"

"We're trying to determine the series of events. Your husband had a special relationship with her." Detective Cabrero stated it like a tawdry fact.

Madeline had always been popular. It hadn't hurt that her husband, Paul, looked like Ryan Gosling. Too bad he was a vapid dick. But everyone still loved him. He was one of the boys. And his assholism was offset by her kindness and overall wonderful personality. "A lot of people had a special relationship with her."

"But no one else was hit by a car around the corner from DeVout." He had her on that one. The club was a home on a secluded suburban street. Not a lot of traffic.

"True. But I haven't seen her in months." She'd seen them at the funeral. The owners of DeVout had asked her to come back to the club, even just to visit, and it wasn't that she didn't want to return. It just wasn't the same without Brad.

"Where did you see her last?"

At DeVout, when she kissed my husband while I watched wasn't exactly something she wanted to say out loud. Not to them. Everyone always judged people in the swinger lifestyle. They never understood. "At the Byrnes' party, December of last year, and then at the funeral."

The quiet cop decided to speak up. "In December, was it a *lifestyle* party?" The way Lucas said *lifestyle* set Harper's teeth on edge. People didn't understand the whole swinger culture—hence the judgment. And from his attitude it was futile to try to explain.

She lifted her chin. She wasn't going to let this guy talk down to her. "Yes."

"Are you still in the lifestyle?" Detective Cabrero was either an excellent actor or he wasn't as offended by her life choices.

"Not anymore."

"Really?" Lucas eyed her with clear disbelief. "They let you quit?" And he was a dumb ass.

"It's not the mob. We can leave whenever we want." Harper sighed and tried to hide the annoyance that wanted to take residence on her face.

Detective Cabrero's lips quirked. "Was Madeline still in the lifestyle?"

"I don't know."

"You didn't talk to her?"

"Not about the lifestyle."

"Why not?" Lucas glared. "Were you jealous? It can't be easy watching your husband with another woman."

"I wasn't jealous at all. It's really very hot. You should try it." She'd loved watching Brad smile. It didn't matter who had been making him smile, because it was all the same. As long as he was happy. She was happy. And he'd felt the same way.

Lucas turned bright red. Idiot.

Harper sighed and decided to explain. Using small words that even Lucas could understand. "The parties aren't just about sex. They *are* about couples, though. When I lost my husband, I wasn't in a couple. And when Madeline and I didn't share the lifestyle, it was hard to find time to meet." It didn't help that Harper spent most of her waking hours working. "You should ask the Byrnes. Emma and John."

Emma and John still threw parties as the owners of DeVout, although they'd stopped asking her to show up a few months ago— when they'd realized she wasn't going to start dating again anytime soon and there was no way she'd arrive alone. She wasn't looking to be part of a throuple.

"Emma and John Byrne?"

"Yes."

"They won't answer our calls." Cabrero ran a finger down the scar along his cheek.

She tried to keep the smile away from her lips, but it was hard. "They generally don't." Emma and John were private, for good reason. They had three kids, and the life-style could lead people into questioning the rest of their life. And no matter what, their kids meant more than anything to them.

"Because they have something to hide?" Detective Lucas narrowed his eyes and she ignored it.

"Because they're busy." And because they had something to hide, but it wasn't murder. People got stupid when they found out about the lifestyle. If the wrong people found out, their life could be destroyed. Run out of town with pitchforks kind of destroyed. Child Protective Services taking their kids kind of destroyed.

Cabrero stood up and handed her a card. "Please reach out if you can remember anything that might help the investigation."

She took it and nodded.

Detective Lucas and his judgment left the room. Cabrero stayed behind, looking puzzled but not scornful. Maybe he wouldn't be as judgmental. Maybe he'd do his job. The detectives assigned to the case last year were closed-minded assholes. Kind of like Lucas. She always felt they hadn't given one hundred percent to the investigation. Like her husband's death was the lifestyle's fault. Like he deserved it. So they'd half-assed it.

Speaking of which. "Why aren't Detectives Sperry and Hanes on this case?" She could honestly say she wasn't upset they were gone.

"Fresh set of eyes." Cabrero's gaze moved to the floor then the wall. A sure sign of discomfort or lying, but she wasn't sure why he'd need to evade the truth. "Are the rumors true?"

"Which ones?" There were rumors about who had been

driving the car that hit her husband. But nothing fit and the cops couldn't substantiate anything, so she'd chalked it up to someone who couldn't handle their booze behind the wheel of a car. Story old as time.

"That no one will talk to me."

Oh that. The lifestyle rumors. "They might, but probably not. It has nothing to do with the murder investigation. People don't understand. They don't approve. So then we get ridiculed, or worse, fired or injured. We have to hide."

"You stopped because of the ridicule?"

Saying goodbye to her husband had been hard, but losing her friends was another level of suck. She couldn't pretend to be happy at the clubs or house parties when reminders of Brad lurked everywhere. "Like I said, the parties are for couples. I'm no longer in a couple."

"Is it true everyone has sexual relations with each other?" The scornful twist to his mouth pissed her off.

"Is it true all cops are racist?"

Cabrero shook his head. "I'll take that as a no." Giving her a nod, he turned and disappeared down the hall. The silence was glorious. But her mind filled up with questions. First and foremost, what happened to Madeline? And did it have anything to do with Brad?

Her chest twisted just thinking the words—thinking about him. Not this again.

CHAPTER
TWO

THE NEXT WEEKEND, Harper sat in her favorite coffee shop grading papers. Large amounts of coffee nearby, just waiting for her. It was the only way to keep her eyes open reading twenty-four three-page essays on *What I Did During My Spring Vacation.*

She focused on Kimber's ode to the video game *Skyrim.* Apparently she'd gotten all of the Daedric Artifacts, but picked the Ring of Hircine instead of the Savior's Hide. Since she didn't like to be a werewolf, it was totally useless.

Kind of like the information in the report. *Wait.* Was that bitchy?

Yep.

Harper took a sip of her coffee. Obviously she needed more caffeine to be less nasty. If it was important enough for the student to write a three-page paper about it, it was important to Harper. Therefore, learning about reptile creatures and Daedric artifacts was worthwhile. For Kimber's sake.

Harper knew it was crucial for her students to see how their lives were a series of stories. But at eight years old, their stories were relatively similar. Then again, she'd take the mundane over and over again if it meant her students weren't living in a terrible environment. She'd read the "locked at home alone and ate bread all week" essay a few years ago. Between notifying the school counselor and dealing with local law enforcement, her heart had broken for the boy.

She fixed grammar on Kimber's paper—although she had no idea whether the reptiles from the Black Marsh were actually called Argonians, let alone spelled that way. She scrawled a smiley face at the top and wrote a little note about Kimber's wonderful storytelling ability and interesting hobby before flipping it over onto the done pile. Halfway through. She slid another essay in front of her and picked up her cup of concentration. Empty.

"Fancy meeting you here."

She turned to the deep voice. "Detective Cabrero."

The scowl wasn't there, but a smile hadn't quite taken up residence on his face. And it was nice face when the anger didn't eat up all the handsome. "Ms. Lange." A tight T-shirt showed off muscles. His badge hung off the belt of his jeans.

He held up his cup. "May I sit?"

"Please." She motioned to the empty chair across from her. "Shouldn't you be out tracking down clues?"

"I should. But I'm running into roadblocks."

"What type of roadblocks?"

He sighed as he ran a hand along the scar on his cheek. "No one will answer my calls."

"Caller ID is a bitch." Yeah, that was a bit sarcastic, but he had to know they weren't going to answer his calls.

"Yes, it is." He laughed. A genuine laugh, complete with smile. He really was doing a disservice to the world only whipping the thing out occasionally. Full pink lips and sparkling brown eyes. If she was into hot, edible-looking men. Unfortunately, since Brad's death, she hadn't been into anything.

"What are you up to?" The detective tilted his head to look at the paper on top of her stack.

"Grading homework."

"Looks exciting."

"It's not police work, but it can be fun." She smiled as she restacked the papers in front of her, mostly out of nervous habit. "One of my students had two separate Easter celebrations, one at each parent's house, and the Easter bunny brought the kid an iPhone in each basket."

"I have no idea how to respond. Is that good or bad?"

Harper laughed. "Not good, but it's not as dire as it seems. His parents are newly divorced. They're too busy fighting to figure out you have to plan the gifts better."

"Sounds like someone with experience."

"My parents divorced when I was a kid." Not something she liked to talk about. "Your parents?"

"Painfully divorced for about twenty years now. Well,

it stopped being painful a while ago. They remarried when I was in high school."

"Each other?"

"Oh, hell no." A cute little dimple appeared between his eyes when he winced. "That's a scary thought."

He took a drink from his cup. The last time she'd seen him, he'd seemed so serious. Today he was downright personable—almost a Jekyll and Hyde situation.

"What are you doing in this neighborhood?" Harper asked. He'd already given a half-answer. "Besides coffee."

"Visiting my mom, in Henderson."

A man who visited his mom. He couldn't be all bad. "How's your mom?"

"Tired, but good." He sighed. "She's in remission. Cancer."

"I'm sorry she had to deal with that, but I'm happy she's in remission."

"She's a fighter. My stepdad is losing his mind. I don't know how he'd survive without her."

"I can understand." She'd stumbled through the loss of her husband for the first six months. Then it got easier, but the tug and pull of the void never really went away. It might have been easier if she'd had parents to rely on, but they'd been gone for a while, too. She'd learned not to even allude to the losses in her life. It sucked all the happiness out of the room. "It's hard going alone after you've been with someone for so long."

Cabrero nodded and turned his focus to the cup in his hand. "How long were you two together?"

Her husband. "We were married two years, dated for four."

Cabrero didn't say anything. Just nodded. And as usual Harper wanted to walk out the door. So much discomfort. So much sympathy.

"Ms. Lange!" a little voice called out. Henry Byrne ran from the front door to Harper's table. His dark-blond hair stuck up along his hairline, as usual.

"Hey, Henry." She gave him a quick hug and a smile. She loved all her students, but some were more lovable than others. Henry— heck, all the Byrnes children were of the more-lovable variety.

"Harper?" It didn't even cross her mind that Henry wouldn't be here alone. She looked up and caught Emma Byrne struggling with a smile. Her dark brown ponytail had been pulled through a brimmed cap, and her all-white outfit was immaculate, even though her cheeks glowed like she'd come from a tennis court. Which she probably had. She looked amazing, yet Harper couldn't help but turn away. They'd been friends, and that friendship had been collateral damage from Harper's year of self-isolation.

Along with all of Harper's friendships.

Emma's husband, John, walked up to the table, his blond hair matted from an obvious morning of getting his ass kicked on the court. He was a force with a tennis racket, but he couldn't beat his wife. Emma had almost made it pro back in the day and had kept that fighting spirit. John's handsome face split into a smile when he saw her, and Harper couldn't help but reciprocate.

Except for regularly scheduled parent nights at school, she hadn't talked to them much since the funeral. They were the owners of DeVout and the face of the lifestyle in their group of friends, which made it hard to look at them without seeing Brad.

"This is Ms. Lange's boyfriend." Henry preened as he looked at Cabrero, like he revealed some secret.

The look on Emma's face said Henry had. "I didn't know you were dating." She looked Cabrero up and down as she held out her perfectly manicured hand to him. "I'm Harper's friend, Emma Byrne."

Cabrero stood as he briefly shook her hand. When he sat down, his fingers inched toward Harper's hand. His brow raised, like he was asking a question.

Unfortunately, she didn't speak Eyebrow.

He looked down, the tilt of his head indicating their hands, now somehow a breath apart. She tilted her head in return—from his eyes to their hands and back again. What was he asking?

He nodded.

What did the nod mean? She'd skipped Confusing Body Language 101 in college. She might have had a clue what was going on.

He hooked his little finger around her thumb, and offered her a smile. Her thumb went numb. Her body went numb. Somehow, she didn't pull away.

Not somehow. She couldn't remember how.

His thumb slid along the side of her hand and her body froze. Holy crap. She hadn't been touched like this in a long time. And her body obviously forgot what to do. Pull away. Run. Sigh. Tingle. She had nothing.

"Don't be mad she didn't say anything. We wanted to take it slow," Cabrero was saying words to Emma and John.

Uh, what? The words didn't make sense. Harper thought she felt his hand in hers. No. No thought. His thumb rubbed along the top of her hand. She knew her hand was in his. What she couldn't understand was why.

"How long have you two been an item?" John looked as excited as Harper should feel—but didn't, since she didn't know the answer to the damn question.

"How long has it been, honey?" Cabrero looked at her like she knew how long they'd been an item. She didn't even know they were an item.

When she didn't say a word, Cabrero smiled. Damn that smile was nice. Cabrero took hold of the conversation, since Harper wasn't speaking up. "Three months."

Maybe she'd speak up if she knew the answer.

"Sounds serious." Emma's blue eyes narrowed as she stared at Harper and Cabrero. Behind her, Henry ran to the counter and stood on his toes to see inside the pastry case. Apparently, the adult conversation was too much for the eight-year-old.

Funny, it was too much for the thirty-three-year-old, too. Especially since Harper was being treated to Emma's angry glare. Emma wasn't a bundle of sunshine, but she was normally pleasant.

Cabrero didn't say a word. Cabrero. She should probably find out his first name if they were dating.

"I didn't catch your name?" John managed to ask the question Harper was thinking.

"Sorry. Alex Coffey." Coffey? Where did that come from? Mr. Coffee squeezed her hand and smiled.

"It's very nice to meet you." John held out his hand and waited for Harper's *boyfriend* to shake it. "You should come to the party we're having tonight."

A Byrne party. Very fun and very in the lifestyle. Part of her would love to go, but the memories. She couldn't get past the memories. "I don't think—"

"We'd love to." Alex— if that was his name— cut her off.

"Oh good." John smiled as he slid an arm around his wife. "We've missed you at the house."

Harper gulped back a knot of emotion. She knew John meant it. It wasn't just the earnestness in his eyes. It was who he was. He was the guy who'd give you the raincoat off his back in a monsoon. And she'd run away from all her friends' kindness. She felt bad, but she just couldn't go back. Not yet.

"You know the address." Emma pulled away from John and turned to Henry. "I'll be right there. Don't touch anything."

"I do know the address, but..." *We're not dating* hung on her lips, but Maybe-Alex wouldn't let her finish and no one else seemed to care...

"I'm so excited to meet your friends, honey."

...including her date.

Maybe-Alex let go of her hand and put his arm around her shoulders, bringing her close. He smelled so good.

Woodsy and spicy. The way a man should smell. She closed her eyes. She hadn't smelled testosterone in so long.

Henry came back, thankfully. "They have chocolate chip scones."

"Let's go pick one out, buddy." John took his hand and headed toward the counter.

"We're on our way to Henry's acting class, so we should head out." Emma nodded in lieu of a wave. "See you both tonight."

The second Emma turned her back, Harper leaned away from her supposed other half. "What the heck?"

"Smile," he whispered without moving his mouth.

"We're dating, Alex Coffey? Is Alex even your real name? Because I know Coffey isn't Cabrero."

"We'll talk." He leaned in, his breath warmed and tickled along her neck. And did she mention how good he smelled? Considering he was so full of shit, that was an absolute miracle.

Emma, John and Henry walked out the door. Chocolate smudged along Henry's face as he stuffed the scone into his mouth. "Bye, Ms. Lange," he mumbled around his pastry.

"Bye, Henry." They all waved as the perfect little family walked out the door.

"So, can we talk now?" Harper leaned away and this time Alex let her.

"Sure. What do you want to talk about?" Alex grabbed his coffee, his face passive like nothing just happened. Like he didn't lie to her friends.

"How about what's your real name, Alex Cabrero Coffey?" Maybe it was all fake. "Are you even a cop?"

"Of course. My name is Alejandro Luiz Cabrero Coffey. I generally just use Cabrero as my last name. It's shorter."

"Okay, then what was all that Alex Coffey nonsense?" She restacked the papers in front of her again. Her hands needed something to do or they'd reach out and smack him.

"An opportunity. I know I sprung it on you, but I'm hoping you'll help me."

"Help you with what?"

He put his coffee cup down and leaned in. Almost conspiringly. "I need to talk to Emma and John Byrne. And I have a feeling I need to talk to a few others in the lifestyle. What better place to talk to them than at a party?"

"How about anywhere else? Call them on the phone. Go to their work or homes. These parties come with expectations."

"I thought the parties weren't all about sex." The arrogance in his arched brow as he fed her her own words would have been cute except for the whole feeding her her own words thing.

"They aren't..."

"Look. They're not answering my calls. Do you think they'll answer if I show up at their door?" Alex took a drink of his coffee and shook his head. He was obviously frustrated about trying to get them to talk, but she didn't see what it had to do with her.

"I answered." Not that she'd had a choice. But would they? Probably not.

"Yeah, but you also dodged my calls. Your administrative assistant didn't lie for you."

"I don't have an administrative assistant, but I didn't dodge your calls. I just haven't had a chance to return them." That was her story. Between teaching and tutoring, she hadn't had a chance to call back. Okay, she'd had a chance; she just chose to binge the Harry Potter movies instead.

Emma and John owned a large casino empire in Vegas. They had people for everything. They probably had an employee to dodge calls.

Harper took a drink of her cooling coffee. "Why should I help you?"

"Because you want justice. This might be connected to your husband. Don't you want to know?"

She did. She wanted to know what happened the night her husband was killed. In the beginning, she'd harassed the detectives daily to find the person who hit her husband and just disappeared. But as the trail grew cold and answers became fewer and fewer, she couldn't find the energy to live in the past. Not when it looked like the answers weren't going to magically appear.

"Look, I get it if you don't want to lie. I'll find another way, but the last investigation ran into the same roadblocks. The previous detectives didn't believe your husband's hit and run was an accident." Cabrero's eyes were solemn, they practically pleaded with her to understand.

"What?" The word stole her breath. Or maybe *"didn't believe it was an accident"* punched her in the diaphragm. If they'd thought it wasn't an accident, why didn't she know? Why hadn't they told her?

"With your husband's hit and run, there were no skid marks. The driver of the car never tried to stop. The detectives working the case came to dead end after dead end and the case went cold. Honestly, it was easier to chalk it up as an accident."

"It was an accident." She didn't want to believe him. People didn't run people down with cars. Not in real life. It only happened in unimaginative books and movies. "But the cop said—"

"He's not on the case any longer." Alex sighed. "I don't think his was an accident and I know Madeline's wasn't an accident. There's a good chance they're connected."

Something about her husband's death had never sat well with her, but the police told her it was an accident. And then they didn't find the car that hit him and the case went cold. And then one day she'd forgotten, and she'd gotten on with her life.

At least she'd tried.

Maybe she should have stayed on top of them. Maybe they would've done more.

"They never solved your husband's case. We have another chance here. We'll go to the party and blend in. They'll talk."

One party. In the lifestyle. She hadn't been to a party in over year. Not without Brad. Her hesitation must have been a neon sign on her face because the detective spoke again.

"I just need to ask a few questions. I need to know if

anyone knows why someone would want to kill Madeline, or if it had anything to do with your husband's accident." He was practically begging. "I want justice for them."

He didn't say it. But it was implied. *Don't you? Of course she wanted justice. There was a time she would've done anything for Brad. She still would.

"One party."

That didn't sound so bad. She could do one party. She could live with the ghosts for one night, but could she pretend? "I'm a terrible liar."

"Then don't think of it as a lie. We'll go out on a date."

Her heart sped. She wasn't ready to date. Not yet. "No. I'll meet you there. I'll practice lying in the shower." Practice lying in the shower. Really?

Thankfully, Alex didn't question her practicing techniques. He smirked as he brought his coffee to his lips and then said, "What time?"

"Seven PM." She had to check the secured website, but she was pretty sure the times hadn't changed. "Give me your phone."

He handed her his cell phone and she called her own cell. Hanging up, she handed his phone back. She slid hers from her pocket and saved his number. *Alex Cabrero.*

"Remember." He clicked on his own screen. "Alex Coffey. Use the Coffey name in case anyone sees the phone."

She deleted Cabrero and entered Coffey. "Have you ever been to a party like this before?" The scent of burning candles and sex was so burrowed into her bones, she could almost smell the sweet, smoky, pheromone sweat just talking about it.

"No. What should I expect?" Alex almost looked leery. Smart man.

"How do you feel about ball gags?" She laughed, as she swore she heard his jaw hit the ground.

CHAPTER
THREE

AS DARKNESS COVERED the Vegas Valley, Harper sat in her car looking at the Byrnes' house that doubled as a club. Just staring. The five-thousand-square-foot house was lit up like a virginal Christmas tree, white lights strategically pointed at windows and trees. It was beautiful.

She was a little early. Which gave her time to think. And thinking was bad. Thinking reminded her of the last night she and Brad had stopped at the house. Madeline and Paul had come with them that night. A couples' date. They'd sat in the house as soft rock played over the speakers.

She'd held hands with Brad as they'd laughed. "Nutmeg," he'd whispered. Her nickname. Because she was a little nutty and sweet. It had been a great night with friends, and a few hours later, he'd been gone. Maybe if she'd known it would be the last time they'd be there, she would've done something different. Taken a picture. Listened longer.

But she hadn't. She'd treated it like any other night.

And now he was gone. She couldn't go back. Not to that night. And not to that house. The house currently sitting in front of her.

Lights danced in the windows of the two-floor mansion nestled in the hills of Lake Las Vegas. She'd parked her car along the street. The driveway was already filled with cars.

The detective would be here any minute. Any minute she'd have to walk in, but she didn't want to. She didn't want to face the past. She wanted to face her flat screen with a pint of Ben and Jerry's and pretend today didn't exist—just pretend none of this was happening. But life never worked that way.

It was sad. She seemed to be mourning Brad longer than they'd been together. Okay. That was an exaggeration. She'd been mourning for a year. But she and Brad had only been married for two years. To be fair, they were two wonderful years and they'd date for year before that. But things hadn't been perfect. Even she couldn't lie to herself about that. But they'd been good years and then he'd been taken from her.

Her car window rattled. Her body jumped. Her thoughts about Brad and the past smacked against the top of the car, with her head. "Ouch." She turned to the noise.

Alex.

"Sorry." He mouthed through a wince from the other

side of the window. She rubbed her fingertips over the pain, trying to avoid messing up her hair.

Another knock. "Are you okay?" She could hear him, so he must have spoken a little louder.

Was she okay? Not really. But it didn't matter. She'd made a promise to help and she kept her promises. It didn't hurt that she wanted to know if Brad's death was an accident or something much worse.

She could do this. For him. It was the least she could do. She owed him so much more.

She grabbed her car keys and slipped them in her Harry Potter tote bag. She probably shouldn't have brought anything with a tweens book on it—maybe a bag without a Snitch on the front. But she needed one big enough to hold a couple bottles of wine and all her adult toys. Not that she needed them for tonight. But she'd tossed her grown-up lifestyle bag after her husband died and she needed her stuff. Her stuff made her comfortable. Less likely to hurl from the butterflies buzzing in her gut. So here she was, looping the straps over her shoulder.

She pulled on her shawl and hiked the bag over her shoulder then opened the car door and angled out. She stood in front of the cop and took him all in.

Alex cleaned up nicely. He was wearing a black suit coat and matching pants. A white collared shirt brought out the light brown in his skin. Maybe he wasn't so bad.

"Are you moving in?" Alex nodded to her bag. When he spoke, all the fuzzy feelings scattered.

"No. I wasn't sure how far we had to go."

"How far?"

"It is a sex club." There was no way they were going to be having sex or anything, but the look on his face made the implication so worth it.

"Harper Specter?" A high-pitched voice echoed through the valley. "I haven't seen you in ages."

Amelia Lopez ran toward Harper with open arms. Her brown skin shimmered beneath the glitter makeup and lights from the streetlamps. Her boyfriend, Jasper, came up behind her, looking more like Casper in comparison.

"How are you?" Amelia's arms wrapped around Harper.

"I'm doing well."

"I missed you." Amelia looked Harper up and down before noticing someone behind Harper's shoulder. "And who would you be?"

"I'm Alex."

"Sorry." Harper felt a little bad for not doing the introductions up front. But to be fair, Amelia hadn't really given her much of a chance and Harper wasn't all that stoked to show off her fake date. Or maybe she didn't know how to navigate the whole fake thing. Or the date thing. "Alex, these are my friends Amelia and Jasper. Alex is my boyfriend." Her throat almost closed on the word *boyfriend*. She hadn't had one of those in years. Were they even called boyfriends now? Maybe they were date-buddies. Did *suitor* come back into style?

She didn't know. And it was all just strange.

"Boyfriend, huh?" Amelia had a goofy grin spread across her face as Jasper shook Alex's hand.

"Yep."

Nope. But as long as her nose didn't grow and she didn't blow the whole thing by rambling, who was counting.

"I'm so happy for you." Amelia pulled her coat closer against the April evening chill. Seventies in Vegas was downright cold to the locals. On the strip, non-locals wore bathing suits and booty shorts. No thanks. That was how you got frostbite on the hoo-ha. "It's so cold tonight. Are you heading in?"

"Yeah, give us a minute." Harper grabbed onto Alex's hand. It was warm and foreign. "We have some, you know, couple things to talk about. You know, since we're together and all."

"Of course." Amelia smiled and turned to Alex. "Newbie, right?"

Harper pulled him close. "Yep. I thought I'd introduce him to the lifestyle. And there's no party like a Byrnes party."

Alex brought her close. Too close. Any words she was going to say stalled on her lips as he squeezed the logic out of her.

"You're in for a treat." Amelia grabbed Jasper's hand. "He's in good hands. See you inside."

Jasper nodded to Alex and then to Harper before he turned around and they headed for the main entrance to the home.

"Are you okay?"

"Why wouldn't I be?" They were just lying to all her friends because one of them might have killed her husband. No biggie.

"You just talked. A lot."

So what? Deception and dishonesty loosened her lips. "I told you I'm a terrible liar."

"You weren't lying."

"Exactly!" Her hands pushed out in exasperation. She stumbled backward but caught herself before her bag or body hit the pavement. "When I try to lie it turns out like that."

Alex laughed, deep and throaty before turning to the sidewalk leading to the house.

"So we're doing this, huh?" His eyes were trained on the front door. It was a normal white door. Metal with a lot of locks. Normal. But the way he looked at it, it might as well be coated in squid ink.

All the exasperation drifted away on his laughter. If she didn't know he was some big strong cop, she might think he was afraid. "Wait, you're not afraid of a few swingers, are you?"

"Afraid, no." He stared at the home. "I'm just not sure what to expect."

"If you didn't know what to expect, why did you take on this case?"

"We don't choose the cases."

"So what you're saying is, if you had a choice, you wouldn't take this case?" Harper pulled her bag over her shoulder. She thought he was different. She thought he wasn't as close-minded as his partner. But weren't they all just the same. "Is it because you don't think those in the lifestyle deserve closure?"

"Not necessarily." He sighed. "I'm just nervous."

"Right." She shook her head. The first time was always the hardest. Changing the subject tended to calm people down. "Do you think that someone in this group killed Brad and Madeline?"

"I'm not sure. Right now, it's the only connection."

And that connection was why she needed to follow through. She owed it to Brad to find out what really happened. She couldn't give him what he'd wanted in life, but she could at least go inside and see this through.

She took a deep breath. One. Two. Three. She had this. "Okay, let's go in." She turned to Alex.

"You look so nervous. Relax." She sighed. Maybe she was deflecting. She was the one who was nervous, but the breath he was holding said it wasn't just her deflection. They couldn't both be jittery. It was her thing. He should get his own thing. "It's just like a regular party. You talk to couples if you want."

"But isn't it more than talking?" There was the fear again.

And the fear—was hilarious. She couldn't help the laughter floating past her lips. He was looking at the house like it stepped on his cat. And didn't that just soothe her nerves.

"It's nothing to be afraid of. Nothing happens that you don't want to happen."

"But this is all about sex?" He stared at the windows, where two guests were standing inside drinking from wine glasses and nuzzling each other's necks.

"The lifestyle is about relationships. There are so many

rules, you're safer inside the house than any other place in Las Vegas."

The look he gave her said he didn't believe. "What kind of rules?"

"Most of the rules are pretty self-explanatory. No means no. Don't overdrink. What happens at the party, stays there." The wind kicked up and a shiver slithered up her back.

"If a person doesn't abide by the rules," she continued, "they'll get banned from this house and every house in the state. It's a small community and everyone talks. I've heard of people getting banned from the houses and the clubs. No one in the lifestyle wants to burn the bridge." Another gust of cool air, and she pulled her shawl closed.

"We should go inside." He rested a hand on her back and her insides warmed.

It was a simple touch along her lower back—probably innocent—yet it felt so good. And didn't she just hate that. She hated that anything felt good. It was too soon.

Her therapist told her when she was ready to move on, she'd know. Maybe her body was telling her it was time. Not with the detective. But with someone new.

After they mingled at the party, he'd get what he needed and she could put this behind her. She could look into dating apps or something. She was pretty sure that was how people did it these days.

She just needed answers tonight. Easy enough.

She hiked the bag higher on her shoulder. Her armor. Her protection from whatever answers were inside those doors. "Let's do this."

HARPER AND ALEX walked up the long path to the front door as it popped open. A man in a dark-blue suit stood in the opening. His scowl was deep until he saw Harper. Jackson. Jackson opened the door wider, and she could see the curved wall blocking the entry and any view into the main parts of the house. The music pulsing from inside was the only indication that anyone else was inside.

"Harper. Haven't seen you around here in a while." His blue eyes warmed.

She couldn't help but smile. Jackson had always been nice to her. Even when she was new and scared, he'd talked her into sticking around the first night—the night when Brad and her had been terrified and thought they'd run away and never return. But Jackson had helped her and she'd stayed. Best decision she'd ever made.

"I'm sorry about Brad." He looked over her shoulder and his smile faded. "And you are?"

"Alex."

"He's with me."

Jackson tried to hide the concern on his face by smiling. But it was there. "Okay then. Nice to meet you, Alex. Harper, do you remember the rules?"

"Yes." It was like riding a bike. At least she hoped so.

"Head around the wall to sign in."

"Thanks, Jackson." Harper walked inside and grabbed Alex's hand. Which was normal, right? Grab the hand of the guy you go to a swingers party with. She'd only attended these parties with her husband, so she wasn't sure on dating protocol. Never thought about it.

They walked around the wall and came up to the bar top. Across the room a fire brimmed in the white stone fireplace. It all came back. The nights sitting around the brown leather loveseats scattered around the room. Talking with friends as they shared wine and dancing. The fun. She couldn't believe it had been almost a year since she'd hung out with everyone.

"Hi. Name?" The woman behind the bar smiled. She held an iPad in her hand. A stylus hung over the top. She must be a new addition. Harper didn't recognize her.

"Harper Lange and Alex Coffey."

The woman grabbed the stylus and tapped the screen. Her dyed red-hair was tied in a knot at the top of her head. "Let me see... Oh yeah, here you are. I'm Symphony, if you need anything. It says here you're returning members."

"I am." Harper knew they kept all kinds of information on the guests in that little iPad. She'd asked Emma to see it once, but her friend refused. It made her wonder what kind of secrets were stored about her.

"Welcome back, Ms. Lange." She turned from Harper to Alex. "Great to meet you, Mr. Coffey. Bracelet?"

Alex looked at his wrist and then looked at Harper. He wasn't wearing a bracelet. But he would, if he wanted to stay onsite.

"Yellow please." Harper figured she'd answer for him.

"Sure." Symphony pulled out a metal box and sifted through the contents. "Shoot, I think I left them in the office. I'll be right back."

She slid out from behind the bar and ran down a side hall.

"What is yellow?" Alex leaned in.

"Yellow means voyeur."

"We're watching?"

"Unless you want a green bracelet so we can participate? But I don't think we're far enough along into our relationship to do a swap. Shouldn't we sleep together before we invite others into our bed?"

Alex's eyes widened and he audibly gulped. Actually gulped. It was kind of cute. And funny. Watching newbies was always fun.

"So, that's a no to swapping?"

"No." Another gulp. "What are the other colors?"

"There's red for a hard swap and orange for a soft swap."

"What's the difference?"

"Sex." Harper smiled as the hostess returned.

"I got them." Symphony waved a handful of bracelets as she ran back to the bar. "I'm so sorry. If I had my way, the office wouldn't be on the other side of the house. Yellow, right?"

"Yellow?" Harper couldn't help it. This was fun. The look on Alex's face as she stared at him, waiting for a reply was priceless.

Symphony held out a yellow band and waited for Harper to hold up her wrist. She snapped the clasp and pulled another band from the stack. "Your turn, honey."

Alex held out his arm and Symphony clicked his shut.

"Okay, you crazy kids. Here are the rules." She slid a piece of paper toward them. "Make sure you look them over. Mr. Coffey, any booze to check in?"

"Booze?"

"We don't have a liquor license. It's bring your own bottle."

Alex leaned in and whispered, "I didn't know."

"We have a merlot." Harper pulled a bottle from her bag.

"Great vintage. I bought this for my mom's birthday." Symphony pulled out a ticket and ripped it in half. She attached one end of the ticket with an elastic string, wrapping it over and over around the neck of the bottle. She handed the other half to Harper. "You'll need that ticket if you want any of the wine. Speaking of, can I pour you both a glass?"

"Please," Harper said while Alex said, "no."

There was no way he'd get through the night without a glass. He was wound tighter than the elastic on the bottle. He was already gulping. And they hadn't even gotten to the tour of the house.

He'd be passed out with the vapors when they hit the prop room. "Make it two glasses."

"Sounds good." Symphony twisted the foil and rotated the corkscrew of the bottle. She levered the cork, back and forth. The cork popped. She grabbed two wineglasses and poured.

Placing the glasses in front of them, she then pressed the cork into the opening. "Would you like a tour of the home?"

"Please." Harper smiled and leaned into Alex. He smelled amazing. Why was she even noticing that right now? "You need the full experience."

Alex cringed a smile. He had to know she was playing with him… a little bit anyway.

Symphony yelled over to Jackson. He was leaning by the front area and staring at his phone. "I'm giving a tour. If anyone comes in, have them sit at the tables."

"Sure thing." Jackson nodded and went back to the screen.

"Let's start with the locker room and the rules." Symphony walked to the room off of the family room. It was built to be an office, with two glass doors opened wide. Two rows of black metal lockers lined the left and back wall. Top and bottom. A round table stood in the center of the room with a huge bouquet of flowers.

Symphony waited for Alex to get fully in the room. "First rule, you must leave with the person you came with."

"Why?" Alex truly looked confused as he brought his wine glass to his lips. Like coming to this party was a prostitution ring without exchanging money. A lot of people didn't understand.

"This is a sex positive club for couples," Harper said, "not for hookups. The couples come here looking for connections together, not outside of their relationship."

"Really?" More confusion. Alex was starting to piss Harper off.

"Really. This is a no cheating zone." Harper was inches away from knocking his widening eyes from his head.

"Is there some confusion?" Symphony looked ready to get Jackson and kick them to the curb. Couples had been kicked out for less.

"Not at all." Harper laughed. "He's joking. He knows how intolerant people can be, so he's just playing around. Pretending to be a narrow-minded asshole. Right, honey?"

Alex almost said something, but he must have noticed the look on Harper's face, so he just nodded.

Good boy.

Symphony stared at Alex like she didn't believe him. But instead of kicking them out the door, she smiled. "Have you done this before?"

"No." Alex's cheeks reddened like he wasn't sure if he should admit it. It was almost cute. But the sheepish grin he gave her as he said, "I'm a little nervous," was definitely over-the-top cute.

Symphony smiled, buying his aw-shucks smile. "Don't you worry. We'll take good care of you.

"Let's start with the tour." Symphony pulled one of the lockers open. "Phones are not allowed. No photography at all. We have lockers to lock up your phone and anything else you want to leave behind. Do you have a locker?"

"No." Harper never had the money to rent a full-time locker, although Brad had one. He'd won it from John during one of the guys' multiple golf outings. She should have thought to bring the keys, but getting the keys and bringing them here would give her a reason to empty his locker. And the thought of going through another one of his personal spaces and sifting through his things broke her heart. With each thing she emptied, she lost him more and more.

She hadn't tossed anything from Brad's office; it was clogging up the second bedroom at the house. When she'd moved from their shared house in the southern highlands to something smaller and affordable in Henderson, she couldn't part with his stuff. It was bad enough she couldn't afford their house. But thinking about all of that while trying to navigate the club was not a great idea.

Harper shoved her bag and phone inside. "Thanks." She nodded to Alex. "Your turn."

He pulled his phone from his back pocket and slid it in the locker. Symphony shut the door and turned a key attached to a leather strap. The door locked. "Keep this with you." She handed the key to Harper.

Harper handed Alex her glass and then slid the leather loop around her wrist. She took her glass back as Symphony moved to the right wall. A framed poster hung on the wall. "These are the rules I showed you earlier. Read them. Know them."

After a few minute pause, Symphony led them out of

the locker room and walked into what was probably built to be a family room. Now it was an entertainment hub. A pool table stood next to another blazing fireplace. They'd added a dart board along the far wall. The rest of the room had high top tables and chairs.

"Does everyone follow those rules?" Alex seemed to find his voice and the red had receded from his face.

"Yes."

"Disagreements must be taken out of the house." Alex must have read the words because he was reciting them like they were sacred. "Have you had any disagreements lately?"

"Me?" Symphony's eyes widened.

"No, here at the club."

Symphony's stance changed from curiosity to skepticism. Of course she was skeptical. The people in this club were private. And strangers asking questions always raised red flags. "Why?"

"I'm just curious."

"We aren't allowed to talk about it."

"Is it fight club?" Alex whispered the words, but not quietly enough.

Symphony angled toward the door. "Excuse me?"

"Nothing." Harper jumped in. There was no way they were going to make it through the night without getting kicked out. He had to know getting these people to talk would take a miracle—or finesse.

"Then let's move on." Symphony looked Alex up and down.

Let's.

"This isn't working." Alex sighed.

Apparently the cop had no idea how to ask questions. Well, not questions at a swingers' club. "You have to have something to offer," she told him.

"What?" The look on Alex's face inferred she wanted to trade answers for a blow job. Although, if that was the case, maybe he wouldn't look so horrified.

"So, Symphony, I haven't been here in ages. How long have you been working the desk?" Harper walked alongside Symphony and leaned in. She was going for conspiratorial bestie.

"Eight months."

"Are the Paskudas still around?"

"Bernard and Karen? Oh yeah."

"Their son still a challenge?" And to say Brody was a challenge was an understatement. Challenge was failing grades or poor hygiene. Brody was a drug addict who stole his parents' living room furniture, *Risky Business* style, and sold it all to a bunch of college kids for a quick fix. Some lucky teens had an original Chagall and custom designed sofa and love seat. Too bad Brody couldn't remember who he'd sold it to. He'd passed *challenge* a year ago and was squarely in *problem.* "He sold all his parents' furniture for a fix last year."

Symphony leaned in and adopted a hushed tone. "I didn't know the specifics, but did you hear they kicked Brody out of the house again?"

"I hadn't heard."

"No one knows what he did this time. Maybe he sold

their bedroom furniture." Symphony looked so upset. Almost like she took it personally.

"Maybe." But given the history, they'd forgive him and the kid would be back playing video games in the million dollar mansion by the end of the month. "Were you here the last time Madeline came in with her husband, Paul?"

Symphony nodded. "I was. Such a tragedy. Did you know her?"

"We were really good friends until I got lost in my own problems."

"I heard about your husband." Symphony laid a hand on Harper's arm. She was so sweet. "I'm so sorry."

"Thank you." Harper held onto Symphony's hand. "It's so hard to lose a spouse. How is Paul doing?"

"I haven't seen him in over a week." Symphony signaled at the family room. "This is the conventional entertainment area. We have a pool table." They moved down the hall toward the kitchen. "The kitchen takes orders for light snacks till nine, or you can come to me for table delivery. But keep the food on the main floor."

"Isn't it illegal to sell food?" Alex pushed open the kitchen door and took a peek.

"We don't sell food. We offer it as part of the membership."

Alex closed the door and followed. "Is the house zoned as a business?"

For crying out loud… "Stop with the inquisition," Harper whispered and elbowed him in the gut. He oomphed. He was lucky she didn't hit him harder. How could they schmooze information from Symphony if he acted like the Spanish Inquisition.

"No, this is a private residence, where private parties are thrown."

"But there are membership dues." Alex was going to out himself as a cop if he didn't watch out with all the questions and all the zoning.

"Sorry, that's a misnomer. They're not dues. They're requested donation amounts in monthly intervals."

She motioned to the dining room as they passed. Twelve chairs sat around a large ornate mahogany table in the center of the room. "This is a great room to eat and get to know everyone." She looked to Alex, probably for his next line of questioning about whether the dining room was zoned for eating.

When nothing came, she turned toward the back stairs. "Let's head upstairs." They walked up the flight and came to a long hallway. Nine doors lined the hall. Professional pictures of the ever-changing Vegas skyline hung in groupings of four.

"We have four rooms available during opening hours." She entered her code into the keypad and the door. "You can give me your credit card downstairs and we'll attach it to a key code. If you need the room, you enter in your code and at the end you identify your donation."

"How does a family live in this house?" The cop managed to pull out a good question.

Harper had wondered the same thing when she'd first attended.

"Emma, John and the kids mostly live in the guest

house behind the house. They hold these parties and rent the main floor and back yard for parties and the occasional movie. Did you ever see *Debbie Does Dagobah*?"

Harper and Alex both shook their heads as they followed her to the end of the hall.

Symphony turned around long enough to see them shake their heads. "That's too bad. It was a good one. The scene between Hands Solo and Duke Skyballer happened right in this very hallway. If you look really close, you can see the grooves where the dick-shaped light sabers hit the wall. It was an epic scene. I think if John is smart, he'll host more movies. It's fun and you get to meet the stars."

The way Symphony talked about Star Wars porn, she obviously got a hard-on for the light sabers. Which if you were going to get a hard-on, this was the place to do it.

CHAPTER
FIVE

SYMPHONY OPENED the last door on the floor. "This is the main room." And main it was.

The master bedroom contained three rows of stadium seating—six chairs each. They stood at the front of the room behind one-way glass. The rest of the master bedroom was on the other side. It had two beds and various flat surfaces. One of the surfaces was currently in use.

"This is the voyeur room. And look, we have one of our regulars already starting." Symphony motioned to the chairs on this side of the glass. "Please have a seat and watch as long as you want."

Harper sat down as Alex leaned against the wall. She gauged his reaction, waiting for a scowl or a grimace. But none came. His face was passive, like he expected to see this, but his eyes betrayed his thoughts. Wide eyes and curiosity. He looked uncomfortable but enthralled. And it took everything in her not to bust out laughing. To avoid that, she focused on the show in the other room. She put her glass next to the chair and just stared.

A man and woman sat on the edge of a table. His suit coat was hanging on a post of the bed. They'd just started. At least Harper assumed they'd just started. Their mouths were joined together, dancing slow and deliberate. His hands skimmed the side of her body. Her breast. Her waist. Slow and soft. It was beautiful.

And boy, did she miss this. It was sexy and sweet. And hot.

She could practically feel Brad's hand on her thigh. This was one of her favorite parts. Watching a couple—or two—have a good time. Not that she didn't want to join, but she loved innocent touches by her husband. Those touches somehow felt erotic as they shared the evocative scene in front of them.

Air whooshed through her nose, but instead of the spiced citrus that was Brad, there was no scent. Nothing. How many times had she sat in one of these chairs as he played with her hair. Not even sexual. Just played with her hair while they watched. It was everything.

God, she missed him.

Tears poked at the back of her eyes. She couldn't be here. Not alone. A hand rested on her shoulder.

Brad.

"Are you okay?" Breath warmed along her neck and her eyes closed. "We could go join them." She swore she heard Brad's voice.

How many times had she asked Brad to join the couples behind the window? How many times had she watched in longing—waiting for him to be ready? So they'd sat and waited, until one day he'd gotten the courage and asked if she'd wanted to join. He trusted her and she'd trusted him to put her first. He always had.

And they'd had so much fun. She missed the fun.

"Harper?" The feelings were there. But the voice wasn't right. "Are you okay?"

Her eyes opened and instead of light hair and ocean blue eyes, she saw dark hair and brown eyes. They looked kind and concerned, but they weren't the right eyes. "Are you okay?"

His mouth was so close, but it wasn't Brad. He wasn't here. Not his hand. Not his voice. She hadn't felt this pull of loss in months. Her heart hadn't broken. Her chest hadn't ached. Not like this, for a long time.

She sucked in a breath, but there wasn't enough room. The air couldn't fit. Her head swirled. She had to get out. She needed air. Fresh air.

She stood up and stumbled to the door. One. Two. She turned the knob and tripped into the hallway. She leaned against the wall. The air hissed through her lips as she leaned over. Breathe in. Breathe out.

"Are you okay?" Symphony leaned down, her face hovering in front of Harper's. "You don't look so good."

Harper didn't feel so good. So, at least, she matched.

"She should sit down."

"She should breathe."

"I'm fine." She wasn't, but she would be.

Alex's hand lifted at the under part of her arm. He might have been holding her up. "Are you okay?"

She'd be a hell of a lot better if they stopped asking her that.

"Have a seat." Alex motioned to a chair that had somehow materialized next to her.

She sat down and sucked in a deep breath.

"Are you okay?"

"I'm fine." If she didn't give a better answer, she had a feeling they were going to keep asking. "I just needed a minute to breathe."

"Do you want to leave?" Alex kneeled in front of her. His hands rested on her knees. It was sweet and intimate. But he probably didn't mean it that way. Which was good. She wasn't ready for intimate.

"We can try this another time."

Symphony smiled. "You don't have to rush into anything. That's the beauty of DeVout. You can take it at your own pace." She must have thought Harper was on the verge of a nervous breakdown because of a sex club. Which was sweet.

"I'm fine. We don't have to leave." Harper nodded at Alex as he quirked up an eyebrow. Like he didn't believe she was fine. He didn't know her well enough to know she used *fine* as a shield.

I'm fine. It's fine. It was all code for "let's just pretend it doesn't exist." It usually took people years to figure that out. Although, Brad never did figure it out. He had other gifts. Thank goodness.

"I'll get you a drink of water." Symphony disappeared down the stairs.

Alex stood up and leaned against the wall in front of

Harper. "What happened in there?"

Breakdown due to latent emotional damage. "It was nothing." Another shield.

"It didn't look like nothing." Alex was staring at her. Harper couldn't look far enough away for him not to see everything. Anywhere her eyes went, his were there.

"There's a reason I haven't been back here in a while."

"Your husband?" It was creepy how much Alex saw. Damn detective. Although that might have been a bit obvious.

"Yeah."

"We have one more stop if you want to complete the tour." Symphony reappeared with a glass of water in her hand.

"We're going to take a raincheck."

A raincheck meant they'd be coming back. Harper wasn't sure she wanted to do return anytime soon. She missed it, but if the past few minutes told her anything, she wasn't ready. She took the glass from Symphony and sipped the water. Her breath was coming in normal bursts. She almost felt human again.

She could handle the club. Just not the main room. She could do this. "No raincheck. Let's finish the tour and then we'll head downstairs to socialize."

"You sure?" The concern on Alex's face was nice, albeit annoying.

Harper took a long pull from the glass in her hand. "Let's do this." She stood up and handed Alex the glass. The air was flowing freely to her lungs as she felt all her faculties return. She was here—in the now.

"The last place we need to visit is the prop room."

Harper forgot about the prop room. The now was looking up. She needed to keep herself calm. She could do this, because even those immersed in the lifestyle were shocked by the prop room.

This was going to be fun.

CHAPTER
SIX

A COUPLE OF MINUTES LATER, they were back at the front bar, Symphony leading the way. "I'll be right with you." She nodded to the guests sitting at the counter.

Emma Byrne stood behind the bar talking to the guests. Her dark hair was curled and flowing down her back. She wore a cornflower dress that brought out the blue in her eyes. "Continue the tour. I've got this."

Harper could tell when Emma noticed her. Her eyes widened as a smile overtook her face.

"You came. How are you?"

"I'm fine." Harper smiled, her shield fully in place. Between the guilt of abandoning her friend and heartache from missing her, she was imbedded in all the feels.

"I'm so glad you're here." Emma smiled at Harper. A warm smile. A smile that said maybe, just maybe, they could find friendship again. "I've missed you."

Guilt snaked through Harper's body overpowering all the emotions running rampant. "I've missed you, too."

And she did. They'd been friends at the club, but they'd been friends outside, too. Shopping buddy. Confidant. Harper not only lost a husband; she lost so much more.

Emma's eyes stopped on someone behind Harper. "Alex, right? The boyfriend."

"That's me." He nodded.

"We have one more stop and then I'll take over." Symphony stood by a door off the front room. She waved her keycard over a scanner on the door and the lock popped.

Harper let Alex rest his hand on her back, guiding her into the room. As soon as she was completely inside, she turned around. She wanted to see his face. Had to see his face.

She almost held her breath. Oh wait, she was holding her breath. And then…

Alex's eyes rounded to Area Fifty-One proportions. He stopped moving and stared, jaw dropping. There it was. She could practically see molars. Success. Harper's heart felt light. Her soul smiled—don't knock it. She could actually feel her whole being smile.

"This is the prop room. We sell everything you might need for a night of fun." Symphony waved at a small two-foot piece of shelving. "Here we have basic hygiene. Everything from mints to cologne." She patted a three-foot-high wooden barrel. "Here are the condoms. We always have these on hand."

"Is that thing full?" Alex looked at the wooden barrel like it was performing close-up magic.

"Not the whole thing. There's a false bottom, so only

the top has individual packets. Below is back stock." Symphony stirred the little ocean of condoms. "We sell through this thing about five times a year. We're independent contractors with Adult Stash Parties and we pass the savings to you. If you want us to come by and do a home party, we'd be happy to schedule one."

Symphony didn't wait for an answer, probably because she could see the blood had drained from Alex's face. She pulled a Vanna White and motioned to the wall of dildos. There were fake penises in every color of the rainbow. Large and small. Glass and bunny-eared. Strapless and vibrating. There was a set of plastic penises that were larger than a glass soda bottle. One package even said *for his pleasure*.

"This one is my absolute favorite." Symphony unhooked one box from the wall and held it out to Alex. "It's incredibly intense and you can use your phone to control it. The ladies love it. Did you want to shop?"

Symphony kept looking at Alex, but his glazed space-eyes were still in place. His hand didn't move, so she replaced the box on the wall and pointed to another barrel on the opposite side of the room. "If you run out of lube, we have packets here. We also have horny goat weed."

"Horny goat weed?" He sounded like he had an entire goat stuck in his throat. Harper didn't laugh out loud, but it was close.

"It's a supplement for male issues with stiffness." Symphony looked down at his package, in case he wondered where the stiffness should occur.

Harper bit back another laugh. "I think we're good."

"Did you want to leave a credit card for donations?" Symphony asked.

Harper turned to Alex, but his eyes were roaming the wall of phalli. "Let's hold off on the credit card for now." Harper smiled as she watched him gawk at the wall. Even she could admit it was a rather impressive wall of dicks.

Symphony headed for the door. "Just holler if you change your mind." As she disappeared, quiet was left in her wake.

Harper watched Alex stare at the wall, but the silence was killing her. "Did you want to buy one?"

"No." He looked in the direction of the largest vibrator on the wall. The Gigantor was large and intimidating—to even the best endowed. "I think I'm developing a complex. I may never get naked in front of a woman again."

The look on his face. He sounded so serious. Harper couldn't hold the laughter back. It was so ridiculous. This gorgeous man—yes, gorgeous—stood in a room of plastic, questioning his manhood.

"How about I get you another glass of wine and we make the rounds? You know, get started on the police work." The whole point of the evening.

"Are you up for an interrogation tonight?" His concern moved from his privates to her private meltdown. It was more fun when he was concerned about himself. She didn't need his pity.

"I'm feeling better." And she was. Nothing like a dildo farm to make a girl feel all warm and fuzzy. Although it probably had more to do with his response. "Are you sure you're up for tonight?"

"Why wouldn't I be?"

"You looked rather devastated by all the" —she nodded to the wall— "competition."

Alex laughed, a deep belly laugh. "I think I'm a bit more satisfying than these things."

She didn't have the heart to tell him how incredible the one with the remote control could really be, so she smiled and nodded. She didn't want to hurt his ego twice in one night.

"Let's get that drink." He gulped.

They left the quiet of the back room and entered the living area. The line to the bar was around the corner. The local high school football game must have let out. All the parents were free to frolic.

Emma stood behind the counter, pulling a bottle of bourbon up to the countertop. She poured two glasses. "We have that new movie you were looking for last week."

"We'll take a look." The man took his drinks and headed over to his wife—at least Harper thought it was his wife, given the rings on their fingers. The lifestyle was a small community, but people did float in and out. They had newcomers to keep things interesting. And since Harper had been out of the game for a bit, there were bound to be newbies.

"What did you bring?" Emma looked at Alex. Like he would know.

Harper handed Emma the ticket. "Merlot."

"Do you have glasses?"

Shit. She left hers upstairs. And since Alex didn't appear to be holding his glass, it must have been left somewhere in the house. Which meant Emma was going to throw a fit. Leaving things around was a no-no. It led to lectures about parents not working here.

"I brought the empties down to the kitchen." Symphony smiled as she checked in the last guests from the line. "They need new glasses."

Symphony tilted her head and gave Harper a knowing smile. Yeah, they both knew the wrath of Emma. At one point there'd been a sign stating to, *"clean up after yourselves. Your mother doesn't work here."* But a few members complained that thinking about their mother at a party killed the mood, so the sign came down and Emma's wrath went up.

Emma looked at the ticket and paired it with its mate. She opened the bottle and grabbed two glasses. She filled Alex's three-quarter full and Harper's about halfway.

Harper looked at the glass. It was her wine, but she was getting stiffed by one of her best friends. "Really?"

"I'm doing you a favor. I'm going to assume you're still a lightweight."

Harper might be a lightweight. She might have danced on a table after two glasses of wine—might—but that happened a long time ago.

"I don't want to have to carry you out at the end of the night." Emma corked the bottle and slid it under the bar. She handed the ticket back to Harper, wrapping her fingers around Harper's. "I need to work on some paper-work tonight, but I'm hoping we can talk later."

"I'd love that." Harper squeezed her hand. She'd missed Emma. The talking and the laughing. The gossiping over ice cream. Things Harper had taken for granted when they'd seen each other all the time.

Harper pulled away and grabbed the glasses. Handing the fuller glass to Alex—Harper's alcohol sensitivity was notorious—she leaned in. "Let's go sit in the family room."

He nodded as they walked away from the bar. When Emma and Symphony had moved on to other couples, she leaned in. "Who do you need to interview?"

"Anyone who would know both victims is priority. But really, anyone who might know something." He looked toward the back office where his phone was locked away. "I need to grab my phone to take notes."

"You can't use your phone. Not for notes. Not for anything. A few years ago, a couple carried their phone around, in case of emergency, and then photos of the house were posted on the web. Not just the house. The people in the house. So, now there are no phones allowed. If you need to be reachable, they allow pagers."

"A pager wouldn't really help to take notes."

"Sorry." She did feel sorry he couldn't take notes, but she wasn't about to draw attention to herself by letting him sneak a phone around. The last one who was caught with a phone was banned for life. She might not hang out here regularly these days, but that didn't mean she wanted to burn the bridge. "You know, there is this thing called paper and pencil."

"True." He took a drink from his glass. "Do you have paper and pencil?"

"No."

"Not even in your Quidditch bag?" That he knew what Quidditch was seemed kind of cute.

"We never really broke out the pen and paper when we were here. There were so many other things to do."

He smiled as he took a deep drink from his glass. They stood on the outskirts of the family room. Soft music came from overhead speakers. Balls clicked and clacked from the pool table. Another couple sat at a table, drinking. Amelia and Jasper.

"Harper." Amelia waved, and stood up so she could wrap Harper in a hug. "You made it inside."

"We did. We just took the tour."

"So, you got to check out the prop room." Amelia didn't say it as a question, just stated as a fact. She was in her late forties. Blond hair from L'Oréal, plump lips from Dior, and boobs from the breast augmentation center. She was gorgeous, with Latin-kissed skin and just enough junk in her trunk to make men swoon.

If Harper was the jealous type, her b-cups would be covered in green. Thankfully she'd gotten over that a long time ago.

Mostly.

"Yes." Alex nodded as the red crawled up his face.

"It's awe-inspiring how many dicks they can fit in three hundred square feet." Jasper ran a hand through long brown hair. If Harper didn't know him, she'd take him for a hipster, complete with beard and skinny jeans. But she knew he had a collection of Prada suits at home for his day job, as president or whatever he was at some construction company.

"Yeah, amazing," Alex mumbled as he brought his wine to his lips. The red wasn't receding, and given the mumble, he was neither amazed nor awe-inspired.

"Not something you see every day. It's really hard to get used to." Amelia's laugh tinkled. She was too damn cute.

And Harper was so not jealous. Just confused. Brad had never gotten along with Jasper, so they'd never really hung out with them, but they were absolutely lovely.

"Am I that transparent?" Alex took another drink. Sometimes a person needed to take a beat when confronted with the limitations of one's prized member— let alone a wall of them, or maybe his inner prude needed to get drunk.

"It's written on the innocent look on your face."

"I've been called many things, but innocent is not one of them."

"Fair enough." Amelia raised her wine glass, filled with equal parts wine and ice, to him before she took a drink. She set the glass down and pointed at Harper's arm. "Nice bracelet. Haven't worn a yellow in a while, huh?"

Harper played with the yellow plastic on her arm. She hadn't worn a voyeur band in a long time.

Jasper's eyes twinkled. "Did you take him up to the main room?"

"I did." Harper couldn't help the smile on her face.

Before she'd lost her shit, his face had morphed into wide eyes and horror—before he'd reined it in. Big strong cop scared of a little intimacy.

"Is anyone in the main room? We were thinking of heading up." Amelia nodded toward the hall with the stairs.

"There was. A new couple. I didn't recognize them."

"There are a lot of new couples." Amelia leaned against the table and motioned to the chairs opposite her. "Have a seat. We have a date in a half hour, but we'd love to catch up."

"Sure." A date? Harper hadn't had a one-on-one date in a really long time, let alone a couples date. She missed those.

"Yeah, new couple—well, new to you. The Yancys."

The Yancys? Amelia and Jasper had been a one-couple couple. They'd been with Madeline and Paul Williams ever since Harper could remember. Although, the Williamses hadn't been a one-couple couple. Even so, Madeline wasn't around any longer. Just the thought made a tear sting the back of her eyes. "I'm sorry about Madeline and Paul."

"Yeah, thanks."

"Why are you sorry?" Alex leaned toward Harper. He might be trying to whisper but his voice carried over the soft hum of the music and clacking of the pool balls smacking each other.

"Amelia and Jasper had been dating Madeline and Paul for a while."

"Three years." Amelia shook her head. "We stopped seeing them about six months ago."

"What happened?"

"I don't know. They changed, or maybe we changed."

"It was definitely them, babe." Jasper wrapped her hand in his. The pain on their face said this had been a hard time. "Madeline became jealous and Paul…"

"Became an asshole." Amelia laughed and the tinkling sound seemed to lighten the mood. "Well, he was always an asshole."

"He was, but Madeline was never jealous." Harper had to agree. Paul was the picture under "narcissist" in the dictionary. And Madeline was under "saint."

"I know. Weird, right?" Amelia played with the condensation dripping from the glass on the table. "That's what we loved about them. But something changed."

"Do you know what happened to cause the change?" Alex asked the question, but that didn't seem to sway Amelia. She was enthralled with the water cascade.

"I don't know. But the last time we went out, she slapped me."

"Slapped you?" Harper couldn't imagine Madeline slapping anyone. She was the person who released bugs when she found them in her home. She couldn't slap a bug, yet she was slapping Amelia?

"I know, right? It was so out of character. Paul was helping me with my golf swing and she accidentally hit me when she slapped his hand away from mine. Well, I'm thinking it was an accident, but that's when we stopped seeing them. We didn't need the drama."

"And I'll be damned if anyone is going to hit Amelia. But she'd been acting weird before then. Right around when Brad died."

Harper's thoughts wrapped around Brad's name. Protected it. It was nice to hear his name, but it twisted at her heart.

"Sorry." Jasper winced, remorse written on the droop in his eyes.

Had she looked upset by his words? She thought she was hiding her shit pretty well. Apparently not. She painted on a brighter smile. Fake it. Fake it, and one day you make it. "No need to be sorry."

Amelia pulled her hand from Jasper's and touched Harper's arm. "Is it hard to talk about?"

Harper looked over at her fake boyfriend and sighed. This was exactly what she didn't want tonight. It was bad enough being here with the ghosts. She didn't need the knowing looks and whispers that haunted her. "I'm fine."

"Hey, guys." A man and woman walked up to the table. "Are you ready?"

"Sure." Amelia squeezed Harper's hand as she stood. "You both should come back so we can talk some more. I have to tell you all about my latest scones recipe."

Sharing recipes. Something Amelia and Harper had done a lot back in the day. "I also have a cheddar biscuit to discuss."

"Deal."

Harper must have finally been making it, because the fake smile on her face fooled her friends. Amelia and

Jasper followed their dates up the stairs without a second glance.

But there was no way she'd be coming back again. Harper loved the lifestyle and she loved being here when she was part of a couple. But not when she was the freak whose husband was gone.

HARPER SAT in the chair and finished her glass of wine. Amelia and Jasper had just gone upstairs and the pool players had somehow left. It was quiet. With the exception of soft music and the man sitting next to her.

"So, do you like being a teacher?" And he was bringing his A-game small talk.

"I do." And she loved talking about her kids. It was hard to let them go at the end of the year, but it was so worth it.

"I like my nephews, but I can't see dealing with other people's kids."

"It's not so bad. It's nice to get them at the beginning of the term and see them change over the year. They grow. They mature. They go from being second-graders with a childish mentality, to being prepared for third grade. There's just something about that age." She took a sip from her glass as she looked around the room. She figured it was safe since no one was walking around. "What about you? How do you like your job?"

"Some days are better than others." He managed to keep his answer vague. Which made sense just in case someone was listening.

"What is today? An 'other'?"

"No, today is definitely one of the better days."

Warmth travelled up her chest. Spending time together hadn't been a hardship to him. Well, spending her night with him wasn't a hardship either. Not that she'd admit she didn't hate it to him. He struck her as a person that didn't do warm and fuzzy.

"What brought you to this place?" he asked.

"You did." She knew what he meant, but she wasn't sure she wanted to get into it. The story wasn't bad, just reminded her of all she'd lost. She tilted back her glass and finished it off.

"I meant the first time you came." Of course that's what he meant. He poured half his glass into hers. It was sweet. And so appreciated.

"Thank you." She twirled the newly acquired liquid.

"Did Brad introduce you to the lifestyle?"

"No. Actually, I sort of introduced him. I was so worried the first time we came. I didn't know exactly what it was, but I had an idea."

"And still you came."

That first night came flooding back. "Emma told me we didn't have to participate. We could watch or just stay downstairs and mingle."

"But you didn't stay downstairs."

The laughter flooded her chest. "You saw what was going on upstairs. How can you not watch? It's fascinating. A little naughty." A new flood was now in her cheeks. She'd learned to enjoy the lifestyle, but it still felt a little naughty—and good. The red heated her face.

"So, what happened?"

"I actually met Emma when I was an assistant in her oldest daughter's class a few years ago. We hit it off. I stayed friends with Emma and she invited me and my fiancé to one of their parties. And we'd been attending ever since."

The first party had been scary and exciting and new. Sharing something so personal and taboo could push couples apart, but it also could bring them closer. That's what it did for her and Brad. They'd found a strength in the secrecy and a camaraderie in the forbidden.

"This place is interesting." The way he said interesting wasn't judgmental, but a part of her wondered if there wasn't a bit underlying his words. "Jasper and Amelia were nice, albeit interesting."

"Interesting how?"

"The conversation. Madeline." He didn't elaborate.

But Harper had a feeling there was more to his point. "And?"

"Could she have been heartbroken when Brad died?"

"Amelia?"

"No, Madeline."

"I'm sure a lot of people were heartbroken. Brad had a lot of friends." Harper made friends at these parties, but Brad made friends for life. All the guys hung out, played golf and scratched their packages—or whatever guys did while hitting the white ball around the green.

"But has everyone's behavior changed?"

"I'm not sure what you mean." And she wasn't sure she wanted to know. Something in his eyes said the question he was asking was going to hurt. Maybe that's why her brain refused to understand. Or maybe he was just being ambiguous.

"Could Madeline and Brad have had a relationship? Maybe they were more than just friends."

"That's impossible." Harper thought back to her relationship with her husband. To Madeline. They weren't any closer than anyone else in the house. She and Brad had had a few make-out sessions with the Williamses, but nothing too intense. Paul was a bit of a dick. And even though Harper tried to enjoy their time together, she couldn't get past his mouth.

Not the kissing. He was pretty good at that. But the speaking. Ugh. Paul would talk and she actually felt like she was losing brain cells just by listening to him. Which was sad because Harper really liked Madeline. Everyone did.

There was no way Madeline was cheating with Brad. It wasn't her style.

"People in the lifestyle don't have to cheat."

He gave her a look—one that said he was thinking something stupid and he was wondering if he should share it. Or maybe that was just her interpretation.

"Just say what you want to say." She sighed and took a

sip from her glass. There wasn't much left and after her earlier gulp, she didn't want to start getting tipsy.

"Aren't they cheating by coming here?"

"No. Cheating is going behind someone's back. There's usually lying involved. We don't have to lie here. Just being here helps a couple talk about things—boundaries and fantasies. You talk about what you're willing to do or not do. Here it's about sharing an experience. Doing things together. Compersion."

"Compersion?"

"Feeling joy because the person you love feels joy. It doesn't matter why they're happy or who brought them joy, just that they are feeling it."

To the detective's credit, he wasn't laughing or shaking his head. He actually seemed to be listening.

"So, there's no room for cheating here. We want our partners to be happy and we don't care who brings them happiness."

"I never thought of it that way."

"Most people don't." She took a drink from her wine glass. "Most people prejudge because they don't understand. They just see movies or hear rumors of horror stories. This doesn't have to be something scary or bad. And when you do it right, it's not."

"And you did it right."

"I'd like to think we did." Harper had been happy with Brad, and she honestly believed he had been, too. They'd had their issues, but everyone does. "When it comes to DeVout we didn't have secrets."

The detective finished off his drink and didn't say a word. But his silence said a lot. He didn't believe her.

"Is it me you don't believe, or is it the whole lifestyle you're questioning?"

"I didn't say a word." He stood up and motioned to her glass. "But everyone has secrets."

She finished the rest and handed it to him.

"We should mingle. Get more information." He headed toward the bar.

She thought about following. She knew she should. They should mingle and talk to as many people as they could, so she didn't have to live this nightmare again. But dealing with the judgment was just another circle of hell.

CHAPTER
EIGHT

HARPER SAT at the table in DeVout for a few minutes, but no matter how much she wanted to stay there and hide, she needed to join whatever conversation was happening across the room. She walked across the room when Alex laughed. Symphony was leaning against the bar, her ample assets resting on the top. *What?* They were impressive. Harper hadn't noticed them before, but from this angle, she couldn't notice anything else.

"Best job I've ever had." Symphony stepped back, making her ample assets shrink down to almost normal size.

"How long have you worked here?"

"Nine months." She disappeared behind the bar and came up with Harper's bottle.

"What did you do before this?" Harper sat on one of the stools in front of her. Might as well join in on the inquisition. It was better than sitting around thinking.

"A few things. I was a waitress at the Rio. I planned

weddings at Caesars for a while." She filled the two glasses, wine spilling over the side as she slid one over to Harper. She wiped down the side of the glass with a napkin. "How about you?"

"I'm a teacher."

"Over at Il Vincitore, right? That's right, Emma mentioned that you were the best teacher in the valley." Symphony said.

"I don't know about the best. She tends to over-exaggerate."

"Do you know her?" Symphony smiled as her head bobbed side to side. "She doesn't give out genuine compliments very often."

It was true. Emma was a wonderful person who could kiss ass with the best of them, but real compliments were few and far between. "So, what about you, Alex?"

"What about me?" Alex took a deep drink from his glass. He was obviously trying to deflect—maybe come up with a fake job. He couldn't just come out and say he was a cop. That would defeat the whole purpose.

"What do you do for a living?"

"I'm a security guard."

"Ooh, where? Anyplace I've been?"

"I don't know where you've been." Alex tipped his glass back and forth as he winked. Winked. If Harper didn't know him better, she'd think he was flirting.

"I've been everywhere, darling." Symphony laughed as she dragged out the word *darling*. She waved at a couple that just walked in from the front hall. "I'll be right with you.

"Okay, you two. Go mingle." She grabbed a towel from under the bar and wiped down the top. "I have to get back to work."

Alex moved away from the chairs and held out his hand as Harper stood up. She picked up her glass and put her free hand in his before following him.

"Where to?" Alex leaned in close. He was letting her take the lead. Which was actually nice. He didn't seem like the type to normally let anyone take his lead.

"Everyone seems to be in the main viewing room. But there's another rush." A line had formed at the bar. A couple of people she recognized. Maybe they could hit up a few of them for the current gossip—see if anyone knew more about the Madeline/Paul relationship. "Let's see if anyone is in the dining room, unless you want to try upstairs."

"I don't know if I can carry you again."

"Exaggerate much?" Harper went to hit him with her free hand, but it wasn't free. Her hand was still in his. She wanted to pull away, but something stopped her— probably because it felt good to touch someone again—even an innocent touch. At least that was her story. Because honestly, she missed the touch of anyone this past year. "You didn't have to carry me."

"But I might if we go up there again." He followed her toward the side hall leading to the dining room. Surprisingly, when they got inside the room, a couple sat at the table with plates in front of them.

Emma and John.

"There you are." Emma stared at Harper—not at

Harper—at her hand in Alex's. "Can I get you something to eat?"

"No, thanks." Harper dropped Alex's hand like it zapped her. And it felt like it had. Or maybe it was the laser-focus of Emma's stare that zapped her hand away.

"Come in and sit down." John dropped his fork to his empty plate. "We were just finishing dinner before things get rowdy."

"Rowdy?" Harper sat in the chair across the table.

"Maybe not rowdy. But we have a date tonight with the Pennebakers."

"The Pennebakers?" They weren't exactly Emma and John's type. At least they hadn't been. They were loud and in your face, while John and Emma were classy. There wasn't another word for it. Emma was all about order and prestige. Not exactly a concern for a woman like Jannine Pennebaker who wore a red rhinestone jacket with a black leather mini-skirt and gold go-go boots—and that was to their daughter's school assembly.

With Emma's white cashmere sweaters and John's Breitling watches—not exactly the couples Harper would see together. But then again, the lifestyle wasn't flooded with fresh couples. Sometimes you clicked with the oddest of bedfellows.

"How are you enjoying our establishment?" John nodded to Alex as he held out Harper's chair and then sat in his own.

"This place is beautiful."

"Yeah, we lucked out finding this house during the recession." He took a drink from the glass in front of him.

If Harper's memory was correct, John was drinking a whiskey sour. "So, what do you do, Alex?"

"I'm in security."

"Fascinating line of work." John took another drink. "What type of security?"

Alex leaned back in the chair. "I'm a guard at one of the properties on the strip."

"Which property? I might have seen you."

"Do you go to the strip often?" Alex was deflecting again.

"I own and operate the Sláinte hotel and casino. So I'm on the strip pretty much every day."

"How about you?" Alex nodded to Emma.

"I'm the CFO of the Sláinte hotel." Emma wore that title with pride. It wasn't every day a woman with a degree in public health, who used to be a gambler, could help run a casino. But she'd kicked her demons and had the five-year pin to prove it.

"Impressive." Alex rested his arm on the back of Harper's chair. His thumb rubbed against her back. He didn't seem fazed by that little touch. He was much better at this pretending thing than she could ever be.

"My wife is amazing," John gushed and Emma smiled. Emma and John were the epitome of the lifestyle. They had it all and made it work. They owned their own company, had three kids, and still managed to run DeVout.

Harper wanted to be them when she grew up.

John finished the food on his plate. "So, where did you two lovebirds meet?"

Meet? We met at school when he started asking questions about Madeline's potential murder. But she couldn't say any of that. Out loud anyway. So she went with the first thing that fell from her mouth. "Golden Knights game."

"Il Vincitore Academy," Alex said at the same time. They really should have gotten their stories straight.

Emma laughed with a hint of confusion and maybe just a tad of skepticism. "Which one? The academy or the hockey game?"

"Both." Harper could feel her eyes getting wider. She should check her nose to see how much it had grown. This was why they shouldn't let her lie in public. Or anywhere, for that matter. "We met at the Golden Knights game during local school night. You know, the academy received a check for the school hockey team. And they ran out of hotdogs. The Golden Knights, not the school." She was rambling. *Mouth, please stop*! "We didn't bring hot dogs. That would be weird."

Alex rested his hand at the back of her neck and her pulse skittered to a stop. Her mouth miraculously stopped moving. She gulped back all the words threatening to spill out and said, "Remember that game?"

"The one where Henry rode the Zamboni?" John smiled.

"Yes." Of course they'd remember that night. They'd practically taped Henry's whole trip around the ice as he waved from the side of the ice-smoothing machine. "That's the one."

"Are you a security guard at T-Mobile?" John wasn't letting this go.

Harper didn't think he would.

"No. I was there with a few friends." Alex took it in stride. Didn't flinch. Didn't have a sign that ready *guilty* on his forehead. Didn't ramble. At all. "Are you big fans of the hockey team?"

"We're season ticket holders." John leaned back. "How about you?"

"My father has season tickets, and he gives them to us a few times a year." Alex nodded toward the main part of the house. "How long have you run DeVout?"

"We started the club ten years ago from our old home in Spring Valley. It was so popular we just couldn't keep up with demand. We were turning people away."

"Good problem to have."

"It can be, but here we have enough rooms to keep the first floor as a traditional type club and the upstairs for more untraditional." John smiled. "We still have to turn people away, but not nearly as many. And it gives the club a sense of exclusivity."

There was a silence as John and Alex took a drink of their respective alcoholic beverages. "So, you don't work at the Golden Knight's arena."

Damn job question again. How did Alex handle all the questions and the lying? All it would take was one call from John to check that he most certainly was not a security guard at any of the casinos. Then he'd keep checking till he figured it out.

Thank goodness Harper wasn't a cop. She couldn't handle working undercover. But she could redirect. "I really love what you did with the place. The changes are amazing." Harper looked at the marble lining the floor. "This tile is gorgeous."

"Thank you. It's been a long road. These tiles were imported from Italy and customs was such a headache. But they're so worth it." Emma smiled and her arms began to move. Emma talking about design or clothes and she was as animated as the inflatable tube-men in front of the oil change place downtown. "We worked with a designer in L.A. He was absolutely amazing. The little touches have made all the difference."

"I like the dart board in the family room. It gives the room a modern sports bar vibe."

"That's what I was going for. Makes the guys feel all safe and cozy. The pool was designed for the women. I can't wait to show you. It's too cold out there now, but there are six beds with netting. It's secluded and romantic. You'll have to check it out once the weather cooperates."

"I would love to." And part of her would love to see it. But the part where she'd have to come back didn't really sit well.

"We should head toward the front." John finished his glass and stood up. "But we should do lunch sometime."

"What a great idea." Emma stood up and smiled. "We haven't gone to lunch in a long time." Since Brad.

John poured two fingers into his glass and uncorked a bottle of wine. "Where should we meet? My work or yours?"

John stared at Alex almost in a challenge. He knew something was up. He had to. He kept bringing up Alex's job. He wasn't going to stop until he had his answer. Alex had to give them something.

"I don't think it matters which one. I'm right down the block at the Blink Hotel." Alex didn't look away. Didn't flinch.

"I know that place well. Do you know Dan Schuler?"

Shit. Shit. Shit. Of course, John would know someone from Blink. Why couldn't Alex have said he worked in security at a club or restaurant. Or maybe he could say he was an environmentalist. John had never claimed any love for the environment and there was a better chance of John not knowing the person. Right. John knew everyone.

"That was before my time. Dan retired a few years ago when Ethan took over. I report to him."

"I haven't met Dan's replacement yet. I'll have to reach out."

"You should. If you're looking for a new security manager, he's the best." Alex smiled. Just smiled. Didn't Alex realize John only had to make a call to validate everything he'd just said? And he was the type to do it.

John checked the Breitling on his wrist. "We should go. It was nice to meet you." He reached out and shook Alex's hand.

Emma hugged him and then Harper. "We have to do lunch. I'll call you."

"Yep. Call me." Harper smiled. At least she thought it was a smile. She should get points for behaving like a normal person. It wasn't that she didn't want Emma to call. She just wasn't sure she was ready to dip back into everything the call meant. The parties. The club. The memories. Her thoughts ran rampant.

Silence. While her thoughts ran, apparently so did Emma and John. Harper looked around only to see them disappearing down the hall and around the corner to the family room.

She was alone with Alex. Again. It wasn't as horrible as she wanted to think it was. She leaned into him. "John will probably call your manager at Blink."

"Probably."

"Doesn't that bother you?" She felt her voice drop as she leaned in close. So close her lips were inches from him. So close she could practically taste him. If she stuck out her tongue, she would taste him. That was an awful thought. "You don't actually work there, do you?"

She'd heard cops didn't make a lot of money. Maybe he moonlighted as a security guard at the Blink. Not that she'd know. Because she knew nothing about this guy. And she'd had thoughts about licking him. She pulled back to a respectable distance.

"Ethan and I graduated from the police academy together. He left the force a couple years ago and now runs their security." He twirled his glass. "I'll text him later. He'll have my back."

"It's good to know people in high places."

Alex just smiled. "So, what now?"

"I saw a few couples that would know Madeline. We could mingle a bit more."

"Lead the way." Alex motioned to the door, and Harper led him off to continue the inquisition.

THE HOUSE HAD FILLED up while Harper and Alex were in the dining room. The family room was bustling. Couples played pool and shot darts. A few danced in a nook near the stereo. People sat at the high-top tables, talking and laughing.

This was what Harper remembered. Fun. Conversations. The upstairs festivities were always a draw and she loved them, but this was the true attraction of the club.

And then she saw him. Brown, slick-backed hair and fake-baked skin. Madeline's husband, Paul, stood by one of the tables laughing. Laughing.

His wife had barely been laid in the ground and he…

Harper hated to judge, but how could he be here? Unless he was here alone. Emma and John had invited her over and over again. Told her she didn't need to bring anyone—just come be with her friends. She'd thought about it back then, but she didn't want the pity. Paul didn't appear to be soaking up pity, so he probably didn't notice the looks and stares.

A woman walked up behind Paul. Long blond hair and a large chest that should have cracked her in half at her teeny tiny waist. Seriously. How did she stand upright with all the weight perched on her front?

She wore tight purple leather leggings and a pink and purple striped tank top that showed midriff when she wrapped her arms around Paul. He didn't pull away. He didn't cringe or rip her twiggy arms from his waist.

What. The actual. Heck.

Before she even realized where she was headed, Harper had stomped across the room and stood next to Paul. "What the hell?"

That might have come out a bit harsh. But his wife's body wasn't even cold. Wasn't there a rule that you had to wait till you cancelled your dead spouse's credit cards before you start sleeping with the local strippers? Unless he was using her cards to pay for the strippers.

No, not even he was that big of a dick.

Paul turned to her. "Harper? What are you doing here?" The stunned look on his face was almost comical.

"Me? What are you doing here?"

"I'm visiting with my friends."

"Hi. I'm Britany." Busty blond held out her long-nailed hand. Something about her felt familiar, but Harper couldn't figure out what. She'd swear she'd never met her. You didn't forget someone like Britany.

Harper shook her hand. Honestly, she hated herself for

it. Like she was disrespecting Madeline's memory just by touching the interloper.

"I'm so happy to meet you. Paulie mentioned you before."

Before? "Before what?" How long had *Paulie* been seeing her?

"You seem stressed, honey." Paul put an arm around Harper's shoulder. "You know what you need?"

Harper didn't ask what she needed. She didn't care what he thought. She had a feeling she knew what he was about to say. And she could barely handle Paul's sex jokes before all this shit happened. Now she was about ready to clock him in the face.

"You need a good dicking," Paul whispered in her ear. "I'm willing to help."

"Paul Williams." Alex came up behind Harper, his face a mask of indifference.

Harper didn't think her face was indifferent. She threw Paul's arm off her shoulder.

"Detective, what are you doing here?"

Well, there went the cover. She'd forgotten that Alex probably had a chance to interview Madeline's husband.

"I need to ask you a few questions."

"Didn't we do this already?" Paul's body went rigid and his attitude went from asshole to…to…what was worse than asshole? Double–asshole.

"We need to do this again." Alex smiled at Britany. "And you are?"

"Britany Waters." Britany inched toward Alex, her

wrist bent as she held her hand to him. "I'm Paul's girl-friend. Who are you?"

"Britany. Stop talking without the lawyer present." Paul looked pissed off.

So sad. Not.

"Aren't you my lawyer?" Britany giggled. The girl wasn't a pro at reading the room, even if she was a pro in any other sense.

"How long have you been Paul's girlfriend?"

"She's not answering that." Paul pulled Britany back to his side and she wrapped around him.

"How could you do this to Madeline?" Harper's stomach bottomed out, landing at her toes. The familiar way this blond bimbo ran her fingers down Paul's side. The way she hung on him like a capuchin. This wasn't a new relationship.

"He didn't do nothing to her. He wouldn't even start dating me till she was gone."

"Britany." Paul shook his head.

"What?" She looked confused. Like she hadn't just handed the cops a motive.

"Can you get me a drink?" He disentangled his arms from hers.

"You have a drink."

He tipped the wineglass back, finishing it off. "Please."

"Sure. Anyone else?" Britany handed her full glass to him.

Everyone shook their heads and off she went.

"We should talk outside." Paul tipped his head toward the room full of staring club members, clearly all excited at the free show. He opened the sliding glass doors and walked through. Alex followed and reached behind to shut the door, but Harper stopped him.

"Stay inside." Alex pulled the door shut—because that was going to keep her inside.

She slid the door open and slipped out. Alex watched her follow him into the back yard. He might have shaken his head. Harper might have not cared.

Alex leaned over and whispered, "I'll do the talking."

She nodded. It wasn't like she wanted to say anything anyway. She just wanted to hear what the jerk had to say.

The first thing she noticed was the remodel. Pergolas surrounded the pool. Gauze hung down the sides and was gathered at the center. It looked like a Caribbean paradise. Emma was right. She'd done a lot of work out here.

"When did you start keeping such questionable company?" Paul took a drink from Britany's glass as he glared at Harper. Like it was her fault the cops wanted to question him about the death of his wife. And like he had room to talk.

"I could ask you the same thing." She nodded toward the house. "Please tell me you're not paying her by the hour."

"She's my girlfriend."

"Even better. Schtupping the intern." Harper could just see him as a stereotype. Wife's gone—or maybe before she was gone—playing hide the gavel with all the legal interns. Promising them a promotion and a pay raise to go with their slap and tickle.

"Britany is an old friend."

Britany was barely legal; she wasn't old enough to be an *old* anything.

"She's helping me in my time of need." Somehow Paul even made *time of need* sound tawdry. Every word he said made her want to go and scrub her skin with hand sanitizer.

"How long has Britany been helping with your needs?" See. She could do tawdry too. Although she hadn't meant to use her outside voice. From the glare both men were sending, she had indeed voiced that question.

It was a good question.

"I don't see how that's any of your business." Paul's eyes narrowed into slits. The glass in his hand looked about ready to burst, given his white-knuckled grip. Alex glared at her, too. The look might have said shut up. It might have said he wanted a cupcake. Who knew? She took French in high school. Not asshole.

"It might not be *her* business." Alex leaned toward Paul. Maybe trying to intimidate the man. "But it is mine. What is your relationship with Miss Waters?"

"Fuck buddy."

What a creep.

"And how long have you and Miss Waters been *buddies*?" Alex cleaned it up a bit, but it was still disgusting.

Paul tipped his glass back before walking to the edge of the pool. The water dipped and the lights slithered back and forth over the surface.

"If you can't answer the question, should I ask Miss Waters?"

Paul sighed. "About a year."

A year? His wife died last week. Harper could do the math here. "You were cheating on Madeline?" Slimy man-whore. She always knew she hated Paul, but she could never quite figure out why. Well, hello. He was a cheater.

"Cheating implies she wasn't aware."

Alex stepped in front of Harper. "Your wife knew about Britany."

"She knew there was someone. She just didn't know her name. We found it best not to get into specifics."

"And she was okay with that?" Harper might have voiced that, too.

"We're all adults."

"There's no way Emma and John let you bring your little pet here." Harper's mouth kept moving. Just shoot her now. Although the way Alex was glaring daggers, he looked like he wanted to. To be fair, if he didn't want her to ask questions, why was he allowing breaks in the conversation to do so?

"This is the first time Britany and I have been to the club." Paul took a generous drink from the glass in his hand. Thank goodness Britany gave him her glass, because pretty soon he'd need the refill Britany was fetching. "The club was always mine and Madeline's."

He looked so upset when he talked about the club and his deceased wife, he might actually believe the words coming out of his mouth. Harper might believe him, if not for the fetching blonde.

"Couldn't wait for the body to get cold before you brought your plaything to the club." Harper snorted.

Unladylike. Yes. Natural reaction to BS. Yes. Yes. "Must not have meant much to you."

Even with the faint lighting of the back yard, Harper could make out the red in Paul's face—the vein in his neck.

"What do you know…" Paul was yelling. Good.

She wanted to yell too. "You're a lowlife…"

"You have a lot of nerve…"

"Harper!" Alex's voice drowned them both out and they stopped talking. "Harper, go inside."

She heard him talk. It was hard not to with the deep cop voice he was using. But she was choosing to ignore him and his *go inside* nonsense. She crossed her arms over her chest and glared at Paul. "I have a lot of nerve?" What a freaking hoot. He was practically a brain stem with all the nerves he had—well, minus the brain.

"You sit here questioning my relationship with Maddie. I wasn't fighting with my wife when she died."

"I wasn't fighting with your wife, either. I haven't seen her in months."

"Yeah, you claimed you were her friend and you just disappeared." Paul shook his head and he looked mad. And he might be right.

Harper didn't know that Madeline and Paul had opened up their relationship—if he was telling the truth. She hadn't talked to Madeline at all. She was a shoddy friend. "I might have taken a step back, we weren't fighting."

"Not with Maddie. But you were fighting with your

husband the day he died." Paul tipped his glass toward Alex. "I bet she didn't tell you, did she?"

Alex didn't say anything, but his narrowed eyes and pursed lips said he wasn't going to be quiet on the subject for long. She didn't know when or where, but soon she was going to get an earful.

"It doesn't matter if we were fighting. It was no big deal. This isn't about me. It's about you," she told him.

"No big deal? You kicked him out of the house because he wanted to see his friends and you couldn't handle not being the center of attention for five minutes."

She'd like to say Paul was lying. She'd like to say that she'd never kicked him out. But it was true. She couldn't remember much about the days leading up to Brad's death, but that she remembered. The center of attention garbage was just that. Garbage.

The question was, how did Paul remember? If she hadn't lived those moments over and over again, the conversation might have slipped from her memory. How many times had she talked with Brad. Hundreds? Thousands? How many of those conversations could she recite from memory? A handful at best.

But how did someone forget the last words she'd ever said to her husband? The last thing you'd said before he died?

CHAPTER
TEN

"ENOUGH." Alex's words were harsh and a vein in his neck was pulsing. The fire in his eyes seemed to be aimed at Harper. "Go inside."

Harper thought about staying. She had just as much right to be there as he did. More so. She was a member of the club. Alex was not. She got him in the door. She deserved to be here. But the way his nostrils flared, she didn't think he'd appreciate her bringing that to his attention.

She turned to the sliding glass doors just as they slid open. Emma and John walked out onto the patio, and they looked about as happy as Alex.

"Who are you?" John's narrowed eyes were focused on Alex.

"I'm Detective Cabrero with Las Vegas Metro."

John's nostrils flared as he glared at the detective. But that wasn't what caught Harper's attention. Emma glared at Harper like she'd kicked her puppy. She didn't actually have a puppy, but Emma looked at Harper like she'd kicked the puppy she had never gotten.

"Did you know?" Emma's words were a knife in Harper's chest. Harper not only wanted to hide, she wanted to disappear and not answer. The answer would destroy Emma.

Harper was an asshole.

But Emma had to understand. "Brad might have been killed."

Emma's face didn't change. She looked disappointed and angry. All things Harper could totally understand. How could she have done this to them? They were her friends.

At least they used to be.

"I'm sorry." John seemed to hold a little more pity in his gaze.

Harper was ashamed to admit she'd take it. She didn't want to alienate her friends.

"Oh, please." Paul snorted. "She probably ran him over."

Harper's hands squeezed into fists as her body went rigid. Heat clawed up her back and scratched at her neck. He kept saying horrible things. Things that had never been true. But people were going to believe this if he didn't stop.

Emma took a step back, glancing from Harper to Paul. "Why would she do that?"

Paul saying, "Brad hated her," nearly drowned out Harper's immediate, "I wouldn't."

Brad what? Lying SOB. Harper lunged for Paul, but her

hands didn't make it to his scrawny throat because someone held her back. The muscles holding her in place were too large to be Emma's.

"See. Violent." Paul stepped away from Harper. Unfortunately, she could still hear his mouth. "Brad's lucky she hit him quick with the car."

Oh no he didn't... She was going to kill him. Laws be darned. She didn't care it was illegal. She didn't care she was proving every word coming from his mouth. She just wanted to hurt him.

Just a little.

Paul snarled his lip. "Crazy bitch."

Just a lot. Alex huffed as he tried to keep her in one spot.

"Step back, Harper." Alex's arms pulled tighter. "Or I'll arrest you. Do you want to spend the night in jail?"

Jail. Not a place she wanted to visit. She'd ever been there. She just never wanted to go. A criminal record and private school teacher didn't really go hand and hand. She'd be an ex-con with no job prospects.

Her shoulders relaxed. No jail for her. Not that any of her scenario was actually based on fact. Vice Principal Steve was working off his second DUI. He wasn't allowed to drive the students anywhere, but driving kids around was frowned upon even without the misdemeanor.

She took a deep breath as Alex slowly let her go. She swore her fingernails retracted as she rolled the stress from her shoulders. Her fight-blocker stepped away.

"Are you okay, Harper?" John rested a hand on her shoulder.

Harper was nowhere near okay. Tears bit at the back of her eyes. Her husband might have been murdered and she was being accused of driving the car.

"What about me?" Paul shook his head as his face took on a red hue. He was getting angry. All that bullshit he spewed and Harper getting two minutes of attention was what finally pissed him off. "Why are you asking her if she's okay? She tried to attack me."

"It's under control." Alex sighed, and his shoulders dropped in resignation. He had to know the interrogation part of the evening was over.

"Now it is. What kind of place are you running here, John? Since when can members to bring police officers into the club?"

"They can't." John looked at Harper with a mixture of aggravation and pity.

"What are you going to do about it?" Paul demanded.

"Detective Cabrero, you need to leave." John motioned to the sliding glass door.

"I wouldn't have come here, but I've left multiple messages." Alex offered in the way of an explanation. He almost seemed upset he'd gotten Harper in trouble. His eyes didn't get the memo as he glared at her to keep back.

"It's a rough time right now and I have a business to run." John turned to Harper. "You need to leave too."

"She should be kicked out of the club permanently."

"Enough." John sighed. "Harper, you have to leave tonight. We'll have to discuss the status of your membership."

John held up a hand when Paul started to whine. He

looked at Harper as if the whole situation was ridiculous. And it was ridiculous. Cops could be swingers too. Just not this one. But still.

Which was why she wanted to argue. They'd invited her, but now was not the time or place. And she was still a member. They were going to discuss things. They'd discuss them later, when there wasn't a cop standing in front of them. She'd just go along. She didn't want to give them any reason to ban her.

She had no intention of returning anytime soon. The faces glued to the windows said that this spectacle would be the talk of the house for the foreseeable future. She'd always be the crazy girl who brought a cop and tried to kill Paul. Although most club members would probably respect her for that last part.

John cleared his throat. "Now, Paul. I believe you brought someone tonight as well. Did you provide the appropriate paperwork for your guest?"

Paul looked like John had stolen his wallet—so that would be a no to paperwork. His stare turned to a glare for Harper. Apparently, his lack of paperwork was somehow Harper's fault, too. Go figure.

"I've been a member for years, John. Come on."

"Everyone here has been a member for years." John sighed and pressed two fingers to his forehead. Looked like one hell of a headache was brewing.

Harper could totally understand.

"Paul, you have to leave."

Paul finished the drink in his hand and shoved it into John's chest. "This is bullshit."

John didn't say a word as Paul walked across the back patio and opened the door. "Get your things. Don't talk to anyone. Just leave. All of you."

Harper nodded and walked through the door, beelining for the lockers. This was embarrassing enough without talking to anyone. The room only had a handful of people, and they were staring. They all had mouths. One would think swingers would have better things to do with their mouths than gossip. One would be wrong.

She gathered her contents of the locker, leaving Alex's phone, and walked through the front room. Symphony held out her bottle of wine and Harper snagged it as she walked past. "Thanks."

Symphony nodded and picked up another bottle. Probably Paul and his undocumented companion.

Harper didn't stick around long enough to check. She walked out the front door. The security guard smiled as she passed him. He must not have heard the drama from the back yard. But he would. Everyone would. She was going to be hearing about that for months. Or longer.

She stomped toward her car. Getting this whole night over with was priority one. Grabbing a pint of ice cream and finding some Netflix was priority two. There was a new series she'd wanted to watch, and now she could. Bonus.

"Do you have something you wanted to tell me?" Alex's voice stopped her and the wonderful Netflix visions in their tracks. She turned around and Alex was spinning his keys on his fingers. Scowling.

Which made no sense. He had nothing to be angry

about. He didn't almost get kicked out of the club, permanently. She did. Breath skittered out of her lungs on a whoosh. All the energy of the evening drained down through her toes.

"No." She shook her head. She was tired of talking and tired of fighting. Even a Netflix show was starting to sound like too much work. "I've got nothing."

"You were fighting with your ex the night he was killed." It sounded so bad the way he said it.

"Yes."

"And you didn't think to tell me."

"I didn't think it mattered. I'd talked to the cops when everything happened with Brad. And it was ruled an accident."

"Did you tell them the two of you had a fight?"

"No. They hadn't asked." She crossed her arms over her chest. "Just like you hadn't asked."

"So, you'll only divulge information if I ask?"

Harper glared at the arrogant man scowling at her. He didn't own scowling. She could do it back. Just watch. She narrowed her eyes a bit more. Her face pinched. She could actually feel it pinching.

His anger didn't seem to ebb or flow. He just stared at her. Like it was her fault she didn't tell him about Brad. Jerk. He wanted information. She had information.

"I wet the bed when I was seven. That's the first time I remember being yelled at when I was a kid. I pulled Jill's hair in third grade because she stole my Hello Kitty lunchbox. I kicked Brandon Pearce when I was in eighth grade because he grabbed my boob. Didn't even ask."

"Really?"

"I know. You'd think by eighth grade he would know to ask, but to be fair, the me-too movement hadn't begun. The worst part, it wasn't even a good grab. It was more of a honk." She held up her hands and tapped her fingers together like she was squeezing an air horn. "Freshman year in high school, I slapped my best friend because she switched our calculus exams. I got my one and only F in that class. Had she asked, I would've given her my exam. She was failing the class and no matter how much I tutored her, it wasn't helping. I wouldn't have let her fail."

Alex shook his head as he pinched the bridge of his nose.

"Don't worry, I just have to get through my college indiscretions and then we can talk all about adulthood."

"Why?"

"You wanted information without questions. I have tons of information. But without the questions, I'm not sure what you want to know."

"I just don't understand." Britany's muted inside-voice rose to outside voice level.

Paul had his arm around her waist. "It's not you they have a problem with. It's me."

"But they never had a problem with you until I came along." She hiccupped. "Your friends hate me."

"They don't hate you. They don't even know you." Paul walked down the driveway and spotted Harper.

How did she know she was spotted? His face took on that red blotchy angry look. Twice in one night. He had better watch his blood pressure. He was a ticking time bomb.

"Why don't you go start the car. I'll meet you in a minute and we'll head home." Paul brushed the tip of his finger along the bridge of her nose. She giggled. If he wasn't such a creep, it would have been darn cute.

Britany ran to the car—her chest bouncing—which should have given her two black eyes. But she seemed to make it there unscathed. She slid into the driver's seat. Rap thumped from inside the car as the ignition kicked on. She sat inside dabbing at her eyes.

Paul turned to Harper. "I hope you're happy. All she wanted to do was fit in, but you couldn't just leave it alone. You could never leave anything alone."

"Did you think maybe you did this? Maybe next time wait till your wife's body is cold before you bring your *buddy*." It wasn't rude to call her that. Not when she was repeating what Paul said. But the way he treated her, seemed like she was more than he let on.

"You don't know anything. You didn't have to take it out on her." Paul slammed a hand through his hair and turned to Alex. "Good luck dealing with her, pal."

Well, crap. Harper watched Paul walk away and she wanted to apologize. Not to him. He was a dick. But he was right. None of this was Britany's fault. And from the look on her face and the tears in her eyes, she got the brunt of it all. It wasn't fair.

Paul walked to the driver's side and waited for Britany to step out. She walked around and waved. Her attempt at a smile so pathetic, but she'd tried.

Harper waved back. The poor girl got stuck in the middle. And it made Harper feel like crap and just... tired. "I'm going home." She headed for her car. She was so done with the detective. Hell, with the whole day.

"We're not done here."

We might not be, but she most certainly was. She clicked the locks and started the engine. She sat and watched Britany slide into the passenger side of Paul's car and before she had her seatbelt locked, Paul was gunning from between two cars and speeding down the road. If that little display was supposed to make him look less suspicious, he was doing a really bad job.

In fact, something he said niggled at the back of her mind. *You could never leave anything alone.*

It was always her downfall. And it was the thing that had gotten between Brad and Paul the week before he'd died. Which gave Paul a motive. Now she just needed to know if he had an alibi. Because she might be done with the detective, but she wasn't done with this investigation. Paul killed Brad. She was sure of it.

And he killed his wife. She just had to prove it. There was just the problem of an alibi. Did he have one? And she had a feeling the person who knew was about to become Harper's new best friend. Well, after Harper begged for forgiveness.

She looked in the rearview mirror as she drove away. The detective stood there watching her taillights. She had to follow through with this because she had a feeling she'd just made the list of suspects. And with her hasty withdrawal, she might even be at the top of that list.

CHAPTER
ELEVEN

THE NEXT MORNING, Harper drove through the tree-lined streets of Summerlin. The houses were large and relatively new. She pulled into the driveway of an ultra-modern home—all angles, dark gray stucco with a black garage door.

She knew it was the house, not only because she'd been there a couple of years ago when Madeline and Paul had bought the house, but because Britany stood by the front door. When Harper had gone through security, they'd mentioned they would check with the owner. Thankfully the owner was Britany.

Which meant Paul wasn't there.

Perfect.

Harper angled out of the car and walked toward the front door. "Nice house."

Britany looked over her shoulder and shook her head. It was not like Britany had much say in its purchase, but she had done some work out front. Where once there'd been stone and cacti, now there was grass and flowering bushes.

"I love what you've done with the yard." A trellis leaned against the side of the house, a red flowering vine crawling up the rungs.

"Thanks. Madeline did most of it, but I added these." Britany smiled and pointed to the layer of pink flowers.

"The colors are beautiful." And they were. Next to the waterfall of red was a row of blue agave grass and a layer of the pink. "Is that Nandina?"

"It is." Britany's face lit with a smile. "Aren't they amazing?"

"They are." Harper was here to butter her up, but on this she wasn't lying. The yard was beautiful. Now was time for the buttering. "I was hoping I could talk to you. I owe you an apology."

"Oh." Britany's sparkle disappeared as she looked to the ground. "You don't owe me anything."

"Of course I do."

The fact that Britany didn't think she was due an apology about broke Harper's heart. Paul might be an absolute tool, but he seemed to have really great taste in women. Really great taste in women who had really bad taste in men.

"Would you like to come inside for something to drink?"

"Sure." Harper thought this whole thing would be harder—maybe a bit more groveling. But why question it when she was getting what she wanted. She followed Britany inside.

The house was still gorgeous, but the doilies and flowers were gone. It had been an interesting contrast—white counters and black cabinets with splashes of color to break up the monotony.

No more flowers. Now it was brightly colored furniture and light-yellow walls. Color popped from every surface, whether it was a multi-colored throw or a bright red vase. It was warm and loud.

Harper wasn't about to get into all of that though. More buttering. "The house looks amazing."

"I know, right. I want to have a designer come in and just gut it all, but we might not stay here. The memories are too much for Paul."

"I understand." That was the first thing she'd done—found a new place to live. The memories were going to swallow her whole if she didn't. It didn't hurt that she couldn't afford the rent any longer. Made the choice super easy.

Well, not easy at all. She'd cried for weeks and drove by the house for months. But the cost made it necessary. And she only felt mildly guilty for having to give up their shared home.

"I try to understand, but I haven't really lost anyone yet. Not even my grandparents."

"You're very lucky." If only Harper had been that lucky. She'd lost her grandparents, parents, and husband. If she really thought about it, she'd think she was a jinx who didn't deserve to be happy.

Good thing she didn't like to really think about it.

"So, the guy you were with last night was pretty hot."

Britany's lips quirked at the side, like she as sharing a secret with Harper.

"Yep." Unfortunately, hot didn't always equate to nice. Especially in the detective's case.

"I don't know how you can date a cop. I've never trusted them. But there's someone for everyone, I guess. How long have you two been together?" Britany thought they were together. Harper thought everyone knew that she'd just brought him into the club to interrogate the guests. Although, there was a better chance of Britany answering the questions if Harper didn't cavort with untrustworthy cops. She didn't seem to mind if Harper dated them.

"Not long."

Britany led her through the high-ceilinged foyer to the kitchen.

"Would you like a drink?" Britany stood at the large white island and leaned against the granite.

"No thanks."

"I make a really great strawberry lemonade." Britany looked so hopeful.

Harper couldn't disappoint her. "That sounds great."

Britany poked her head in the fridge and pulled out a plastic container and a jug. She scooped some strawberries into two glasses.

"So how long have you and Paul been dating?"

"We've been dating on and off for a year."

The answer matched Paul's. He wasn't lying about that. "What about Madeline?"

"She knew." Britany cut a lemon down the center with a smack as the knife hit granite.

"She knew about you?" Skepticism tinted Harper's voice, but this didn't make sense. Paul acted as if Madeline knew and was okay with the whole situation. Harper would like to think she knew Madeline better than that.

"She didn't care."

"You heard her say she didn't care?"

"No, we never really met." Britany squeezed a lemon into the first glass. She twisted another lemon and cut it down the center. She pressed it into the second glass. "That's not true. We actually did meet last year at the Sláinte hotel Christmas party."

"The one at Club Limerick?" Harper and Brad had gone to the party since Brad had been the Realtor on a land acquisition for the expansion of the hotel.

"Yeah, were you there?"

"We were." And then it hit Harper. That's where she knew Britany from. The Christmas party. The one where Madeline had broken down and cried about her and Paul losing their connection. She'd never mentioned there was a Britany involved. She'd said they weren't communicating because he was out of the house so much.

Harper assumed it meant he was working. She'd told Madeline to take him away from work. She'd suggested a great resort in Mexico. Madeline had cried, wiped her eyes and said she'd give it a try.

They'd never gone to Mexico. Not that Harper knew about. A few days later Brad had been killed and Harper had lost contact with her old life.

"I don't know." Britany stirred her glass, the strawberries swirling to the top.

Harper must have gotten so lost in her own thoughts that she'd missed the preparation. But the look on Britany's face said she was lost too. Making the drinks by rote.

"I don't think she knew who I was, but she was so nice when I walked up. Once I said my name, she turned cold. It's like she knew. But I don't know how she could. Paul said they didn't discuss the names of their friends. But if she didn't know, why the change?"

"Maybe she didn't want him to see other people."

"Maybe." Britany slid a strawberry wedge on the side of the glass and slid a plastic straw inside before handing Harper the drink. It really was beautiful. The strawberries had sunk to the bottom, leaving a pink pool with the pink tinging the drink incrementally up to the yellow top.

"I don't know how she couldn't know with Brainiac. Although, I always felt like she wasn't the nicest of people. Like it was okay for her to play, but not Paul. Even though they agreed. Hell, Paul didn't even want to do it. It was all her. Then she'd get upset."

Britany was rambling and honestly, Harper had no idea what she was talking about. "Who's Brainiac?"

"Her boyfriend."

"I thought they didn't share names."

"That's why I only know him as Brainiac. I never found out his real name. I don't think Paul even knows." She picked up her own drink and took a pull. "I don't think she would tell him."

"He told you she was lying to him?" None of this sounded like Madeline. Lying. Hiding. Cheating. That was all Paul. And this poor girl was so blinded by him, she couldn't see he painted the picture he wanted her to see.

"Yeah." She swirled her straw in the drink. Pink mixed with yellow and then her gaze flew up. "How is it?"

It? The drink. Harper brought the glass to her mouth and took a swallow. Tart of the lemon and sweet of the strawberry mixed together. "Delicious."

Britany glowed with pride. It was sweet. This woman was sweet. And she obviously believed every line of bullshit Paul had fed her.

Britany stirred her drink as Harper took another drink. "Does everyone hate me?"

"Who?"

"Everyone at the club?" Britany was swathed in self-esteem issues. "Although Amelia was nice to me."

"Amelia is nice, but why would everyone hate you?"

"I saw the way they looked at me. They blame me. For Paul and Madeline. They know it's not his fault, so it must be mine."

"They don't blame you." They did blame Paul. Harper didn't want to get into that right now. Britany seemed to have drunk the Kool-Aid—the same crap Madeline drank. She couldn't stop making excuses for the guy either.

Harper sucked down her lemonade with a smile. Well, her mouth was too busy drinking to smile, which meant it was also too busy to start bad-mouthing Paul.

She didn't need to badmouth him, He knew how Harper felt, but Britany didn't deserve the massive complaining session Harper wanted to bestow upon her. One that started with "are you crazy for believing this guy?" And ended with "blink twice if you're here against your will."

Surprisingly, she seemed to be here of her own volition.

"I would really like to hang out for a while longer, but I have a mani-pedi in a half-hour."

"That sounds like fun." And it did. Harper couldn't remember the last time she'd gotten her nails done.

"You should come with me." Britany's eyes sparked to life. All the heaviness of the former conversation was gone.

"I don't have a reservation." And it would probably be impossible to get one this short notice. Which was kind of a bummer. If someone had told her last night that she'd be disappointed she wasn't getting a mani-pedi with Paul's side piece, she wouldn't have believed it. But here they were.

"So, they can get you in." She bounced up and down and waved her phone. "I texted Reynaldo and you are totally in."

"Great." And it was, except she'd have to pay for it. "But I think I have to pass."

"Why?" Britany's face drooped like she just found out there was no Santa Claus.

Harper stared at her hands—jagged nails with overrun nail beds. A manicure would fix the knives on her fingertips. She wanted to tell her the truth, that she couldn't really afford it. She was barely able to cover her rent these days. But it just sounded pathetic—even to her—and she was the one living it.

"Come on. He's a whiz with cuticles. You'll never see them so vibrant. And he's really discreet. It wasn't until Madeline died that I found out he was seeing her every Friday for years." Britany walked into the hall and pulled her purse from a closet.

"She did?" Madeline went to the spa every Friday? There were quite a few things Harper didn't know about her friend.

"Apparently, she had a standing appointment and then about a little over a year ago, she just stopped showing up regularly. Kept the appointment but rarely came in."

"What happened?"

Britany's head tilted to the side. "I don't know. I didn't think to ask. Maybe Reynaldo knows."

Those were the magic words that would get her to shell out a hundred bucks on nail polish. "Let's go."

"I'll drive." Britany led her through the kitchen and out the side door to the garage. Two cars sat inside the three-car garage. One hid under a giant tarp. It looked taller than the car Britany had just chirped to life with the fob in her hand.

"What's that?" Harper nodded to the tarp she wanted to peel back like a Christmas present. But she needed to stay on the good side of the woman that would help get answers.

"Madeline's car." She frowned and shook her head.

"May I see it?"

Britany bit her lip, like a war was going off between her

ears. "Paul doesn't like anyone to touch her car." Which meant Harper really needed to see it. He was hiding something. He was always hiding something.

"Anyway." Britany smiled. "We don't want to be late."

No, wouldn't want that. Harper climbed in the passenger side and stared at the front of the car, willing the tarp to rise in game-show fashion. But it didn't move.

The little red sports car purred to life and they sped out of the garage as the door opened.

The garage door closed and they were off. But this wasn't over. Harper was going to get a look at that car no matter what it took.

CHAPTER
TWELVE

THE LOW HUM of tinkling music met Harper's ears after the door to the spa closed. Gone was the blinding sun; in its place, soft lighting and warm tones. A light wood desk stood off to one side with white fabric chairs surrounding a wicker table. Women sat in bright white robes hiding behind the pages of their magazines.

Harper followed Britany past a four-panel screen covered in cherry blossoms to the front desk. On top of the desk bamboo plants sat in varying sizes. The room was an ode to relaxation. All it needed was a large sand garden with a rake to fully complete the picture.

"Namaste." The woman behind the counter placed her hands on the black and gold kimono and nodded in a small bow. Her unnaturally strawberry-red hair shimmered in the soft light.

"Namaste, Cynthia. We have a consultation with Reynaldo." Britany's pep was somehow muted by the earth-tones. Her voice was barely above a whisper.

"Very well." Cynthia poked at her computer and looked at Harper. "And you are?"

"HARPER LANGE!" Harper didn't yell, nor did she talk all that loud. But the look on Cynthia's face, and the shush on her lips said she might as well have.

"This is a relaxation spa." Cynthia pointed at the sign above the desk. *Please observe silence.* "We have people meditating."

"Sorry." Harper cringed and lowered her voice to barely a whisper. "Harper Lange."

"Yes. You have a last-minute appointment." The glare deepened. "And you didn't come in early to choose your color and fill out paperwork."

This must be some pretty important paperwork that it required the evil eye.

"That's my fault. We wanted to come in together." Britany looked worried, like this peace toting woman might block their mani-pedi.

And if the look on her face said anything, Evil-counter-lady wanted nothing more in life than to ban them from their relaxation services. But instead of lifting her charm-bracelet covered arm and pointing at the door, she handed Harper a clipboard. "Fill this out."

Harper stood looking at the clipboard. No one told her there'd be homework, but it was the price to pay for information—oh, and healthy cuticles.

Grabbing the clipboard, Harper read over the questions. Or at least she tried to.

"Now," Evil-counter-lady barked. Which was quite the feat in a hushed whisper.

Harper nodded and started filling in the spaces. Name. Date. She wasn't sure if anything she was writing was true, but getting words on paper was more important than accuracy at this point. At least her scribbling had gotten the dog to quit barking.

A practically teenaged attendant walked through a back door and held it open before whispering, "Britany."

Britany leaned over and smiled. "I'll see you back there."

Back there? Harper was an adult and she could handle herself, but she thought they'd go back together. Apparently not. Britany disappeared behind the door and Harper was left holding the clipboard.

She flipped over the pages left. Three. Three pages of questions. *Have you ever had gels or acrylics?* Yes. *Any nail issues?* Who the hell knew.

The teen had come back and stood in the doorway. She whispered, "Harper. Did you choose your color?"

No. Harper grabbed her half-filled in paperwork and walked to the door. She hadn't even finished her spa-day homework. Who had time for color? "Pink?"

"Which pink?" The teen waved her arm at a wall of nail polish in the back corner that was concealed by a short wall. She hadn't even noticed it when she walked in. But now, all she saw was fifty different variations of pink.

"Let's go clear instead." There was only one variation on clear. Hopefully.

The teen grabbed a clear bottle from the wall and waved her through the door.

The soft tinkling music shadowed Harper as she

followed the girl inside and past soft peach walls with white carpet. They walked into a room lined with black pedicure chairs.

The teen stood next to the chair where Britany was leaning her head against the head rest. Water jets swirled at her bare feet.

The teen looked over the paperwork as she motioned for Harper to get into the chair. "Is all of this correct?"

Harper thought about saying no. What would they do? Kick her out for falsifying pedicure documentation? She had a feeling this place might actually do that.

"It's all correct." The bowl of water was filling as Harper sat in the leather chair and pulled off her shoes and socks. She slid her feet in the warm water as the girl turned off the spigot and started the jets.

The warm bubbles circled her feet and soothed the ache she didn't even know was there. Massage rollers spun up and down along her back, slowly kneading her muscles. So relaxing. Her eyes closed as the soft hum of music barely echoed past the gurgle and hiss of the jets.

"Hey, sexy momma." A man in black fabric pants and snug yellow tank walked up to Britany and air kissed her cheek with a whisper.

"You flirt." Britany batted her lashes as Reynaldo—Harper assumed it was Reynaldo—took Britany's hand and fondled her fingers.

"These look amazing." Reynaldo brought her finger to his face like he was trying to gauge the cut and clarity of her nails.

"Then I guess I can go home." Britany lifted her butt

from the seat and tried to pull her hand away, but Reynaldo must have grabbed on tighter.

"Oh, honey, they don't look that good. Sit your ass down." Reynaldo ticked his tongue. "You have beautiful hands."

Britany giggled and a blush colored her face. "You're going to make Paul jealous."

"Girl." The *ur* part of the word seemed to last forever. "He should be jealous. You are super-fine and he's..."

"Don't be a dick." Britany slapped at his arm.

"Me?" Reynaldo pointed to himself and widened his eyes to innocent bunny rabbit before laughing like an evil hyena. The laugh died on his lips when he turned his attention to Harper.

Britany must have noticed that his attention was no longer on her. Or she just noticed the silence. "This is the friend I texted you about."

"Hi, friend." Reynaldo picked up Harper's hand and turned it side to side. Scrutiny. "Hmm..."

What "hmm" meant, she had no idea. She wasn't sure she wanted to know. He wasn't cringing or screaming, so there was that. But she knew her cuticles—you couldn't miss them. They were taking over her nails. So the noise coming from his chest probably wasn't good.

He dropped the hand without so much as one "girl." He grabbed a bottle of nail polish from behind Britany's head. "Feeling lilac today?"

"It's my signature color."

"I thought violet was your signature color." He shook the bottle and the beads inside mixed the ingredients.

"It is, but lilac is my serious signature color."

Reynaldo's eyebrows jumped as Britany laughed.

"How's Marquetta?" Britany rested her head on the back of the chair.

"She's crazy as a crackhead in a police evidence locker." He dropped to a stool in front of Britany and pulled her foot from the bubble bath. He started trimming and scraping at Britany's toenails. "She wants peacocks now."

"Peacocks?" Britany's eyes grew.

"At the reception."

Harper's question of "why" came out at the same time as Britany's, "That's amazing."

"Apparently one of the Housewives had them at their wedding." Reynaldo must have heard Harper's question. "I just want to get married. Nice church. Family. Maybe a cake with a bride and groom on top. I don't need all this crap."

"What you call crap, we call necessities." Britany was all on board with peacocks. Why did anyone need peacocks? For anything. Unless you're a television network—or you were Britany or Marquetta. "We dream about our weddings our whole life."

"Have you dreamt about your wedding, Brit?" He pulled her other foot from the bath and drained the water, before attacking her foot with pedicure tools.

"I have," Britany gushed.

"How about you?" He looked over at Harper, expecting an answer. She didn't want to admit to it, but she'd had a book filled with ideas starting with her first potential fiancé that she'd cut out of "Tiger Beat."

"I dreamed about it." And cut out pictures and created a book. She still had the darn thing.

"In your dream, were there peacocks?" One of the teens showed up with two bags full of pink wax and handed it to Reynaldo. He slid a bag over Britany's feet and twisted the top around her ankles.

"No."

"But wouldn't that be awesome." Britany leaned forward as Reynaldo attached the other bag to her other foot. "The peacock opening its feathers. All bright colors next to the white of the dress."

"It would be nice." Even Harper could admit the bright blue and green contrasting against the stark white would be striking.

"Nice enough to hand over a thousand?"

"Dollars?" Britany said the word Harper was thinking. No matter how gorgeous, it wasn't worth a grand.

"Not pesos, honey."

"For one bird?" For a thousand bucks, there should be multiple, and they should wear little neckties and carry drinks to the guests.

"One bird for two hours."

Two hours?

"You don't get to keep them? Maybe walk them on little peacock leashes." Harper kind-of wanted to walk a peacock now.

"That I would pay for." Reynaldo laughed. "So, Brit, how was the party Paul took you to? Did you meet all his friends?"

Britany's lips turned down as her gaze moved to the floor.

Shit. The poor girl just wanted to be accepted. And Harper had been so focused on Paul, she'd been a jerk.

"Did Paul ditch you?" Reynaldo pulled the plug on Britany's foot tub and swore under his breath. "I knew that guy couldn't be trusted."

"No." Britany tried to pretend not to wipe away a tear. "It was just very overwhelming to meet all his friends."

"You sure?" He looked skeptical. Smart guy.

"Absolutely." The chirp was back in Britany's voice. If she hadn't watch it happen, Harper wouldn't believe the girl had been on the verge of crying a second ago.

"Hey." Reynaldo fiddled with the wax bags and then used a towel to soak up loose water around the tub. "Did you hear Jenna quit?"

"Ooh, I loved the way she did my hair." Britany pouted but kept talking. "But her brother was getting out of jail. Maybe they moved away."

"Like Gretchen."

"I never met Gretchen." Britany and Reynaldo talked, back and forth saying names that Harper didn't know. There was barely a breath between the words—a gossip-dance between the two.

And then he was standing up, opening his hand to Britany. "Veronica, can you start a hand soak for Britany."

Britany, who was without pink bags—when did those disappear?— but somehow had white flip flops on her feet followed Veronica out of the room. The other chairs were silent. The room was empty as Reynaldo moved his stool in front of Harper.

Reynaldo gently cupped the bottom of her foot and set it on the top lip of the bowl. He rubbed the foot semi-dry and grabbed a metal torture device. He brought the clippers to her toes and started snipping. He was so gentle. "So, how do you know Brit?"

How did she know Brit? That was a loaded question. She couldn't mention the club. She wasn't sure if he knew about it and she wasn't about to break the first rule of sex club.

"I was friends with Madeline."

Reynaldo's clippers stopped mid clip. "If you were friends with Madeline, why are you out with Britany?"

"My husband was friends with Paul. Just curious about the new woman."

He nodded and finished clipping her damp nails, pulling out a nail file. He filed the ends of the freshly cut nails. The board tickled against the wet tips of her toes, but she held back a giggle.

"Befriending the enemy."

"She's not the enemy." No matter how much Harper wanted to hate her and call her the enemy, she just couldn't find a reason. She was sweet and just wanted to be liked.

"No?" He switched feet and began to tickle her other toes. Why was this so damn ticklish?

"No." She squashed the urge to pull her feet back and slap his hand. Between the tickling and calling Britany the enemy, the slapping seemed like a good idea. But she managed to refrain. "Britany and Madeline aren't the enemy. Paul is."

A burst of laughter rumbled from Reynaldo. "That he is."

He pulled out a giant filing board with a handle and cupped her ankle. The board ran back and forth on the bottom of her foot. "So, you didn't drink the Kool-Aid?"

"Which Kool-Aid?" Harper's shoulders relaxed. No more tickling.

"The Paul-is-awesome Kool-Aid."

Paul was the furthest thing from awesome, and the fact he attracted good women spoke to some sort of blind devotion. Or drugs.

"I'm not Paul's biggest fan." Understatement. "But I didn't see you at the monthly meeting."

"There's a meeting? I'm in." Reynaldo dropped the large file in the foot sink as a bag appeared at his side. The pedicure was almost over and she hadn't asked one question. Although it was fun to talk crap about Paul, that wasn't why she was here.

Reynaldo slid her foot into the plastic bag and pink goop slid between her toes and stung her raw skin. The sting disappeared and only warmth was left.

"So, you were friends with Madeline."

"You could call us friends. She came for a mani-pedi once a week." His eyes took on a faraway look. "We talked about everything. She was the one who reminded me that if I loved Marquetta, I should put a ring on it."

"Did she talk about Paul?"

"Why do you think I hate the man?" He shook his head

as he slid her other foot in a bag of goop. "He never treated her right."

"What did he do?"

"Well, you probably know, but he didn't take care of her. She never would have started seeing that other guy if he took care of her."

"The other guy?"

"She called him B." He emptied the foot tub and wiped down the area.

Brainiac. "Did she say anything else about him?"

"Weren't you friends with her?" Reynaldo peeled the first bag off her foot. "What's your name again?"

"Harper Lange."

He moved her foot to the lip of the tub and peeled off the other bag. Didn't say anything, just worked. He turned on the foot sink and rinsed off her feet. "She mentioned you." His tone was so serious and all the bubble was gone from his movement and his eyes. The smile was gone too.

"Did she say bad things?" Harper couldn't imagine Madeline saying a bad word about anyone.

"She told me about your husband." He used a fresh towel and dried her feet before pulling out a bottle of lotion and massaging it into her skin. "I think she took it pretty hard. She started missing appointments."

"When Brad died?" Britany said Madeline had started acting weird a few months before she died, but she hadn't mentioned it had started back then.

"Yeah. She started talking about having one life and making herself happy. She talked me into proposing to

Marquetta—best decision I ever made. And I think I talked her into leaving that tool she was married to."

"You did?" Could Madeline have been ready to leave him? Maybe for the other guy. That couldn't have sat well with him.

"Yeah, told her to run to B and don't look back."

"Did she leave him?"

"I don't know. She had been cancelling appointments, but a few weeks after that, she was cancelling more and more appointments. And when she would actually show, she wouldn't talk. Just said everything was okay."

"Did she say why she was cancelling appointments?"

"She said something about going to California."

"What was in California?"

"I don't know. I assumed it was the boyfriend." Reynaldo shook the bottle of nail polish and opened the top. He quickly painted her buffed and moisturized toenails.

She didn't have much time. The room was still empty —thank goodness—but when they moved to the manicure room, she couldn't exactly ask questions in front of Britany. She had to go for quality. So, what were the important ones?

Shit. She didn't know. So she'd go for quantity and hope for the best.

"Why did she want to leave Paul?"

"He wasn't treating her well." He shook his head. "It got worse about a year ago. I figured she was just fed up with him. I'm so afraid the same thing will happen to Britany."

Harper could admit she was afraid of the same thing. The woman was sweet and Paul was Paul. Hell, he might have run down his wife. But it didn't explain the connection to Brad.

"It was that party."

"What was that party?" Harper might have missed what he was saying.

"That hotel Christmas party."

"At Sláinte?" The party where Madeline broke down and cried. Where Britany was first introduced. The party seemed to be a turning point.

"Yeah."

"Madeline cried at the party. She said she and Paul were losing their connection." Harper thought the whole night was weird, but when she'd talked to Madeline the next day, she chalked it up to drinking too much. But maybe something else was going on. "Did she say anything to you?"

"No. She'd gotten tight lipped about everything and it just got worse." He capped the polish and set it off to the side. "She kept talking about life being short."

"She met Britany at the party. Could that have sent her over the edge?"

"She knew Paul was seeing other people."

"But knowing and actually meeting her competition are two different things."

"True." Reynaldo held open white flip flops and slid her foot inside slowly, so her tacky nails wouldn't smudge. He slid on the second flop and lifted to his feet. "She just changed. Things changed."

She stood. Someone had to know what really happened the night of the Christmas party when Madeline's world turned upside down. There wasn't anyone from the party to ask. Madeline and Brad were both gone, and she'd rather not talk to Paul unless required.

She needed answers. She just wasn't sure where to find them.

CHAPTER
THIRTEEN

TWO HOURS LATER, Harper's fingers were buffed and shiny. She was sitting in Britany's car, as Brittany pulled next to the tarp-covered car in Paul's garage. Maybe not a car. It looked more like the height of an SUV. She'd only really know if she could get a look at it. That tarp was calling for her to pull it off like Jason Momoa's t-shirt. She had to get alone with the vehicle.

She just couldn't do it in front of Britany. The girl thought Harper hated her last night—and she hadn't been far off the mark. But Britany was sweet and she was cool to hang out with. Harper didn't want Britany to think she was using her. It might have started that way, but she really liked the woman.

She slid her phone from her pocket and dropped it between the seat and the door. She'd realize it was missing and have to run back. *Oops. My bad.* Not a lie since her phone was currently wedged in the gap.

Harper followed Britany into the house.

"Do you need to leave or would you like another lemonade?"

She couldn't believe the words that were about to come out of her mouth, but she really did want to stay. It might have to do a little with the dropped phone and somewhat the lemonade, but it was also the company.

"I'd love another lemonade."

"Great. Do you want me to show you how to make it? We got distracted before." Britany's smile was filled with expectation.

"Sure." No matter how distracted, Harper could probably figure out how to put strawberries and lemonade in a glass. It wasn't like she needed to take notes.

Or did she…on her phone.

"I'll take notes on my phone." Harper felt at her hip. "Crap. I think I dropped my phone in your car. I'm going to run and grab it."

"I can get it." Britany literally jumped toward the back door.

"Oh no, why don't you get all the ingredients we need for the drinks, and I'll get my phone so I don't miss any steps."

"Great idea." Britany pulled two glasses from the cabinet.

Definitely a great idea. Harper ran for the back door and slipped inside the garage. Darkness overwhelmed her. No windows. No lights. She felt along the closest car, running her hand along the hood. She followed the windshield to the door handle. She lifted and the light spilled from inside of the car. But it wasn't bright enough to make it to the tarp. And Harper needed to be able to see.

She looked at the front floor and next to the seat. Nothing. This was where she dropped the phone. It had to be there. She slid her hand between the seat and frame.

Or not. Shit.

Harper kneeled and pushed her hand in farther, fingers bumping against something cold. Metal. She slipped her fingers under the seat and goo squished between them. Wet coated her nails.

Still no phone. Which wasn't necessarily a bad thing. She didn't want her phone anywhere near the goo.

She pulled her hand out and looked at the wet. Wasn't blood. Maybe clear? Definitely gross. She rubbed her hand along the carpeted floor of the car, getting rid of the goop.

She ran her other hand along the gap toward the back seat. She felt the hard case of her cell phone, pulling it to the front. Turning it over, she ran her hand along the top. There was no sticky. Thank goodness.

She swiped up and turned on her flashlight. The goo on her fingers was clear. Who knew what it was. Not that she had time to figure out. She needed to move the tarp. Walking toward the covered car, she leaned down and gripped the edge of the cover. This was it. She lifted the fabric and it locked in place.

The front hooked on the bumper. She pulled the material out from under the front bumper and levered it over the metal.

"What are you doing?" A male voice that she shouldn't recognize came from the house door.

She dropped the cover and jumped back before turning toward the sound. Her cellphone was aimed at the detective. "I was looking for my phone."

Detective Cabrero stood in the doorway. He looked good for a jerk. Black jeans and white collared shirt. The top two buttons were left open showing just enough skin to make her want to run her fingers along his jaw and lower. He was staring at her phone with a smirk on his face. "It's in your hands."

"Well, I just found it." Jackass.

"What's under there?" Alex hit the light switch near the door. "You could turn off your phone now."

Harper could have turned on the light if she had been able to see it. She'd been in a hurry. She slid her phone light off. "Toaster."

"What?"

"You asked what's under the cover. It's a toaster."

"That is one large toaster." He walked up and leaned over Harper. His face so close. His body hovered over hers.

He smelled so good and his lips were right there. They were right by her face. And did she mention, he smelled so good. Mint. He tasted like mint. At least she figured he did. He was close, she could smell him. And he smelled like man and spicy outdoors. She leaned away. No matter how much she wanted to dive in and take another sniff, this was no good.

He inched closer. Her body hummed and her stomach roared to life— She honestly couldn't tell if it was a good thing or a bad thing. She didn't want him to kiss her. Did she? But still he moved closer. He leaned in, his breath a ghost along her lips. Her eyes fluttered shut. Waiting for impact.

Nothing. She opened her eyes as he leaned toward her. His stare was on her, but his body was aimed at the car. She followed the muscles in his arm to his hand—which wasn't on her. Grabbing the material, he lifted the cover.

The left front fender gleamed a crumpled blue. Dents and dimples lined the front toward the Ford emblem. The cracked light was jagged. He pulled the material farther.

"What are you doing?" Paul stood in the doorway.

Caught again. Harper stepped away. "Nothing."

The detective hadn't got the memo on how to behave when caught red-handed. You jump back and lie. They taught that in kindergarten.

"I was looking at this car. What happened here?" Alex went with truth. Go figure.

"Where?" Paul walked in the garage. He looked pissed.

Alex pulled the tarp back. "What happened to the front bumper?"

Paul's face fell. "It was my wife's car. She hit a deer a few months ago."

"You didn't get it fixed?" Alex eyed the damage.

"I tried, but she yelled and cried." Paul tapped his hand on his leg.

"Right." Harper stopped her eyes form rolling. "Like she didn't want to get her car fixed."

"You weren't here." Paul glared at Harper, moving closer. The implication was clear. She'd abandoned Madeline. And she had. "You didn't see what she was like."

"I was dealing with a lot."

"So was everyone else." Paul stepped back and raised his arms. He almost looked ready to cry, but Harper knew him better than that. "You need to leave."

"I have some questions." Alex dropped the tarp.

"I'm not feeling up to answering them right now." Paul glared at Harper and moved to the light switch on the wall. Instead of hitting the light, he hit another button and the garage door began to rise. "You both should leave."

Leaving didn't seem like the best idea. Harper had had a good day with Britany and she didn't want to just ghost on her. "I need to say goodbye to Britany."

"Why?"

"She's my friend." And she was. And it was shitty to just run out the door without saying goodbye, after they spent all afternoon together at the spa. They'd talked about peacocks and weddings. If that wasn't bonding, Harper didn't know what was.

"Bullshit. You don't know how to be a friend."

Harper's eyes watered.

"That wasn't necessary." Alex stepped between Paul and Harper. If she didn't deserve it, she'd be impressed.

"It's okay." Harper laid her hand on Alex's arm. She turned to Paul. "Just tell her I said goodbye. I don't want her to think I just left."

Harper ran toward her car, anger and sadness coated her movements. She hadn't meant to hide away and block out her friends. But she hadn't been ready to talk. She hadn't wanted to be "cheered up." And every interaction after Brad's death was someone trying to lighten the mood.

She didn't want the mood lightened. And maybe that meant she'd cut them out, but she hadn't known what to do. She'd had to take time to feel all the hurt. She had to take time to heal. If anyone would have understood, it was Madeline.

But she wasn't here. So, Harper couldn't even ask her. She couldn't even apologize. And she had to live with that.

"Hey." Alex jogged toward Harper's car. The garage door shut behind him.

Harper stopped before she could whip open the door and run away. It was feeling like a two-scoop of ice cream kind of day.

"Are you okay?"

"I'm fine." The sad thing was today started out so well. She looked at her fingertips. Filed to perfect little ovals— well, as perfect as one can get with imperfect nails. They were shined to a sheen.

"You don't look fine."

Harper didn't normally focus on how she looked, but she could admit that hurt a bit. "Thanks." Hopefully, she didn't say that with too much sarcasm. He didn't deserve to know how much he annoyed her—or hurt her feelings.

She should have just opened the door and driven off when she had the chance. Now Alex stood between her and a clean getaway.

"I didn't mean it like the way it sounded." Alex leaned against the door blocking any chance of escape. "I meant the way he treated you was pretty brutal. He had no right."

"But he's right. Madeline was having a hard time."

"You didn't know…"

"I should have known. I should have asked. I was her friend and Reynaldo knew more about what she was going through than I did. She didn't tell me anything."

"The hairdresser?" Alex's face was a mix of confusion and terror.

"How did you know about the hairdresser?"

Alex smirked. "I'm good at my job."

"You are." She attempted a smile, but Paul's words kept wringing at her chest.

"You know," Alex lifted his hand and moved apiece of hair from Harper's collar. "Maybe she didn't want to weigh you down with her problems."

"That makes it worse. She didn't feel comfortable enough to reach out. And I was so self-absorbed, I didn't even know what was going on. Paul was right. I'm a shitty friend." A tear slid down Harper's cheek, and honestly, she didn't care.

"You were dealing with a lot."

"Apparently, so was Madeline." Harper shook her head. Suddenly, she was exhausted. "Look, I appreciate you trying to defend me, but there is no defense. And right now, all I want to do is go home." Ice cream and maybe a bath. An escape into a book sounded good about now.

Alex stepped away from the door. "Are you going to be okay?"

"Sure." She attempted a smile and she must have done

a pretty good job because he opened the door for her instead of offering cheerful platitudes.

He didn't offer pity or anything else either. Which she appreciated. She didn't need anyone else's emotion. She had enough locked inside her chest, bursting to get out. Harper slid inside the car and clicked her seatbelt.

"Have a nice night." Alex closed the door slowly.

She would try. But she had a feeling a nice night was not in her future.

CHAPTER
FOURTEEN

THREE HOURS, one nacho platter, two glasses of wine, and three scoops of ice cream later, Harper was questioning everything again. Not just questioning, but making a list. She needed to remember everything, and it wasn't easy. Maybe because it had been a long time ago or maybe it was the glasses of wine.

She came by her lightweight reputation honestly. Although, she'd eaten her bodyweight in chips and cheese, so she wasn't as drunk as one would expect. So she was holding the pen in a horizontal position. Success!

It just wasn't writing anything useful. Failure!

Of course, it might not be so hard if she'd written anything down a year ago. To be fair, she'd been busy dealing with the death of her husband. Which was the subject of Paul's reprimand today. And he hadn't been wrong. Completely.

Yeah, she'd been overwhelmed with Brad's death. And

yes, she hadn't been there for Madeline. But they'd talked on and off for months and Madeline hadn't said a word.

That wasn't Harper's fault.

And Paul making it seem like it was a shitty thing to do. Or maybe he was just diverting her attention. Madeline's car had been in an accident. Maybe Paul had been driving. Maybe he hadn't had a chance to get it fixed.

She needed to find out what type of car hit Madeline. A Ford SUV hadn't hit Brad, but that didn't mean Paul hadn't been involved. The way he behaved today said he was hiding something.

She took a final pull from her wine and walked into the kitchen to pour some more. The bottle was empty. Bummer.

She should be getting lost in a good book while soaking in a giant tub filled with bubbles, but instead she was rehashing every word and every action. Living with the ghosts, hell, practically interacting with them. But she needed to do this. She needed to figure this out. If Paul killed Madeline, or… oh crap. Harper's chest ached. If Paul killed Brad, she had to know. She had to make sure he paid.

She grabbed the corkscrew and another bottle from the wine rack on the counter. She twisted the corkscrew, popping the top on the bottle in her hands. She sniffed the cork and paused. Fruity and delicious. She needed this. She needed to numb the pain.

If Paul had hit Brad, he took everything away from her. It was hard enough dealing with the loss when it was an accident—a cosmic fluke that left her without a home and vulnerable.

Harper filled her glass until only the lip of the glass wasn't touching liquid. If she played her cards right, her lips would be touching that liquid. She slowly lifted the glass, slurping at the jiggling liquid before it sluiced over the side. Her tonsils welcomed the fruity nectar.

If Paul took it all away without one backwards glance, she was going to be devastated. He knew Brad. They were friends.

The doorbell rang. At least she thought it was the doorbell. She might have had so much to drink, she was starting to hear bells.

Another ring. Not her imagination. She shuffled across the tiled floor. She looked through the peephole. Alex. He was still in a white collared shirt but the shadow on his face said it was after five o'clock.

The collared shirt was still unbuttoned at the top, and his skin looked good enough to eat—well, at least good enough to lick.

Good enough to lick? She must have been less sober than she'd thought. Which meant she really should not open the front door.

"Hi, detective." She licked her lips, wishing he was doing the licking. Although, they did taste rather fruity from the wine. Num.

Her body leaned up against the door that had somehow opened. She wasn't quite sure how. But now the peephole wasn't distorting the view, and he looked even better. His hair was messy in that sexy I-been-doing-manly-things-all-day look. And the wine in her veins was warming her body—she wanted him to warm her body.

Bad.

She smiled in a flirty way she'd seen on television. Her bare arm stretched out over her head, her hand on the door. Her yoga pants just below the navel. Yeah, she had a midriff if she stretched far enough—and she knew how to use it.

Well, she used to have one. And she used to know how. Now she wasn't so sure. She ran a hand down her stomach. Mostly flat. Yep, still mostly got it. She pulled her body longer along the door.

She could just imagine the view. She pouted her lips like a porn-star pro. She was bringing sexy back.

"Are you okay?" Alex tilted his head and looked at the top of the door. "Do you need to reach something above the door?"

Her arm dropped, her midriff no longer feeling the soft breeze as her shirt fell back into place. "No. It's fine." The alcohol slowly left through her toes in mortification. Her arms crossed over her chest. Sobriety swirled in her head, but the booze kept fighting it back. "Is everything okay with you?"

"Yeah." He looked confused.

She was confused too. "Why are you here?" That might have come out a bit harsh. But he interrupted her happy little buzz with his disinterest in her sexy come-hither.

"You were upset earlier. I wanted to see how you were holding up."

"I'm fine." She had been a few minutes ago. Now she

was mostly mortified. But his words cut through the humiliation. *I wanted to see how you were holding up.* He was sweet.

"I'm good."

"Good." Alex kicked at the ground, his hands in his pockets. His eyes looked everywhere but at Harper. If she didn't know any better, she'd say he was the one embarrassed. But his face wasn't the color of neon, so nope, that would be her.

Not that she could see her face, but she could feel it. One could probably fry an egg on it.

"Well, I should go then." Alex looked at his car in the driveway but didn't make a move.

"You could come in. I'm just drinking a little wine." And overanalyzing the day. She kept that tidbit to herself. People didn't always understand her need for closure. But she liked things tied in a neat little bow or she couldn't move on. Which was one reason she'd had such a hard time starting over again when Brad had died.

"I don't want to interrupt."

"Please. I'm on the second bottle. Save me from alcohol poisoning." She smiled and moved to the side.

Alex nodded and slipped inside. Goodness, he smelled good. Which wasn't good. She was practically a married woman and she didn't want to do anything she'd regret. And this man had regret written all over him.

She closed the door and backed away. Wine. Wine fixed everything.

"Would you like a glass?"

"Sure." Alex walked into the house and she could practically see his cop mind cataloguing everything he saw. The honey-colored cabinets and white floor tiles. Her kitten spoon rest and the floral curtains above the kitchen sink.

"Nice place."

"I think so. Have a seat." She motioned to the large pink couch in the living room, then the stools next to the raised counter separating the kitchen from the living room. She walked around into the kitchen and poured another glass of wine.

He lowered himself to one of the stools next to the counter.

"I hope you like Malbec." She poured an appropriate amount of wine into the glass and placed it on the raised counter in front of Alex.

"I don't think I've ever had one." He brought the glass to his lips and sipped. He smiled. "That's good."

"Do you normally drink wine?"

"On occasion." He swirled the liquid in the flute. "I'm more of a vodka guy."

"Straight?" She'd tried that once. It was like battery acid slicing down her throat.

"On the rocks." He laughed. "I take it you aren't a big vodka drinker."

"No." She didn't even have any on hand. Not anymore. When Brad died, she'd gotten rid of the useless booze. It wasn't like she was hosting parties or anything. "Have you had dinner?"

"Yeah, I ate at the precinct. Candy machine granola bar."

"That sounds awful."

"Come on, it's the dinner of champions."

"Still awful. I made nachos for dinner, if you want me to make up a plate."

"Nachos?" Alex's eyebrow popped up.

"Pulled pork, cheese, and jalapeños."

His eyes sparked. There was interest. He shook his head and that spark diminished. "I don't want to put you out."

She pulled out the leftover pork and cheese and started the oven. "I offered." She layered tortilla chips on a pan and sprinkled the cheese and pork on top before sliding it in the oven. "So, why didn't you get a chance to eat dinner?"

"Busy day."

She dried her hands on the kitchen towel and leaned against the opposite counter. She grabbed her wine glass and watched as Alex looked around the room. He didn't say anything, but her house was clean and he wasn't scowling. Good signs. "So, what does a busy day consist of for a Las Vegas Metro detective? Were there police chases and interrogations?"

Alex's chest rumbled with a deep laugh. "My day isn't that exciting."

"Are you sure? I've seen *Law and Order.*"

"*Law and Order* makes it look a lot more interesting than it is." He took a drink from his glass. "Today, I hit fast forward for four hours. I sped through most of seventeen hours' worth of parking lot footage."

"They didn't cover that in *Law and Order.*"

"No one would watch it. The show wouldn't last long if everyone fell asleep."

She opened the oven and checked the nachos. Done. She pulled the pan out and slid the chips onto a plate, then spooned a couple of jalapeños on top. "Sour cream?"

"Do you have to ask?"

Reaching into the fridge, she grabbed the tube of sour cream. She squirted a line around the center. She loved the squirty-bottle. Normally. But when a hot guy was staring at her as the bottle farted, she questioned her choice in condiment delivery. "Sorry."

Alex laughed as heat pooled in Harper's cheeks.

She had to change the subject before he started making jokes or refused to eat it because of the white spatter that accompanied each fart. Why did she buy this damn bottle? The case. If anything would get his mind off the inappropriate squeeze bottle, it was work. "Did you find anything on Madeline?"

"Nothing yet."

She slid the plate in front of him.

He picked up a loaded chip. "This is good," he said once he finished chewing.

"Thanks."

"Can I ask you something?" He took another bite and might have even groaned. It was adorable—and he'd asked a question.

"Sure."

"You don't like Paul."

"That's not a question." Although she could imagine what the question might be.

"Why not?"

"How to say this." Why not? It was hard to explain. She'd tried to explain it to Brad. Brad had loved the guy. She just didn't understand. "Paul is smarmy like a shady car salesman. Not a regular salesman who's working nine to five to pay for his family. No. He's selling cars made with bicycle parts and rubber bands. Everyone thinks his cars are great. But I don't see it."

"What do you see?"

Harper attempted a sip of wine that morphed into a gulp. Discussing Paul seemed to have that effect on her. "I see a guy who treated his wife like crap and expected her to just take it. I see a guy who would sell his mother for success. I see someone who's hiding something. And I need to know what it is."

Alex nodded as he dug into the pile of nachos on his plate. The food disappeared like he had a vacuum attached to his mouth. Harper took another drink. She really had to stop drinking. Thinking about his mouth as a vacuum was way too distracting.

She needed another distraction. She pulled the empty pan from the top of the stove and placed it under the tap of the sink, she hand-washed it and dried it with the towel.

The silence gave her mind time to clear. She was acting like a horny teenager who'd never been alone with a man before. That wasn't her. She wasn't this person. She just had to remember she was taken. She turned around. Alex's plate was empty.

"That was amazing, Harp. Thank you."

Harp. She shouldn't, but for some reason her name shortened on his lips felt familiar and nice. *Taken, remember?* It's just a name. "I'm glad you liked it. I haven't made dinner for anyone but myself in a long time."

"Since your husband."

"Yes."

Alex took his wine glass and walked toward the shelves in the living room. He pointed at a framed photo. "Is this him?"

Harper crossed the room so she could see the picture. "That's him when we were dating."

"He looks happy."

"He was." She picked up the frame. They'd just watched DJ Marshmello at the Electric Daisy Carnival. Brad was sweaty and dirty, his golden hair spiked all over, and smiling bigger than she'd ever seen him smile. His eyes actually sparkled—or it might have been the overhead lights. She snapped this picture as they were leaving the motor speedway.

Alex's body had somehow moved behind her. His front to her back. Heat soaked through her T-shirt and warmed her insides. It had been so long since she'd been this close to a man—well, except the other day when he stood by her. But somehow this felt different. This was all him and it felt good.

"Were you at the EDC?" His breath warmed along her neck. His lips were so close to her skin and she wasn't hating it.

Stop!

She was looking at Brad's picture, for heaven's sake.

She should be missing *him*. She should be feeling *his* body in the heat at her back. She shouldn't be enjoying Alex—or anyone else.

"Uh, yeah." She stepped forward, out of breathing range.

"With that DJ…"

"Marshmello." It was the night Harper knew she wanted to spend the rest of her life with Brad—or at least the rest of his life. They'd had so much fun. She ran her finger over the frame. If she'd had her picture taken that night, her face would have looked just as happy as his.

How things had changed.

"Who is this?" Alex picked up another frame.

"My mom and dad. They died when I was twenty."

"That must have been rough."

"It was, but I was in college. I had a place to live and I had a scholarship. So many others have it so much worse." She settled the picture of Brad back into place on the shelf—where he could watch her.

Where she could watch him. "Brad and I had that in common, but he'd had it so much harder. His parents abandoned him and his sister when he was four. He always said we were perfect for each other. We were alone."

"That's nice." Alex's face had taken on that pity-concern look Harper knew so well. Part of her wanted to slap the look from his face. She didn't want that look anywhere near her. But another part wanted to hug him because the reaction was normal and kind.

She hadn't felt kindness like this in a while. Not that it

was anyone's fault but her own. She'd been so busy pushing people away, she'd forgotten she needed them. Or at the very least wanted them. Brad smiled at her from the shelf, and guilt and sadness gripped her heart and exploded like a nuclear bomb. Shrapnel poked at the back of her eye.

"Thank you for dinner." Alex. He was watching. And she was losing her shit.

"Of course." She wiped at her eyes and smiled. "Thank you for checking on me."

"Any time." He walked to the front door, trailed by Harper.

She leaned against the door after he opened it. The night air nipped at her face, but she still had a question that needed an answer. "What type of car hit Madeline and Brad?"

Alex shuffled his feet, like he was thinking about his answer or maybe he just wasn't going to give her a response. "It was two different cars. A blue BMW was seen at the first accident."

"The car in Paul's garage was a Ford. Could they have been wrong about the BMW?"

"Maybe. I don't see how a BMW could be mistaken for a Ford, but an X5 isn't that different from an Escape." His eyes looked at the ground. Something was on his mind. Before she asked him what or tried to pull it out of him, he ran a hand down the back of his neck. "You know I have to ask."

Ask? "About what?" The past couple days had been insane. What could he possibly want to ask about?

"Did you fight with Brad the night he died?"

Oh, that. She hated bringing up old news. Old heartache. But she couldn't lie. She was so bad at it. "We did."

They'd been so happy. He had been killing it at work. He'd sold some large buildings in the area. Their sex life had been amazing. They'd been fixing up the house. Three bedrooms and large backyard. She should have known this would become an issue.

"About?"

That was the discussion she didn't want to have. Part of her wanted to redirect the conversation, just like the detective had done less than a minute ago. Don't think she didn't notice how he didn't fully answer her question.

But with every diversion, she looked more guilty. The detective stared at her. Expectant. That was the word. Disappointing him would just lead to more problems. And Lord knew she didn't need any more problems.

Just rip off the Band-Aid. She sucked in a breath and held it. "I can't have children." The words escaped from her body and she wanted to pull them back in. But her body was the problem, wasn't it?

"From what you've said about him, I'm sure he understood."

She wanted to believe that so much. She wanted to smile when she thought about her marriage, but it had been teetering on the edge of a blade. It had always amazed her how honest they could be about the club and expectations. She could tell him anything about her body.

Anything, but the one thing that would change their relationship.

"I didn't tell him." A tear fell down her cheek. "I didn't know at first. I only found out shortly before he died. And then I just changed the subject when we talked about kids. I told him I didn't want them."

"Why didn't you tell him if you knew?" Alex almost sounded judgmental. But little did he know that she judged herself way harsher than anyone else ever could.

"I didn't know at first. And it's not that I didn't want them, I just couldn't. Don't get me wrong, when I was young, I didn't. I wanted to have fun and travel. But working with kids every day and seeing happy families. Seeing the parents look at their kids with such adoration. I wanted that, but I couldn't have it." She wasn't a monster. "We'd always said how we didn't want kids. We'd agreed. I didn't know he'd change his mind. I didn't know I'd change my mind,"

"He told you he changed his mind?"

"No, but something changed."

"What?"

"I don't know." She thought back to those last few months. He'd pulled away from her, just an inch. They'd still been happy and had enjoyed the life they'd built, but there was just something. Something off.

"Then it shouldn't have been an issue."

It shouldn't have, but something changed a little over a year after she'd worn the white dress. And day after day, she could feel him pull away. She could feel something shift. He'd bring up kids, more and more, and she'd change the subject.

Like right now. She had to change the subject. And since they were in this bubble of honesty... "Am I a suspect?" The weight of the words nearly crushed her.

"Should you be?"

Wasting time on her issues would not lead to answers. "No. Brad and I were happy. We had some things to work out, but we would have. We had trust and honesty." Mostly, anyway. She'd hidden a few things, but that was only till she could figure out how to tell him.

Alex nodded, staring at her like needed to see every piece of her. "No."

"No?" No what?

"You're not a suspect."

Her knees wobbled at the conviction in his voice. The belief. He didn't think she was a murderer. Hooray. Not exactly the making of a friendship, but it was a step towards trust. Which meant she needed to share more information, or at least ask.

Alex tilted his head to the side. "How did Brad find out about it?"

"What? That I couldn't have kids?" She continued after Alex nodded. "He didn't. I was going to tell him, but Madeline called and invited us to DeVout. He said yes without asking me if I even wanted to go. Granted, normally I would have been all over it. But not that night. I wanted to talk and get it all out in the open."

"Why not just tell him and cancel the plans?"

"I don't know. It felt like I shouldn't say anything if we

were going to go out and see our friends. But an hour or so later Madeline called back to cancel. She said something about Paul having to work late."

"So, you had the chance to tell him."

"I had the chance." Harper didn't want to say the next part. It made her look so bad. "But I didn't."

"Why not?" Either Alex was a great actor or he wasn't judging her. Not yet anyway.

"I chickened out. I was so scared he'd leave." Scared didn't even cover it, she'd been terrified to tell him—to lose him.

"So you kicked him out?"

She shook her head, but the regret from that night wouldn't leave. "I wasn't exactly thinking clearly. All I saw was that I was going to scare him away and I'd be left alone. I should've been stronger, but I was lost. Sad. Scared."

"He might have surprised you."

"He might have." She nodded and believed he might have, but that didn't stop the tears from falling. "But how could I ask him to forgive me for something I couldn't forgive myself for."

"Was it your fault?"

"When your body doesn't work the way you want it to, it feels like it's your fault." She couldn't think about this any longer. She didn't want to think about the anger she'd felt or the disappointment she'd swallowed. She couldn't give Brad a child, but she could find answers for him.

And the questions were mostly about Paul. "Do we

know what happened to Madeline's SUV? Was Paul telling the truth?"

"I'm not sure."

Harper blinked. Not sure? "Can't you just look?"

"Not without a warrant."

A warrant. Of course, she'd seen *Law and Order*. "How do we get a warrant?"

"We?"

Did she say we? "I meant you."

His chest shook with laughter. "I submitted the paperwork today. I'm just waiting for the judge to sign."

"And what about Madeline?"

"What about her?"

"What type of car was used in her accident?" If he thought she'd forget about how this whole conversation started, he was sadly mistaken. She needed to know the type of car.

"Green Audi."

"Maybe it's the same person. They're both German cars." It sounded logical in her head, but she probably should have kept that one inside.

"There are a lot of German cars on the road." His logic was why she should have kept that to herself.

"But how many were used in a hit and run?" She repeated his words from yesterday. The cool Vegas evening air ran up and down the hairs on her arms. She wrapped her arms around herself, trying to keep the warmth inside.

Alex leaned in and pushed a whisp of hair from her

forehead. Just the slightest touch, but it felt electric. "True."

He was so close. Only a few inches from Harper's lips. She could practically feel him. Haze clouded her vision as he looked her up and down. She thought for sure he'd close the distance. Too bad she wasn't sure if she wanted him to or not.

Well, her body wanted him to wrap her in his arms and kiss her like crazy. Her brain was still trying to figure out if that just made her crazy.

He stepped back. His eyes no longer caressing her body. The moment passed. He sighed as he ran his hand down the scar along his cheek.

That scar. She reached up and ran a finger along the jagged edges. "What happened?" The gesture was too personal, but she couldn't stop her finger from trailing.

"Fight in a high school with my best friend."

"Let me guess, over a girl."

"Isn't it always." Alex smiled as a chill crawled up Harper's spine causing her to shiver. "You should get inside."

"Why? I have more questions."

"Personal or about the case?"

"The case." She smiled. Although, she had some personal questions she would have liked to throw his way, too.

"It's cold, and we can talk tomorrow."

Tomorrow. He wanted her to help with the case, like *Castle* or some USA Network comedy-drama. Maybe that last *we* wasn't too far off the mark. "Really? I have so many ideas. Once we know that it was Paul's car, we can look at his business dealings for motive."

"Hold on." Alex pulled his keys from his pocket and laughed. Laughed. At her. "*We're* not looking into Paul. Once I get the warrant, if something turns up, I'll look into Paul."

Harper wanted to slap him or shove him or pull a Three Stooges routine that ended with kicking him in the balls. "So what am I supposed to do?"

"Do what you normally do. Teach. Grade papers. Let me take care of this. If I find out anything, I'll let you know." He sauntered to his car like he owned the block, and paused after he opened the door. "Trust me. This is my job." He waved and slipped into the driver's seat.

Trust him.

Like she'd trusted the last cop on the case. Like she'd trusted a man who wasn't breathing down Paul's lying, backstabbing neck.

Wait for a warrant? See if something turns up?

His judgment was faulty. And Paul was sneaky.

She needed more information about Paul and Madeline and the club. And she knew exactly who to talk to. The hub of everything DeVout—well, that would be Emma and John—but Harper couldn't get them involved. She couldn't drag Emma into this, not unless she absolutely had to.

Emma wasn't exactly Harper's number one fan right now anyway. But Symphony? Working the front desk, she probably knew a whole hell of a lot.

And tomorrow Harper would find out what.

ON SATURDAY, the sun blinded Harper as she stood by the black metal railing circling the edge of the small back porch of Symphony's apartment in North Las Vegas. Two chairs with red cushions and a bistro-style table sat in the center of the stone pavers. When someone named Clara led her inside the condo, Harper tried to kill her with kindness but Clara wouldn't die.

"Want a drink?" Clara stood at the door in pink scrubs. Apparently, Clara was the roommate. Gorgeous blond hair pulled back in a ponytail didn't take away from her angular features. Her face was as severe as the scowl perched there.

"No thanks." Harper smiled at the model standing guard at the door. She nodded at the pink scrubs. "Are you heading to work?"

"Yeah." Clara didn't elaborate, just pulled out her phone and stared at the screen.

"Are you a doctor?"

"Vet tech."

"So, you like animals."

"No. I failed my nursing exam." Clara didn't laugh and it wasn't April first, so not a joke?

"Really?"

"No." Clara tapped at her phone. "I work with animals every day, but I don't like animals."

Still no laughing, but Harper swore she saw an eye roll.

The back door slid open and Symphony walked out in spandex shorts and a T-shirt that said Zombies Eat Brains. "Sorry, I had my weekly call with my mom."

"No problem." Harper smiled because Symphony was actually talking and smiling back. Unlike Clara, who might or might not hate animals.

"You're not being nice." Symphony wrapped an arm around Clara, who rolled her eyes. Good to know she rolled her eyes at Symphony, too. Made Harper feel less special. "My roommate is just mad because we were supposed to go out for coffee before she headed to work."

"I'm sorry. If I'm interrupting your plans, I can come back." Harper really didn't want to wait, but she also didn't want Clara glaring at her. And caffeine was obviously important.

"No. I'm already running late." Clara kept her eyes on her phone as she turned to the house. "Gotta bounce."

"Bye, Clara."

Clara raised a wave to Symphony as she walked through the apartment and out the front door.

"Take a load off." Symphony set two bottles of cold

coffee on the table before she pulled out one of the chairs and sat down. "I brought you a drink, if you'd like."

"Thank you." Harper pulled out a chair and sat down. The sun was crawling higher in the sky, slowly burning off the morning chill.

Symphony opened her bottle and took a drink. "No problem. What questions do you have for me?"

"Is it that obvious?"

"You showed up at the club with that hot cop, and now you're here."

True. Didn't exactly take a rocket scientist to figure that out. "I was hoping you could tell me how Madeline was acting before she died. Was she acting weird?"

"Define weird." Symphony took another drink. "We got one guy who dresses up as Elmo and his wife chases him around the room with a paddle."

"Really?" The sex rooms weren't supposed to have cameras. "How do you know that?"

"Too many people complained about not being able to tell if the rooms were empty. So about a year ago the Byrnes installed cameras out in the hallway to show when people leave. Elmo ran out of the room one night laughing as his wife yelled for him to come back in the room."

"So the cameras are just in the halls?"

"Yeah. They couldn't get away with recording people in the rooms. Can you even imagine?"

Nope. That would never fly.

"Anyway," Symphony said, "Madeline was so nice when I first started. She's the reason I still have the job."

"Really? Why?"

"A few weeks after I started, I forgot to lock up my phone."

"Oh no."

"Oh yeah." Symphony slid her nail under the label on her bottle, pulling it back piece by piece. "The thing started ringing during a party."

"Did anyone hear it?" If anyone heard that phone, it was a miracle she was still employed.

"It must have been on the megaphone setting. I swear, everyone heard it." Symphony's head popped up and her finger stopped mid pick. "Not just during the party. There happened to be a lull in the conversation. I'm wiping down a table and *Dirty Deeds* from AC/DC starts blaring from my pocket."

"'Dirty Deeds?'" Not exactly a quiet song.

"Yes. It was so damn loud, I thought time stood still as everyone just stopped and stared. Literally. Glasses stopped mid-drink. Eyes glued to me."

Harper couldn't help but laugh. She could just imagine everyone in the room frozen in place.

Symphony giggled. "It was awful. Emma ran up to me and I swear, if she could've zapped me into cinders, she would have."

"I'm surprised Emma let you stay on."

"Oh please, she would have fired me, but thankfully Madeline was at another table with Paul. She jumped up and asked if that was her phone. She forgot to take it out of her pocket...yada, yada. I gave her my phone and she put it in her locker."

"Madeline actually took your phone?" She must have

been committed to the whole act.

"She did. She kept it in her locker until they left that night." Symphony's lips curled at the edges. "I thanked her, but I don't think she really understood how much I appreciated that."

"I'm sure she did."

Symphony took a drink and returned to peeling the label. "Yeah. I guess you're right. I'm sure she understood. That's just how she was. Kind."

"She was kind." Harper had been on the receiving end of that kindness over the years. It was the reason none of this made sense. Who would—

"How could anyone have hurt her?" Symphony finished Harper's thought.

Exactly. "That's what I don't get." Unless it was Paul. Which begged the question. "Were Paul and Madeline having problems?"

"Not when I first met them." Symphony tilted her head and peeled, lost in thought, maybe. "I mean, they weren't exactly warm and fuzzy with each other. But they didn't yell or anything. Not at first. But I caught them a few times."

"A few times?" Knowing they'd fought somehow scared Harper more than anything. She was sure Paul was a creep, that wasn't in question. But a murderer? If he did this—really did this—everything she knew changed. He was Brad's friend. She knew Paul. She'd kissed Paul— before she knew what an ass he was.

But if he fought with his wife. If he killed her. That was

more than an ass move. That was a felony and ruined all of their lives.

"Being on the main floor all night, I see a lot of things. And I saw them fight a few times. Not drag-out fights, but they were angry."

"About what?"

"I didn't hear them all, but the last one was about how much time she was spending away from the house. Saying it started with Brad. Something about going away with *him*."

"Who's him? Brad?" And why were they fighting about Brad? What did he have to do with anything? Madeline wasn't running around with Brad.

"Oh no," Symphony said, "the him couldn't have been Brad."

Not that Harper believed for a second Madeline and Brad had something going on. At all. But now… "They were fighting after he was gone."

"Exactly." Symphony beamed like she hadn't planted a seed of doubt.

Not that it was her fault. And not that there was any doubt. Harper had known Brad. He wasn't sneaky and had never hidden anything from her. Not one thing. Like the time he showed her his infected hangnail. Some things should be hidden. Keep the illusion alive. "But do you know why they were fighting over Brad?"

"I don't know. Paul said something about she'd changed, after he, you know."

"After his death?"

"Maybe." Symphony finished the bottle of coffee. "Probably. They didn't really say."

Of course they didn't. "Did you ever meet the him Paul was talking about?"

"No. You know how the Byrnes are. They'd never let Madeline bring someone else to the club."

"True. I was just hoping you might have seen this guy."

"Sorry, I never met him. But Paul said they stayed the weekend of her birthday at the Hotel del *Colorado*, or something like that."

"Hotel del Coronado?" It was where Harper had spent her honeymoon. The Del was in San Diego and gorgeous and probably haunted.

"That's it."

A loud ring came from inside the apartment. Doorbell.

"I'm popular today." Symphony smiled and got up from the table.

Harper opened the coffee and took a sip. Perfect timing. She needed a minute to think. She still didn't know who Madeline's new guy was, but apparently they were going to San Diego. To the Del.

It had to be a coincidence that Harper had been there, right? It still didn't make her feel all warm and fuzzy. But it had to be a coincidence. She didn't have time to think about that now. This was about Paul. How would Paul have felt if Madeline was on the beach in San Diego with some guy?

Harper could admit, if that were her husband, she'd be

pissed. So that just enforced the jealousy/ anger angle. When at the club, there's a sharing component but it's sharing *with* your partner. Once the partner was removed from the situation, it wasn't the couple sharing, it was going behind the partners back. It was cheating. Maybe Paul didn't like to be left out. Or maybe Paul didn't like the guy she was with—although her cheating kind of blew Harper's mind.

She stared past the back railing at another building that looked the same as the one she sat next to. Rows of apartment homes sparkled under the rising Vegas sun. The sliding glass door opened behind her.

"Was Paul mad?" Harper asked without turning around.

"About what?" The voice was male.

Harper turned in her seat. "Where's Symphony?" she asked, and her breath stopped in her lungs. Alex's brown hair was wet and he was wearing a button-down shirt with the sleeves rolled up over his forearms—and what lovely forearms they were. He'd look good except for that darn scowl was back.

She seemed to be having that effect today.

"Hi, I brought you another coffee." Symphony walked through the sliders carrying three bottles. She must own stock in cold coffee—or she should.

"Why are you here?" Alex leaned against the railing and accepted his bottle from Symphony. "Thanks."

"I live here." Symphony twisted the cap and somehow didn't laugh. Like she didn't know he was talking to Harper. With an attitude.

Symphony pulled out her chair but then stopped. "Do I need to go downtown?"

Alex didn't move his glare off Harper. "No. I want to know why you're here, Harper."

Symphony must have realized she was off the hook because she stopped talking. Between the look on his face and the way he said Harper and not Harp, she knew she was in trouble.

"I'm talking with my new friend Symphony." Harper lifted her lips in the sweetest smile she could muster.

"Like you were talking with your new friend Britany."

"I'm friendly. Sue me." And she was friendly, but she was also looking for information. He didn't need to know that—but he didn't strike her as an idiot, so he probably already knew.

Alex folded his arms over his chest as he turned to Symphony. The glare disappeared and his tone shifted to not-asshole. "Why is she here?"

"Gossip." Symphony smiled. "Did you know that the first company hired to install the palapas in Emma and John's backyard was fired for stealing a television?"

"No way." Harper pretended to be appalled. She wasn't quite sure what a palapa was, but she knew the rest of the words, and fired for stealing was universally bad. "A few years ago, they had a cleaning man who would come in and steal the silver."

"I heard about that." Symphony bounced in her seat. "I have to count the forks every night before I leave work because of him."

"Do they put out the silver? I thought they'd stopped—again because of him."

"No, they're made of cheap stainless steel. One step away from gray plastic." Symphony laughed. "I used one on my chicken tenders a few weeks ago and it bent. Bent. I'm telling you, plastic would hold up better. But Emma still makes me count them."

Harper couldn't help but laugh. Not at Symphony's story about cutlery, but the look on Alex's face was priceless. His eyes were narrowed and he kept looking back and forth from Harper to Symphony. Like he didn't believe that they were sitting around gossiping.

"Sorry. I'm sure you didn't come here to discuss forks, Detective." Symphony looked so innocent. She was now Harper's favorite person.

"No, I don't care about forks." He leaned back on the metal rail like he was watching a tennis match. He kept looking from Symphony to Harper, but there was nothing casual about it. He was probably waiting for them to slip up, or at least for someone's nose to grow. "I think we should talk in private."

Here it goes. He wanted to yell at her in private. She must have done something wrong.

"Okay." Harper replaced the cap on her barely touched coffee and stood up.

"Not you." Alex angled forward. "I need to talk to Symphony."

"I can stay—"

"No. I think I can handle it." He moved closer. "This is my job."

A slap would've hurt less. To be fair she wanted to slap him. But she refused to give him the satisfaction. Angry, back-stabbing cops didn't deserve her attention.

"I'll go." Harper picked up her bottle and opened the sliding glass door. She turned to Symphony, who appeared to be watching Harper and the cop like a high-rated sitcom. Well, a sitcom minus the laughs. "Thank you for the coffee and the chat."

"Anytime." Symphony smiled like she meant it. And she probably did. She was sweet. And even though their day was cut short, she had given Harper a place to start. The Del. It had been a while since she'd been there, but they had to have video. The problem was how to get to it.

CHAPTER
SIXTEEN

TWENTY MINUTES LATER, Harper pulled an overnight bag out of her closet. Not that she thought she'd be there overnight. But San Diego was almost six-hours away by car and it was almost eleven AM. The responsible thing would be to call in for work tomorrow, just in case.

Well, the responsible thing would be to stand back and let the cops handle it, but when she'd done that in the past, it hadn't worked out so well. So calling in with a sniffle and fever was where she was at.

If she drove up, walked into the hotel and said, "Show me the tapes with the Brainiac" —and they did— she could be back home by midnight. But nothing was ever that easy. Especially since she had no idea when they'd have checked in—other than Friday. Hell, Symphony never said they actually checked into the hotel. The hotel had a fabulous steakhouse. Maybe Madeline drove there just to meet for dinner.

Probably not. Did she mention six hours? No woman

was going to drive six hours for a steak with a man without getting her own steak braised.

Harper tossed pajamas, socks, and a T-shirt that would match the blue jeans she was wearing into the overnight bag. Then she shoved a bathing suit in the front pocket. What? There was an ocean, and if she had a few minutes, she could jump in for a minute or two. She was human.

Whether Madeline stayed the night at the hotel or not, she'd be on the camera footage. It was just a matter of Harper getting her hands on it. *How* was the question. She could pretend to be a cop, but that was felony-inducing. Ending up in jail in California would make it hard to call in sick to work.

She'd have to think some more. Thankfully, she had a six-hour trip ahead of her to do all kinds of thinking.

The bag swung against her thigh as she moved through the living room and dropped the bag on the kitchen counter. Road snacks. You couldn't drive for six hours without snacks.

Her doorbell rang just as she took a couple of cans of diet Pepsi out of the fridge. She slid the cans into the bag and grabbed her keys. Once she dealt with whoever was at the door she'd hit the road.

She opened the front door. The detective. Who else would it be? She should have looked through the peephole and gone out through the garage. Damned hindsight.

"Going somewhere?" Alex stood in her way like those giant poles at the front of big box stores, except he had a vein pulsing in his neck.

"I'm going for a drive."

"With a bag?"

"It has my license." Not a lie. It totally did. Harper shifted the bag from one shoulder to the other. "Did you need something?"

"Why were you at Symphony's house?"

He might have told her to trust him, but since *she'd done enough*, well... "I just wanted to talk to a friend. That's not illegal."

"It is if you're hindering my investigation."

"How am I hindering it? I talked to her and then you talked to her." And he might have gotten more information from Symphony, but it probably would be in bad form to ask what she'd said.

"I thought we agreed you'd trust me."

"I never really agreed." And she sure as hell never trusted him. Well, maybe she'd thought about It, but thankfully that never came to fruition.

He sighed. "Fine. What did you two talk about?"

Apparently, it wasn't bad form for him to ask. "What did she tell you?" She crossed her arms over her chest and the bag swayed on her shoulder. It almost slid down her arm, which would suck because that would ruin the whole power move.

"Ceasefire, okay." Alex ran a hand down the side of his face. The frustration evident in his tell. He seemed to run his hand along the scar on his face whenever she pissed him off. "Look. We're on the same side."

She seemed to piss him off a lot.

"Are we, though?" She didn't move her arms. She didn't move at all for fear she'd do something to hurt the man. "I got you in the door at DeVout and apparently that wasn't enough for you."

"You got me kicked out."

"For one night. I could've been kicked out for good. Those are my friends." She might not be regularly participating, but that didn't mean she wouldn't want to in the future.

"Well, you wouldn't have been in danger of being kicked out if you let me handle it like you said you'd do."

"When did I ever say that?" Harper frowned at the same time a frown crossed his face. If she didn't know better, she'd think he might actually have a few hurt feelings. But that would imply he cared what she thought.

"Last night, we agreed I'd look into the case and you'd trust me."

"I..." She had, hadn't she?

A smug smile curved his lips. "Exactly."

"I couldn't just sit here. I needed to do something."

"I get this is personal. I just thought we had come to an agreement to let me take the lead." He laid a hand on her arm.

She stared at his hand. Contemplated shaking it off.

"I'm sorry." He took his hand away. "We are on the same side."

Sort of. They might be on the same side, but that didn't change the power dynamic. She couldn't go off on her own or he might decide she was a suspect again. "True."

"Let's share intel." Alex sighed. "Symphony mentioned how Madeline and Paul were fighting at DeVout."

"She mentioned that to me too."

Alex nodded and blew out a breath. "She also said that Madeline spent Fridays in California."

"She mentioned that." Harper pursed her lips. He couldn't know where she was headed. She didn't want him tagging along. No offense, the guy was okay. But this wasn't about him.

"At a hotel in San Diego. The Hotel Del Coronado." He was fishing. For what, she had no idea.

"Yep."

"What are you hiding?" He nodded to her bag. "Where are you going?"

"Nowhere." This was her lead. This was her hotel with Brad. There were hundreds of hotels along the coast of California and Madeline had been going to this one. Why this one? Why Harper's hotel?

"Harp, really?" Alex's face was a mixture of annoyance and anger. One hand played at his hip where his handcuff case hung. And his body still stood between her and her car in the driveway. If she had been smart she would have parked her car in the garage for a couple reasons. One— because it was way too hot in Vegas with the noon sun beating down on the car seats. Two—because she could've pretended to not be home.

"Fine." There was no way she'd get out of here with him blocking the way, or worse, with her stuck here in cuffs. "I'm going to the Del."

"In San Diego."

"Yep." Short answers. Don't let anything slip.

"Why?"

"Madeline went there on Fridays."

"But she's not going to be there." Alex scowled, but it looked more like confusion than anything else.

"I know that." It's not like she was an idiot. She understood how death worked. And then she saw it. Pity. He was pitying her. Screw that. She'd had enough pity to last a lifetime. "I'm not going there to find Madeline, but they have cameras on the main floor. If I can get access to the footage…" She shrugged.

"How do you know that?"

This was why short answers were the way to go. When all else failed, play dumb. "Know what?"

"How do you know they have cameras on the main floor?"

"All hotels do." It was only logical.

"Harper?" Alex didn't seem to be buying the logic. And the pulsing vein in his neck said he was very close to reaching for those cuffs—and not in a fun way.

Fine, ugh. "I've been there."

"When did you go? With whom?" His jaw ticked. He knew how she was going to answer. He had to.

"My honeymoon. With Brad." This looked bad. She knew it. And now Alex knew it, too.

"So, of all the hotels in all the world, Madeline and her boyfriend went to a hotel you've been to."

"Yes. It's a hotel. People stay there. It's not unusual." It was just a coincidence. She didn't believe it, but she just had to make him believe that she believed it. Or something like that.

"So you're saying it's a coincidence that Madeline and her boyfriend—whose name we don't know—drove over three hundred miles on Fridays and stayed in the exact same hotel as you and your husband."

This was why she didn't want him to know. She knew he'd lose sight of the real issue. "Madeline had been seeing someone for the past year. It couldn't be Brad. He's gone." She tried to control her voice. She heard the catch on the word *gone.*

And given the return of pity to Alex's expression, he'd heard it too. "I'm not trying to be an asshole, but didn't Brad spend Fridays in San Diego before he died?"

"He was on a project in California," she told him. She knew San Diego was in California, but he was in *California* for work. "It's a big state."

Alex nodded, and he held up his hands like he was talking a jittery cat off a tree branch. "It's a big state, but, Harp, you have to admit this is a huge coincidence."

"But he went for work." He couldn't fake work.

"Where in California did he go?"

Harper breathed out hard through her nose. "All over. LA, Oakland…"

"San Diego?"

"Yes." That's how he knew about the Del. He'd stayed there when visiting a client back when he first started out in real estate. Not that she'd tell Alex that. He was already too far down a rabbit hole that she refused to acknowledge—without proof.

"Maybe we should hold off on the field trip to San Diego."

Another reason she shouldn't have told him anything. "Why?"

"How are you going to get the camera footage?"

"I was going to figure that out on the way there."

"There's nothing to figure out. We'll need a warrant." Another thing they needed a warrant for. That was starting to be her least favorite word.

"Can we get one?"

Alex's lips tipped up at the sides. "I'll submit the paperwork today, on one condition." He held up a finger and just stopped. Just left her hanging.

Are you kidding… "What's the condition?"

"Wait. Come with me to lunch."

The wait part was expected. But the lunch?

"There's this great burger place down the road," he added.

"Farmer Boys?"

"You've tried it."

"Who hasn't?" She pulled her purse from the bag. "But just so we're clear, if you don't have a warrant by Friday, I'm going on my own."

"If I don't have a warrant by Friday, I'll drive you myself."

Harper stuck out her hand and smiled. "Deal."

Alex took it and shook. Warmth spread through her fingers and zipped all the way to her toes. With one touch. If he could have this effect just touching her hand, she was in trouble.

A lot of trouble. The thought of being stuck in a car with Alex for six hours made her body burn. And she hadn't felt this way in a long, long time.

CHAPTER
SEVENTEEN

MONDAY AFTERNOON, Harper sat at her desk—knee bouncing and her eyes glued to the door. After a great burger and fries with the detective yesterday, she'd agreed to meet him after school today to talk to Brad's coworkers.

She was not looking forward to this. She hadn't seen Brad's coworkers in a year. Not to mention it would probably be a dead end. She had known Brad better than she knew herself. But she wanted to be in on the investigation, and if that meant a trip down memory lane—again—she'd do it.

One of her students raised his hand, but didn't wait for Harper to acknowledge him. "Ms. Lange, Bobbi is looking at my paper."

"Bobbi, keep your eyes on your own paper." Harper glanced at the clock. Ten minutes left, and then her date. Not a date, a police interview. She wasn't sure which terrified her more: that she immediately thought *date* or that it was actually a police interview. Both were equally scary. "Time to hand in your papers."

Henry ran to her desk and handed in his paper. He smiled as the other kids ran up behind him and fought to get their papers in the tray next.

"Slow down," Harper said. "Remember, I grade from the top. The last one in gets graded first." Henry immediately dug to the bottom of the pile and put his on top. Naturally. "All right, let's get ready for the bus or it will leave without you."

The last few kids slid the papers onto her desk, and ran for their lockers against the front wall. Yes, she tried to scare children so they'd stop wrangling over their papers. To be fair, it worked. "Don't forget to have your parents sign the permission slip in your bag."

A chorus of *okay* and *yes* came from over by the lockers. She'd learned a long time ago to make them put anything that needed to be sent home in their bag at lunch time. The end of day was pure chaos, with students bumping into each other like molecules, and it was too easy to forget things.

The final school bell rang and the kids flooded out into the hall, taking with them all the yelling and banging. Her own desk thumped as she yanked the drawer open. She was as excited as the kids for the bell. Well, maybe it wasn't excitement. More like nerves.

"Am I early?" Alex walked in the door as the last few kids left the room.

"Nope. We're going home." Henry smiled as he hiked his backpack over his shoulder and gave Harper a look.

The look was smug. Although, he was eight, so how smug could he be?

"Henry, right?" Alex nodded at the kid.

"That's me." Henri preened. "You're Ms. Harper's boyfriend."

Boyfriend. They weren't playing that game anymore, so she was curious how he'd answer.

"I am." Interesting. "You're Ms. Harper's student."

"I am." Henry beamed, like he was the only student in the world.

"You'll miss the bus." Harper nodded to the emptying hallway, and Henry ran out the door. The room was suddenly quiet as the yells of recently paroled students faded beyond the windows of the classroom.

Harper shoved the student papers into her bag before she slipped the strap over her shoulder and picked up her purse.

"Ready to go?" Alex slid his finger under the strap of her bag. "I'll take this."

She dropped her shoulder and let Alex remove the weight. He wrapped the strap around his hand and let it hang it at his side. It was sweet, like being back in grade school.

"So how was your day?" Alex held the side door as Harper slid through.

"It was good. Only confiscated one cell phone today. I think that's a new record."

"Are they allowed to have phones in school?"

"They're supposed to leave them in their lockers." She shook her head. "They never do."

"Maybe you should have DeVout handle your phone confiscation process, and then you'd never have problems." Alex laughed as he opened the passenger door of his Chevy crew cab pickup for her. He was carrying her bag, opening doors. Chivalry was alive in kicking in Las Vegas today. "It's like Fort Knox. No one is getting anything in or out, even if they wanted to."

And that chivalry had Harper all distracted, in a parts-tingling and mind-swooning kind of way.

Gosh, Harper missed chivalry. Just the thought of all she'd missed over the past year made her a little bit sad. She climbed into the passenger seat and waited as Alex shut the door behind her.

Alex opened the driver's side back door and set her bag on the seat. "Sorry, that wasn't funny."

What wasn't? Oh yeah, the phone confiscation and DeVout. Harper laughed—maybe a little too loud. "No, sorry, that was funny. I'm just distracted."

Alex slid behind the wheel and started the engine. "So what has you distracted?"

She was not answering that one. The words *self-pity* and *pathetic* would not be leaving her lips today. "Do you know where we're going?"

"Brad worked at Commercial Realty Pros over on Boulder Highway."

She should have known he'd know where Brad worked. He probably had a file and everything. A file she wanted to see. But since he probably wouldn't hand it over, questions would have to do. "So what else do you know about Brad?"

Alex turned onto Lake Mead Parkway.

Harper wasn't sure if he even heard her ask the question. He made no attempt to answer. Just concentrated on driving and merging with traffic.

"I know that Brad was a Realtor," Alex said finally. "I know he made the newspaper because of some big land deal for the Sláinte Hotel. He played golf. He was a member of DeVout."

That pretty much covered everything about Brad. He was simple. But Alex did forget one thing. "He also had an amazing wife."

Alex smiled as he turned onto Boulder Highway. "I figured that went without saying."

The parking lot was nearly empty when they pulled in a few minutes later. The Commercial Realty Pros sign hung over one glass front door, the red letters bright against the sand-colored stucco. A few Mercedes-Benzes, BMWs and Lexuses were still parked in front, but most of the spots were empty. Probably off showing properties or schmoozing with other foreign car owners over two fingers of cognac.

Alex parked in a spot at the far corner of the lot as a jalopy with smoke trailing from open windows rolled by. She could never understand why they put a multimillion-dollar real estate company in this neighborhood. Not that it was bad—there were very few bad neighborhoods in Henderson. But this was smack dab in the middle of a few apartment complexes with section-eight housing.

It just didn't match. But from what Brad had said when

he'd joined the team, the cheap rent matched the owners' desire to keep their money. So, there was that.

"Ready?" Alex opened his door but wasn't moving. Probably because Harper hadn't even made a move for her door. The last time she'd looked at this building, she had been bringing Brad his lunch, the one he forgot on the counter at home.

She hadn't been back since. Why come back when he wouldn't pop his head out of his office? Why enter the building when he wasn't going to kiss her on the cheek and try to talk her into sticking around and help him eat his lunch?

Yet here she was. "I'm ready." She almost checked her nose to see if it grew.

"If you want, I can do this alone. You can wait out here."

She ran her fingers over her face. Nope, didn't grow. She just sucked at lying.

Being in the lot reminded her of Brad. Going inside wouldn't change that. "No. I got this." She slipped out the door. She could do this. She'd handled DeVout—with only a minor meltdown.

She should have known that at some point she'd have to go to all these places. But she'd been so content in her own little world, avoiding everything from her past. Then this. She walked up to the front door and tried to forget when Brad would hold her hand as he'd escorted her to her car.

Harper shook her head. She couldn't think about it anymore. She couldn't look at the door, the building, the lot, and see Brad. She couldn't look at every little thing and miss him. She needed to move on.

Her chest actually ached thinking about it. And maybe today wasn't the day to move on. She just had to do it. Soon. Today she'd focus on staying here and now. And not see Brad everywhere she looked. Today she'd help interview Brad's oldest friend. Tomorrow she'd deal with the rest.

CHAPTER
EIGHTEEN

ALEX OPENED the glass door to Commercial Realty Pros and held it for Harper. "Ladies first."

"Thanks."

A woman in a black skirt and dark red collared shirt stood behind the desk just inside the door. She was either pregnant or carrying all her weight in her belly. "Harper?" The woman frowned, and then her face brightened. "Harper Specter. I haven't seen you since—since" —the funeral— "in a while."

Harper smiled because it was the polite thing to do. She could not remember who this woman was, but apparently she'd met her. "It's so nice to see you again." Little white lie. Hopefully, she'd gotten better since she'd lied to Alex outside. Otherwise, she'd hurt this poor woman's feelings.

"I really miss Brad." The woman leaned over the desk. "He was one of the best agents here." She shook her head. "Don't tell anyone I said that."

Harper mimed zipping her lips. "Your secret is safe with me."

The woman looked behind Harper and smiled. "Who's your friend?"

"Sorry." Harper stepped to the side. "This is Detective Cabrero."

"Detective Cabrero. Las Vegas Metro." Alex glanced at Harper, obviously realizing she didn't know who this woman was. "And you are?"

"Bonnie Schmidtgall." She rested her hand on her stomach and rubbed.

Yes! Bonnie. She'd started a few weeks before Brad had passed. Her face was fuller, probably from the bun cooking in her oven. No wonder Harper didn't recognize her.

"What brings you to the office? Wait, you came for Brad's things." Bonnie hobbled behind her stand-up desk and opened a large drawer. She pulled out a cardboard box and handed it to Harper.

"Thanks." Harper juggled the box until it miraculously disappeared from her hands. Alex smiled at her as he easily propped the box in one arm. "We're here to see Lydia."

"Of course. I'll go get her." Bonnie wobbled toward an open door but didn't have to go very far before Lydia walked out in a bright red dress, all smiles. Harper had missed Lydia, one of Brad's best friends from college. She'd hired him when he was buried underneath college debt.

"Harper Specter, as I live and breathe." Apparently no

one got the memo that Harper had gone back to her maiden name. And she was too tired to explain.

Lydia wrapped Harper in a hug. Six inches shorter than Harper, she had twice the energy. She smelled like a flower bed, but Lydia's Betty Boop body was as squishy as a mattress. At one point, Harper had been jealous of Lydia's relationship with Brad. But then she'd gotten to know her. It didn't hurt that Lydia was a lesbian who had basically been married to her college girlfriend before women were allowed to be married.

"How are you doing?" Lydia pulled away, and then immediately smashed Harper back into her chest. "I've missed you."

"I missed you, too." Harper wanted to cry. She hadn't come by to see her friend—because yes, she'd become friends with Lydia over the years—and that should have made her feel awful. But she wouldn't let it. She'd made a promise to focus on the here and now. "How's Chrissy?"

Lydia's wife had been dealing with some health issues before the accident. Hell, she probably was still dealing with them, since Huntington's didn't just go away.

"She's hanging in there." Lydia's lips turned down. "She has good days and bad days. It's been an adjustment. You should come on by. She'd love to see you."

And Harper would love that, too. Just seeing Lydia brought back so many memories, but it also felt comfortable and familiar. Like friends and home. God, Harper missed having that. "I will. I promise."

"Are you still working over at Il Vincitore?" Lydia took Harper's hand and led her into her office.

Harper wasn't sure, but she thought she heard Alex following them. "I am."

Lydia let go of Harper's hand and waved at the chairs in front of her desk. "Have a seat?"

Harper sat. Lydia walked behind her desk, and Harper saw the moment she noticed Alex standing in the doorway.

"I'm sorry." Lydia came around to the door and held out her hand. "I'm Lydia Hess."

"Detective Cabrero, Las Vegas Metro."

Lydia looked from Alex to Harper. "Is everything okay?"

"Yes." Alex nodded. "We just have some questions in regards to Brad's case."

Lydia's eyebrows stitched together as she sat down behind her desk. "Is his case reopened?"

"We have new information and we're just revisiting his file." Alex sat in the chair next to Harper. "We need to ask a few questions."

"Of course. Whatever you need." Lydia crossed her legs and leaned back against the chair.

"How did you know Brad Specter?"

"We went to college together. We met in Marketing 101. He tried to pick me up with a wink and a Snickers."

Harper had heard this story many times. And each time she laughed.

"Snickers?" Alex looked confused. And who wouldn't be? Since when did a grown man use Snickers candy to pick up a woman?

Lydia smiled crookedly. "He asked if I wanted a Snickers, because like him, it really satisfies."

Alex smirked. "He didn't."

"He did." Lydia's laugh was tinkling and contagious.

"And you still became friends with him."

"Right? I was young and dumb." Lydia's laughter faded. "Over the years, he became my rock. When my first girlfriend dumped me for the lead singer of a rave band, he helped me egg her car. When my brother died in plane crash, he helped me pack up his house and set up the funeral arrangements. When my wife was diagnosed with Huntington's, he let me cry on his shoulder, so I could be strong in front of Chrissy. He was a good friend."

"Sounds like it." Alex leaned forward in his seat. "Right before the accident, Brad was working in California. Why was he in California?"

"California?" Lydia's face blanked. "Oh yeah, California. He helped one of our clients buy land in San Diego, but that was months before he died."

"He was still going to California up until he died." Harper tried to hide the squeak at the end of the sentence, but there was no way they didn't catch it. She swore she heard dogs bark in the distance from the sound.

Lydia shook her head. "Brad found the client a warehouse in April."

"But he said he was going to California every Friday." Harper remembered. She had a fricking red rose for every time he left.

"I don't know…"

"Ms. Hess, did Brad come into work on Fridays?"

Lydia bit at her lip and fumbled with the edges of papers on her desk. "No."

Alex might have wanted to ask the next question, but Harper beat him to it. "Where was he?"

"He said he was taking time to play golf with a friend."

"Which friend?" Not that it mattered. She thought they told each other everything. She thought she knew Brad better than she knew herself. But he'd gone golfing on Fridays and didn't tell her. Why wouldn't he tell her?

"Paul." Lydia couldn't even look Harper in the eyes.

"Do you know why he was golfing every week?"

"I figured he was going after new business. Paul set him up with the Peridot sale, and I thought he was looking to create more of those five-figure opportunities."

Peridot. The sale that landed him in the newspaper, but it wasn't a five-figure type of deal. "Five figures? He didn't make five figures on that deal."

"He did." Lydia nodded as she turned her chair and pulled a manila file out of a filing cabinet. She slid a piece of paper across the desk to Harper.

A contract. Peridot. Twenty-five thousand dollars. "Twenty-five?" She couldn't even repeat the rest. She'd never seen this money.

"That was his commission."

Tears stung the back of Harper's eyes, but she pushed them back. Her husband was off golfing with friends and hiding money. He'd lied to her. Why?

"I take it you never knew about the money?" Lydia handed Harper a tissue.

Harper took it and dabbed at her eyes. Pushing the

tears back wasn't working. Her eyes were as big of a traitor as her husband.

"I'm sure it was nothing." Lydia's smile looked forced. "He probably just forgot to tell you. Maybe he'd had big plans to surprise you."

"Maybe." Harper squeezed her eyes shut and patted them dry. No more. She just had to ignore the idea of Brad and his lying and whatever the hell else he'd been doing while they were joined together in the holy bond of matrimony. "I'm sure that's what happened."

Alex asked Lydia a few more questions. But they didn't matter. None of it mattered. Harper knew all the answers to those questions. She couldn't get her mind off the ones she didn't know.

Why was he taking every Friday off, and was it with Paul like he told Lydia? Or was he lying to his boss, too? Why hadn't that money appeared in any of their accounts when he'd died?

Harper had had nothing. The accounts had been anemic at best. She'd had to leave their home and find her own place.

So that money was not in her possession. Which led to the question, who had it?

CHAPTER
NINETEEN

TEN MINUTES LATER, Alex held open the passenger door as Harper slid inside. He put the boxes on the back seat. She'd forgotten all about Brad's things.

Lydia had smiled and tried to play off the whole golf thing as innocent, but who was she kidding. It didn't matter if he was playing golf with Mickey Mouse. He hadn't told his wife. No one lied to their wife unless they were doing something sneaky, right? There was nothing innocent about that.

"I'm sure he was just golfing." Alex turned the key and the engine sparked to life. He backed up and headed for the exit to the lot.

"So, what, you're lying to me now, too?" That might have come out way harsher than needed, but she deserved to be a little harsh right now. Her world had been upended. Again.

"No." Alex pulled into another spot and parked. "Look at me."

Harper didn't want to look. She wanted to cry. But that damn promise to herself meant no tears. And the fact that Alex wasn't proceeding with whatever thought he had meant he was waiting for her. She tilted her head so she could see Alex and swallowed back the lump clogging her throat.

"I don't know what Brad was up to, but we'll figure it out." Alex turned in his seat and watched her. When his eyes were on her like this she felt like she was the only person in the world.

He continued. "Sometimes people need time away to deal with something. I know you don't want to think about it, but could Brad have known about your medical situation? Maybe he figured it out."

"I don't think so." There was no way for him to know. "Unless he went to visit my gynecologist."

The terror on Alex's face at just the thought of visiting a gynecologist was almost comical. "We'll go with a no on that. Was Brad anxious or worried about something?"

"No." She'd always thought Brad was happy. Maybe not ecstatic, like he'd been at the Electric Daisy Festival. But that wasn't normal happy. That was the elusive happy that happens a couple of times in someone's life. But maybe he was searching for that again. Wait. That wasn't the only thing he'd been looking for. "The only thing I can think of was he'd stopped looking for his family."

"I thought he had no family."

"He was abandoned, but it was never determined what happened to his parents. He'd tried to look for them, but he kept hitting dead end after dead end. He couldn't take the disappointment any longer, so he stopped."

"Did that upset him?"

"Yeah, for a while. But he seemed to get over it. At least I thought he had." For months after he gave up the search, he'd been quiet and distant. But he'd slowly gotten back to normal.

"Why did he decide to look for them?"

"Lydia's wife Chrissy was diagnosed with Huntington's disease. Her grandmother completely lost all her faculties and she was looking at the same fate. It got him thinking about his parents and his sister and whether any diseases ran his family. He started looking, and one path pointed to his parents dying, but he couldn't be sure it was them. So then he focused on his sister. But nothing. The adoption agency burned down right after he was adopted. The agency had been in the process of putting everything on computers. Apparently, they had been behind the times. It became so hard for him to deal with the disappointment, so he stopped looking." And she hadn't wanted to push him.

"I'm sorry. That must have been hard."

"It was." She'd felt so helpless to help.

"Maybe he was handling it worse than you thought. Maybe he needed a friend."

A friend that wasn't her. "Paul."

"Paul." Alex reached over and slid his hand in hers.

The warmth of his palm slipped through her body, warming her chest. She wanted to feel guilty—because,

because— this felt so good. She was married. Well, not anymore. It still felt weird. And good.

He stroked his thumb over her wrist. "I should probably talk to him, but if you want sit this one out, I'll keep you posted."

Talking to Paul was about as high on her list as rehashing all of this old news. But she needed to know if Brad had really been on a golf course every Friday—and why. And why the hell he hadn't told her. "I really want to go."

"I understand." Alex nodded as he let go of her hand, staring out the windshield. "Since we're going to talk to Paul, I want to ask you a question."

The hesitancy in his voice and the fact that he felt it necessary to preface the question with an announcement about the question told her she wasn't going to like it.

"Fridays. I'm sure Brad was golfing, but I'm going to have to find out if it's true." Alex sighed. "If he wasn't golfing with Paul, I'm going to be looking into the Madeline angle. Can you handle that?"

No. "Yes. I need to know."

"Could Brad have been with Madeline?"

The possibility Harper had refused to consider. But it hung there like a huge elephant. Sword. Whatever. The elephant of deception. That was a thing, right? Clogging up all the air in the room. "I'd like to think no, but now I'm not so sure."

"Do you trust Paul to tell you the truth?"

"No. I don't know. But they were friends. If anyone would know why he was taking off on Friday, it would be

Paul." And didn't that thought scare the crap out of her. Her whole marital memoir in the hands of a jerk.

Thirty minutes later, after braving rush hour traffic, Harper and Alex stood at the front door of Paul's house waiting for the doorbell to stop dinging and someone to answer the door. Someone had to be home because someone had answered the call from the security gate. Although if Paul knew she was in the car, he probably would have said no.

"Paul might still be at work." Which would suck. Although then she'd get to see Britany. Which wasn't all that bad.

"Maybe, but I'd rather talk to him in a relaxed environment. I show up at the office and lawyers circle like sharks."

The door flew open and one of those sharks stood in the doorway holding a short glass with amber liquid. "Harper and the cop. Why are you here?"

"It's so nice to see you too." Harper couldn't help the sarcasm. Paul just had that effect on her.

"I'm sorry, did I incorrectly imply I was happy to see you?" Paul glared at her.

Alex said, "Mr. Williams, I was hoping to ask a few questions."

"About?" Ice clinked as Paul took a drink from his glass.

"About Brad Specter."

Paul stared at Harper, and she expected the word *no* to fall from his lips. But instead he said, "Come in."

Harper followed Paul into the sitting room and perched in the L of the large white couch. Alex sat next to her.

Paul chose a chair on the other side of the room. "What do you want to know?"

"Before Brad's accident, did you spend any time with him?" Alex leaned forward, his elbows on his knees.

"Not anything unusual. We saw him at the Byrnes' parties."

"Did you golf with him at all?"

"We hadn't golfed in months. I tried to get him to go, but he had other plans." Paul shrugged, looking confused.

Join the club. Harper was all kinds of confused.

"What is this about?" Paul focused on Harper, but he didn't seem angry. He almost looked sad.

"Paul, did you meet Brad to go golfing on Fridays? Starting around May before he died?"

"No. Should I have?"

"Are you sure?" Harper thought the words, but Alex managed to say them out loud.

"I think I would know if I took time away from my practice to golf with one of my best friends."

"Do you know if he was golfing with anyone else on Fridays?"

"If he was, I would have been with him."

"Paul, where else could he have gone?" Harper heard the desperation in her voice. She didn't care. "Please, if you know anything, let me know."

Paul shook his head. "I don't know anything about Brad golfing on Fridays."

Harper felt a lump in her throat. He didn't know about golf. "What about anything else? Was he cheating on me?"

Paul stared into the glass before taking a sip. He stood up and stared out the sliding glass door. "I don't think so, but I don't know."

"Oh." The lump in Harper's throat grew into a ball that made it hard to breathe. She swallowed, but she couldn't move the object. He didn't know. He didn't know if Brad was cheating. All of a sudden she didn't either.

"Shit." Paul continued to stare out the door. "He was going to Pahrump."

Pahrump? Why there? Pahrump was the middle of nowhere. There wouldn't have been any reason for Brad to spend any time forty minutes south of Las Vegas.

"How do you know that?" Alex's back was now ramrod straight.

"My wife was acting weird. She and I shared everything, and then it was gone. She couldn't look at me. We were a shell." Paul threw back the amber liquid in his glass like he had to catch it before it ran out the door. He turned to Harper. "It started when Madeline got pregnant."

Harper had no idea. "When?"

"The summer before Brad died. We were so excited. She was glowing." His eyes glazed.

Harper's throat closed. Madeline had been pregnant. Why wouldn't she have told Harper about that?

"What happened?" Alex watched Paul put the glass down on a side table.

"In September, she started bleeding. I rushed her to the hospital, but it was too late." Paul cleared his throat. "We lost the baby."

"Oh, god. I'm so sorry." Harper couldn't keep her promise not to cry as a tear slid down her cheek. "Why didn't she say anything?"

"She was heartbroken. She didn't want to talk about it —even with me." Paul gave a small smile, but it didn't eliminate the heartbreak tearing across his face. "The doctor said we could try again, but she had an abnormality that meant she probably wouldn't be able to conceive."

Oh god, that must've killed Madeline. Like the word *endometriosis* about killed Harper. They were in the same childless boat.

"She threw herself into work."

"Where did she work?" Alex kept him talking.

"She was the CFO over at Sláinte. She'd spend day and night there sometimes." Paul picked up his glass from the table and stared at the ice. "It took her spirit. Her laughter. She pulled away. She stopped enjoying sex and she stopped wanting to date other couples."

"Did that anger you?" Alex was still in full cop mode.

"No. I was having a hard enough time dealing with it myself. I always figured we'd have kids." Paul shook his head back and forth like he was trying to Etch-a-Sketch all the bad thoughts away. "I gave her space. And then she started acting weird. She wanted things I couldn't give her."

"Like what?"

"She wanted me to hurt her. Like, really hurt her. In the bedroom. I tried but I couldn't." Paul walked to a bar in the far corner of the room. "Want anything?"

"No thanks." Harper's answer mingled with Alex's "No."

"More for me." Paul sighed as he filled his glass. "I couldn't even make her happy. She said she needed something more."

"What did she mean by more?" Harper's heart was breaking for her friend. Heck, even for Paul. Their relationship always looked so solid—even though he was a jerk. She seemed happy, but apparently it wasn't as it seemed.

"Someone who could hit her. Not like simple flogging, or things we'd done in the past. She wanted real physical pain."

"What did you do?"

"I tried." He shook his head, and swiped the corner of one eye with his thumb. "I really did, but I couldn't. I...I couldn't watch her cry. I couldn't be the reason. I asked her to see someone. To find a therapist to talk to. But she refused. And then she found someone else. Someone who could meet her needs."

"Who?" Harper had an idea where this was going, but it didn't stop her from praying it wasn't Brad. *Please don't be Brad.*

Paul faced Harper. "For the longest time, I thought it was Brad."

Her stomach lurched.

"Was it?" Alex asked the question. Harper couldn't get the words past the heaving.

"I don't know. I kept hoping he'd tell me when we'd go out. But he was always too fucking busy. He wouldn't meet for golf, wouldn't do dinner. What the hell was I supposed to think?"

"So what did you do?" Alex stood up.

"I hired a PI. Figured she'd find out if Brad was meeting my wife. She followed him for a week, but he died before she could get anything. All she said was that he went to a place in Pahrump, but she'd lost him."

"What's in Pahrump?" Harper wanted to be mad that Paul had her husband followed, but somehow, right now she wanted to hug him. If he could tell her what the hell was going on, she'd literally wrap her arms around him.

"I don't know."

"Did the PI ever find out who was with your wife?" Alex asked.

"No. Once Brad died, I just couldn't do it anymore." Paul shook his head. "I couldn't live like that. I couldn't keep being jealous. I loved Madeline and wanted her any way she'd have me. And Brad was just gone. Life's too short. That's when I started getting serious with Britany."

"I apologized to her." Harper didn't know why, but she thought he should know that.

Paul smiled. A true smile. "Thank you for that."

"No need to thank me. She's nice."

"She is." Paul took another drink. "I wanted to work things out with Madeline. She was my wife. But she just didn't care. After she lost the baby, she just stopped —being."

"I'm so sorry, Paul." And Harper meant it. "For everything."

Paul nodded. "Thanks."

"Have you thought of anyone else that might want Madeline or Brad dead?" Alex kept the interrogation on track.

"No." Paul stared into his glass almost like he wanted to drown in it. "Any more questions?"

"I think that's it." Alex headed toward the front door as Harper stood.

"We'll find who did this." Harper wasn't going to stop till they did.

Paul emptied the glass down his throat. "Let it go."

Was he kidding? "Let what go?"

"Just let the police do their job. You're not going to like what you find." Paul headed back to the bar and grabbed the bottle of bourbon. "Trust me."

She wasn't sure if he was concerned for her or if that was a threat. But since it was Paul, it could go either way.

A HALF HOUR LATER, Harper sat in front of her house—in Alex's car—trying to get away. "I'll be fine."

"Are you sure?" Alex drummed his fingers on the steering wheel. "Today was a lot."

A lot was an understatement. She didn't even know where to begin describing what an understatement that was.

"Are you going to be okay alone?"

"I'll be fine. I have a bag of donuts and Netflix. My night is set." Part of her wanted to say no and invite him in her house—eat donuts and have him help her forget that today ever existed—but that wouldn't be good for her right now. She needed to be away from men. All of them.

She probably didn't need the donuts either, but she was only human.

"Okay." He looked concerned, like she was going to OD on sugar and start foaming at the mouth. The sugar thing might happen...

"Look, today was shocking, but I'll get over it."

"Did you know?"

Did she know what? Did she know that Friday golf was a lie? No. Did she know that Brad had money he hadn't told her about? No. There was so much she didn't know. "Can you be more specific?"

"That he was lying?"

"Something was off, but I didn't think anything of it. He'd gotten upset about not being able to find his family before. It was a cycle. He'd look, find nothing, and then he'd quit. He'd get upset and eventually feel better."

"Why did he keep on looking?"

"I don't know." She was so tired. Tired of talking and tired of thinking about Brad. "I should go in." She slipped off her seatbelt and opened the door.

"Thanks for coming today."

"Thanks for letting me tag along." It might have been painful, but it was good she found out the truth. At least that was what she kept trying to tell herself. Harper stepped out of the truck and took a deep breath. The cool, dry air energized her.

She opened the back door of the truck and took Brad's personal effects box out of the back seat. Walked up the front walk. Opened the door. Went inside. Silence met her as she locked the door. Alex's headlights bounced off the wall and skittered away.

She was alone. It sounded like such a good idea in the car.

She dropped her purse and the box in the living room and headed into the kitchen where a bag of coconut crunch donuts was waiting for her. They were old and mini-sized, but who cared. A donut was a donut.

She filled a wine glass half full of rosé and took a few gulps from the bottle before grabbing a mini-donut and eating it over the counter. Don't judge. She'd had a bad day. Another gulp. Another donut. Her chest tingled with warmth and her belly was happy.

Harper reached in the donut bag. Empty. Crap. There went dinner. She picked up her glass to go sit on the couch, but it was so sad. Glass half full. She could fix that. She tipped the bottle over the glass. Empty.

She wasn't quite sure how long she'd been standing at the counter, but apparently it was long enough to polish off a bag of mini donuts and a bottle of wine. Most of a bottle of wine.

So not a good sign.

She took the glass and flopped onto the couch, only spilling a little wine on the floor. She draped her arm over the end table and slapped at the top, looking for the remote.

Her cell phone rang as something hit the floor with a rattle. Probably the remote. She'd take bets on that, but there was no one here to make it interesting.

Her phone rang again. She braced her feet and shoved one hand in her pocket for her phone, while trying to not spill any more of her drink. If she stood up this wouldn't be so hard, but standing up was overrated. So were cell phones. It rang again.

Who the hell used cell phones for calling anyway? No one she knew, that's for sure.

She finally extracted the stupid phone and accepted the call. "No one I know would call me on my cell phone."

"Where would they call you?" A woman's voice. It almost sounded like Britany.

"Britany?"

"Yep." There was a clicking noise— a turn signal?— and other voices in the background. "We're coming over."

"Why? And who's we?"

"We need to find out what was in Pahrump, right?"

"How do you know about that?"

"Paul." Britany sounded like she was smiling. Harper wanted to slap the happiness off her face. Britany continued. "He told me what happened, and I was worried about you."

She was just too sweet. There would be no slapping. Harper loved Britany. How did that happen?

"Ask her if she ate. Ask her," another voice asked in the background.

"I will," Britany said, or at least that's what Harper thought she said because it was muffled. Her voice unmuffled as she asked, "Did you eat?"

"Mini-donuts and wine."

"So, that's a no. We'll be there in thirty." The line went dead. Apparently they were coming and there might be food. Probably a good thing. Harper needed something to counteract the wine in her veins.

Too bad Britany mentioned finding out what was in Pahrump. Harper wasn't sure she was ready for that. She wasn't sure what she'd find, and she was scared Paul was right. Because, really, what were the chances she'd like what she found?

A short time later, somebody knocked at Harper's front door.

She wasn't sure how long it was. Not long enough. She was still trying to find excuses for not talking about Pahrump. *We can't talk about Pahrump on even days of the week. We can't talk about Pahrump because Vegas will get jealous. Speaking its name makes Voldemort appear.*

The last one popped into her head while she was channel surfing and hit a Harry Potter marathon on one of the cable channels.

Given all that, she obviously needed more time.

Another knock.

She didn't have time. She stumbled to the front door and whipped it open. Britany, Symphony, Amelia, and Emma stood on her front porch.

"Let us in." Symphony looked Harper up and down as she held out a bag of food. She didn't scowl, but Harper had a feeling she could see the wine that hadn't quite made it in her mouth.

Harper ran a hand along the front of her shirt to erase any spills. She looked down at the pink stains along her Gilmore Girls tank top. Oh, and now she wore ratty shorts, too. When had she changed into her pajamas? It was a mystery.

"We brought wine and food." That was Emma, in her perfectly pressed off-white pants, complete with a neatly tied brown fabric belt. Her light pink V-neck cashmere sweater hung casually off one shoulder. She scowled, probably at Harper's ratty shorts.

"Looks like you already found some wine." Britany took the glass from Harper's hand. She knew it was Britany because she was wearing purple. Okay, it was Britany's signature color and all, but were there enough clothes in purple to wear it all the time?

Harper would ask, but the only wine left in the house was walking away.

"I ran out." Harper stumbled while she followed her glass to the kitchen island and sank onto a stool.

"I see that." Symphony set a paper bag on the counter and took out some black plastic containers.

"What's for dinner?" Harper reached for one of the lids and Symphony slapped her hand. "Hey!"

"Wait till we pull out plates." Symphony was all punked out, in black skinny jeans with red suspenders hanging down the sides and a cut-off T-shirt announcing she fought like a girl in red and black tiger print. Her black platform boots looked like they'd seen some military action, except for the whole platform thing. "Have you found any plates yet?" Symphony asked Amelia. "She looks like she's going to gnaw my arm off."

"Who?" Harper rubbed at her stinging hand. Symphony was mean.

"You."

Harper refused to pout. "I'm not gnawing anything. I just wanted to see what kind of food you brought."

"Thai." Symphony took more food out of the bag.

"I like Thai."

"I know. I told them." Amelia set four plates on the counter.

Emma sat on a stool and waved at the kitchen cabinets. "Why are your plates all the way over there?"

"So maybe I'll be too lazy to grab one and skip eating." *Duh.*

"Has that ever worked?" Amelia added wine glasses to the crowded counter.

"There was that one time… no. I just ate a Twinkie," Harper admitted. "But it could work, and it's that hope that makes it all worth it."

"Hoping is half the battle." Symphony opened containers, and peanut and garlic permeated the air. She lifted a pile of noodles onto a plate.

Harper's stomach rumbled. "Are those garlic noodles?"

"Yep." Symphony slid the plate across the counter.

Harper smiled when her wine glass appeared at her elbow. Filled. They were all angels.

Before she could take a sip, Emma snatched it from her hand. "Eat first, lightweight." Emma handed Harper a fork. "Eat. Then more wine."

"You're no fun." Harper spun her fork in the noodles and brought a bite to her mouth. Salty garlic perfection. Another bite. Egg and peanut sauce. Her stomach smiled.

She hadn't realized how hungry she was. Who would have thought a couple mini donuts didn't make a dinner? She took a few more bites as the three other women gathered around the island and began eating their tofu satay and rama noodles.

Symphony leaned in when they all down to nearly clean plates. "So, it's time to start talking. What happened?"

Harper finished her bite and looked up into expectant —sympathetic— faces. Today she'd take the sympathy. Had she mentioned it had been a rough day? "I'm going to need the wine to get through this."

Amelia handed over the glass. "You earned it. Now speak."

Harper took a deep drink, and then today's headlines came out. All of it. Madeline's Friday excursions to San Diego with her Brainiac. Brad's lying, and his trekking to Pahrump.

"Did you have him followed?" Emma's blue eyes widened. Her sympathy had been overtaken by something that looked like shock without the awe. More like awful.

In their circle, one that embraced and expected trust, being suspicious was not exactly popular. The lifestyle was all about strong relationships and trust.

"Not really." Harper took another drink and looked over at Britany. How much had Paul told her? She didn't want to ruin another relationship or cause any friction.

All of that must have been written on her face because Britany smiled. "Don't worry, Paul told me what happened. He tells me everything."

"Really?" Harper couldn't believe that Paul was honest with Britany—to that degree. And all this time she thought he was a tool. Yet he spoke the truth to his girlfriend while Brad didn't.

Paul was still kind of a tool, though.

Harper took another drink. "Paul hired a PI. He thought Madeline was sleeping with Brad."

"Wait." Emma's eyes widened to saucer proportions. If Harper had a teacup, she was sure it would fit. "Paul sent a PI after Madeline?"

"Not Madeline. Brad."

"Then He broke Madeline's trust as well as Brad's. He didn't ask the questions. He sent in a private detective to trail her." Emma's pale face was splashed all over in red splotches. She looked at the other women, who were staring at her. "Obviously their relationship was in question, but they didn't stop coming to the club."

"This has nothing to do with you or the club," Harper told her. "They were having troubles and they were dealing with it. Paul's human." *Crap.* Harper almost ran to the window to see if pigs were flying. She was defending Paul.

"Are you defending him?" Emma pulled her dark brown hair back into a ponytail and secured it with a hair-tie from her wrist.

Yes, she was. So disturbing. It had to be the wine. "Maybe I am. He was going through some things, and he did some things he regrets." Harper had given Emma that hair-tie bracelet to her for her birthday a few years ago. "You kept it."

"Of course I kept it." Emma shrugged. "I figured eventually we'd become friends again."

Harper didn't want to have this conversation, especially in front of other people, but she couldn't stop the words from coming out. "Did we stop?" She almost didn't want to know the answer because then all hope was lost, but deep down she needed to know.

"You stopped calling. You stopped taking my calls. I assumed we stopped being friends." Emma's lips curved into a frown. If she was a crier, Harper could imagine she would've started to tear up. Harper was crier.

Tears welled and slid down Harpers cheeks. "I just needed some space. Every time I saw anyone from the club or even from my old life, I couldn't handle it. I just saw…Brad."

"Don't you think I know that? Why do you think I was so happy to see you and Alex together? To see you move on. But that was a lie, wasn't it?"

"I am so sorry I brought a cop to the club."

"Do you think I care about that? I'm not happy, but that was nothing." Fire brimmed in Emma's eyes. "You lied to me."

"I know."

"Here I thought I was going to get my friend back. That you'd want to go out to dinner or see a movie. That you were ready to move on. That you were over him."

"You wanted me over my husband?" Harper's voice rose, but she didn't care. One of the hardest things she'd been through, and Emma wanted her to just move on. Like it was oh so easy.

"I'm sure she didn't mean it like that," Amelia said.

Emma sighed. "I didn't want you over him. I wanted us to be friends again. I miss you."

Maybe it was the wine or maybe it was Emma's disappointment, either way Harper's heart cracked in her chest. She knelt on the chair and leaned over the counter to wrap her arms around Emma. "I miss you, too."

"We can't go that long without seeing each other again." Emma squeezed Harper closer.

The counter dug into Harper's thigh, but she didn't care. This was the best feeling in the world. Being here with Emma. Even though they were crying, she didn't care. She missed having a friend. She missed hugging. She missed Emma. And they really couldn't go this long apart again. "Agreed. I've felt so alone."

And Harper had been alone for so long. She wanted to believe it was easier, but bringing up the past didn't make life easier when she had to avoid life to do it.

"Can I get in on this?" Symphony joined in. "You're not alone."

"Me too." Amelia leaned over the counter and held out her arms.

"Get in here." Emma waved to Britany, and they all came together in a big hug-fest. After a minute they each peeled away, wiping their eyes with the back of their hands. *I'm not crying. You're crying.*

But they all were. Even Emma.

"You're not alone. We're all here." Emma lips turned up in a watery smile.

Harper looked at her group of mismatched friends and

couldn't help but smile back. They were here. Together. With Britany. She didn't get the impression that Britany had been friends with any of them. "How did you all get here?"

"Britany drove." Symphony poured herself more wine before she took her plate over to the sink.

"No. I mean, were you all hanging out?" Not that Harper could say anything if they had been. Maybe they were all BFFs now. They all had lives while Harper was busy hiding from hers.

Red swept Britany's cheeks. "Paul told me everything and then he got called in with some emergency at Sláinte." She finished off the last little bite on her plate and handed it to Symphony, who rinsed it and put it in the dishwasher. "I swear you guys work him like crazy."

Emma shook her head. "We have some HR issues. I have four meetings tomorrow to try and fix it. Not like I plan on getting my hands dirty on any of it. That's why we hire HR staff."

"That's too bad." Britany's voice pitched up. "Anyway, he told me about the PI and Madeline and Brad. Then he told me that he'd had to confess to you about all of it. He felt terrible. So instead of staying home, I called Symphony. She's the only one who really talks to me at the club. I thought she might know your address."

"She doesn't," Harper said. At least she didn't think she had.

"I didn't," Symphony confirmed. "But I figured Amelia would know, so I called her."

"And I called Emma." Amelia smiled.

Britany raised her glass in a toast. "And that's how we all ended up at your doorstep."

"I'm glad you came." Harper couldn't even imagine getting through tonight alone. Mostly because she didn't have to—thanks to her friends.

"We need to talk about the topic at hand."

"Which topic is that?" Harper took the bottle of wine and headed to the living room. She set the bottle on the table and dropped onto the couch. This time, no spilling. Success.

"Why was your husband in Pahrump?" Emma lifted Harper's legs from the couch and sat down, resting Harper's feet in her lap.

"He'd been there for a land deal," Harper said, "but it closed a couple years ago and he hadn't been back. Or I thought he hadn't."

Emma hummed. "But if there's nothing else there, that's got to be it."

"It can't be a land deal in Pahrump." Britany sat on a side chair. "The big casinos won't go near there right now. Even the one that they built was closed about a year and a half ago. There's no way they'd build in Pahrump again. It completely drained them. Wait, you don't think he went to one of those brothels, do you?"

A brothel? Brad? No. No matter how much she didn't know Brad, she knew he wouldn't go to a brothel. He didn't need to. She gave him all the freedom he needed to explore sexual relationships. They both had that freedom.

"Why would he go to a brothel? That's just stupid." Amelia seemed to be getting mad on Harper's behalf.

Harper wasn't sure she minded, but Britany looked offended. Harper shrugged. "I don't think he would go to a brothel."

"If it's not a land deal, why Pahrump?" Symphony asked from the kitchen.

"If only there was a way to track where he was." Britany slid her shoes off and curled her toes over the edge of Harper's coffee table.

"Does it matter though? He's gone, why sully your memories?"

"I guess." Harper didn't want to sully anything, but she had to know. And something kept poking at the back of her mind. *If only there was a way to track where he was.*

If she could've tracked him. Found out where he was. Maybe just see where he had been. Holy shit.

"I have his phone."

"How will that help?" Amelia curved her feet underneath her and leaned against the back of the couch. "You can't really look at his phone and see where he's been."

"Doesn't the phone have to be active to check location on Google maps?" Symphony took a drink from her glass.

It was Harper's turn for her face to heat fire engine red. "I haven't turned it off."

"Wait. What?" Emma had that look again. Judging. Maybe a bit like Harper was crazy.

"I like to listen to his outbound voice message. I don't have any voicemails from him left. It's all I have."

Emma rested a hand on Harper's arm. "Of course. But that must make it hard to move on."

"Go grab the phone. Let me see what I can do."

Symphony smiled. Her words didn't say it, but her soft tone had pity written all over it.

"Sure." Harper walked down the back hall, passing the second bedroom and its locked door. She didn't have time or energy to think about that. She turned into her bedroom and pulled Brad's phone from the charger on her nightstand. Yes, on the nightstand. She tapped the screen to life. The last app she opened still shone. His contacts were opened. The name Nutmeg.

Her. She missed being called Nutmeg. She missed so many things. Taking a breath, she closed the app and ran into the living room.

"Okay. I got it." Harper sat down on the floor and stared at the picture of her on the home screen. "How do I check where the phone has been?"

"Open the map." Symphony leaned forward.

"Which map?"

"Here give it to me." Symphony took the phone and clicked around the screen. "Here. It's in Google maps. What date?"

"Some random Friday. Two years ago."

"It looks like the phone hasn't moved much this month." Symphony poked around.

"I haven't taken the phone out of the house." Harper was barely turning it on these days. Just when she needed to hear his voice.

Symphony poked and swiped. Then her lips turned up into a smile as she bounced. "Found it!"

Harper grabbed the phone and read the screen. "It says he was on Homestead Road in Pahrump."

Amelia's lip turned up. "What's on Homestead Road?"

"Does it tell you what's there?" Emma's breath was in Harper's ear.

"Maybe he was buying fireworks? I hear they have a good selection at those mega stores." Britany was leaning over, her face next to Harper's.

"Or maybe he was looking to buy you a horse." Emma was on the other side.

"A horse?" Symphony was looking over Harper's head.

"What the hell else is in Pahrump but fireworks and horses?"

"They have some pretty good brothels." Symphony leaned against the back of her chair and took a deep drink of wine.

"How do you know that they're pretty good?" Emma's tone had a bit of a bite.

"What? My ex was into sharing." Symphony was full of surprises.

"I don't think it's sharing if he was going from girl to girl."

"Who said he was the one going from girl to girl?"

"You were going from guy to guy?" There might have been a bit of appreciation in Britany's tone.

"Not really." Symphony shrugged. "I'm fluid. I enjoy the company of men and women. And my ex liked to watch."

"You know we offer that at the club without going to the bargain basement." Emma may have been trying to be helpful, but it just came out as judgmental. Perhaps it was the bargain. Or the basement.

"We didn't know about the club or we would have been there. Well, we might have. We probably wouldn't have been able to afford it back then."

"But you can now. Why not invite him to one of the parties?" That excited gleam was in Emma's eye.

"Long gone. He got a job in Chicago and I didn't want to leave Vegas."

Emma's face dimmed. Another couple who wouldn't be attending her parties. "That's too bad. I'm always looking for new blood at the club." Her excitement with new couples was starting to get a bit suspect. They'd have to talk alone at some point and figure out why that was such a high priority.

"Well, I'm glad you're here." Britany smiled and held up her glass.

Amelia smiled. "Me too."

"Me three." Harper stared at the phone, willing it to give more information. "What do I do about this?"

"I don't think you should worry about it. Brad was probably just checking out a good golf course." Amelia's smile held sympathy.

"That's got to be it. But you could go check out the place tomorrow." A sparkle twinkled in Symphony's eye. "Bring that smoking detective and you could make a day of it."

"Yes. Go to brunch and buy fireworks. Check out Homestead. It could be romantic." Britany was getting that faraway look in her eyes.

"He wouldn't want to come."

"Oh pu-lease." Symphony laughed. "He was completely adorable and all over you."

"He didn't touch me." Much.

"He might not have touched you, but his eyes were ripping your clothes off. I practically came just watching the two of you." Symphony was way too excited about Harper's love life. Not that she had a love life right now.

"Stop." Harper hid her face behind her hands because crawling behind the couch would be way too obvious.

"She might have an interesting way of saying it, but she's right." Emma walked into the kitchen and grabbed another bottle of wine and started filling glasses. "But I wouldn't suggest doing anything with this cop. Just move on."

"Why not with the cop? He's dreamy." Britany was ever the romantic. "And he likes her."

"He lied to all of her friends. And he made her lie to all of us." She said it like Alex held a gun to Harper's head. "That's not the type of guy you want to start a long-lasting relationship with."

"Maybe." Britany didn't sound as convinced.

"You're right. I can't do lying. Not with everything I'm finding out about Brad. I just couldn't lie to the person I love. Never. I won't do it." Harper knew that to her core. She'd definitely learned a lesson.

"You don't have to lie." Britany smiled. "But it's okay to move on."

They were right. She'd hidden away for too long. It

was time to join the land of the living. She lifted her glass. "To moving on."

"To moving on!" Amelia clinked her newly filled glass to Harper's and everyone joined in before taking huge gulps.

Moving on? Was the clink of the glass legally binding? Because moving on sounded scary. It felt disloyal. And worst of all, it broke her heart all the way to her core.

CHAPTER
TWENTY-ONE

HARPER'S EYES didn't want to open and the fuzz coating her tongue told her that might be a good thing. The outside world was probably filled with sunlight and noise—things she didn't want to deal with right now as her head pounded.

Oh wait. That was the door.

A voice croaked in Harper's ear. "Somebody get that."

Harper turned her head and a rogue blonde wig worn in a windstorm blocked her view . Britany pushed her hair back, revealing her greenish face, when there was another knock.

The doorbell rang next. Dammit.

"Is someone going to get that?" Symphony called from the couch. Her leg hung over the edge. Where was Emma and Amelia? The darn bell rang again.

Harper stood up, her back barking with a lock and twinge. That was what she got for sleeping on the damn floor. She slowly stood to a fraction of her height and wobbled forward.

Somehow she managed not to step on Britany. Total win in her book. She tripped around the kitchen island and opened the front door.

"Sorry if I woke you, but I come bearing gifts." Alex stood on the front porch with a bag and a carrier holding two cups of coffee. "I brought you coffee."

The man was proving to be a nice guy.

"I also brought donuts." He wasn't a nice guy, he was a saint.

She looked down at her wine stained t-shirt—that incidentally was way too tight to be worn without a bra. And she was definitely not wearing one. But then again he was carrying donuts, so priorities. She opened the door and let him inside. "Thank you so much. I need that."

"It looks like it. Rough night?" He was staring at Harper with sympathy and maybe a bit of regret.

Although that might have been her. She ran a hand through her hair and it snagged. So much regret. "Come in."

"Who's here?" Britany lifted her head and groaned. "Why is it so bright in here?"

"Detective. Nice to see you here first thing in the morning." Symphony smiled, and her hair was not a mess. Her face fresh. How? Just how?

He put the bag and the coffees on the counter. "First thing? It's ten AM."

"No it's not." Harper found her phone on the floor.

9:50. Close enough to ten for him to be right. "I'm supposed to be at school."

"Oh, don't worry, you sent an email." Emma appeared. She, too, didn't look like a rat took time to nest in her hair.

She sent what... Harper opened the mail app on her phone. "When did I send an email?"

"Last night. Don't you remember?" Emma walked into the kitchen and opened the bag on the counter. "No coffee?"

Alex slid the cup holder close. Smart man. "I'm sorry, but I didn't know there would be a bevy of women."

"There's a whole bevy here." Symphony stepped over Britany and leaned on the counter. "Anything good in there?"

"Just two donuts." Emma took out a chocolate long john.

Harper's favorite.

"What's left?" Symphony reached in the bag and came out with a chocolate sprinkle.

Harper's other favorite.

"There's still one left." Emma handed Harper the bag.

"Thanks for leaving me one." Harper looked inside. A chocolate covered cruller.

Harper's other other favorite.

Of course, eating the donut without offering it to one of her guests who was practically passed out on the floor would be rude. "Britany, want a donut?" Harper whispered, but of course Britany heard it.

"What?" She sat up, rubbing the remote button impressions on her cheek.

"Do you want a donut?" Harper's clutched the bag, hoping Britany said no.

"Yeah." Britany's eyes went wide, and she clapped a hand over her mouth. There was no way she would be eating. Harper could practically taste the chocolately goodness.

Britany stood up and took a deep breath, the green ebbing from her face as she stumbled over to the counter. "Do you want half?" Her hand dove into the bag.

"You can have it."

Alex smiled as he sipped his coffee. Coffee. Harper looked across the counter, and in the carrier sat the remaining cup of coffee. Her coffee.

She reached for it and nearly slapped Emma's hand. She would scream "mine," but again with the rude. Then again, the last time she decided not to be rude, she lost three donuts.

"My coffee." Harper glared at everyone within touching distance of her cup.

Alex laughed and hid it in a cough.

"Wow." Emma snapped her hand back. "Geez. You don't have to bite my hand."

She didn't bite. "You stole my donut."

Emma smiled. "I'll take you out for breakfast, and I'll buy you another one."

"Don't you need to get to work?" Harper couldn't believe she'd blown off work. She never blew off work. She had over thirty days of time off that she'd accrued over the last few years because she was always there.

Emma nodded. "But I could go for breakfast."

"Don't you have that big meeting about all that HR stuff?" Amelia appeared out of nowhere.

"I thought you might have left." Harper offered Amelia her coffee. She could always get another one.

Thankfully, Amelia turned her down. She was a little disheveled but she looked like she'd had a late night—bags under her eyes, Clothes a little crumpled. How was it Harper looked like she'd been run over by a steamroller before she'd gone swimming in a vat of wine?

Emma looked at Amelia and then nodded to Brittany. "Yeah, I should probably get to work. Are you able to drive?"

Britany smiled, but between her Elphaba impression and Medusa hair, there was no reason for that girl to be on the road.

"I'll drive." Symphony picked up Britany's keys from somewhere. "But we should probably hit the road. Harper's got her road trip and I'm sure your husbands are worried about you."

Alex's eyes narrowed. Probably because he caught the whole road trip thing. They—her and Alex—agreed she wouldn't drive to San Diego, but they hadn't talked about Pahrump. But he didn't know that. Which was probably why he was giving her the old side-eye. She wasn't sure she even wanted him to go with, but she was very sure she didn't want to ask him in front of the girls. Getting turned down with an audience was not her idea of morning fun.

"Paul's not worried. We had phone sex last night." Britany finger-combed her hair and gathered it over her head in a pony.

Wait. What? "You had phone sex. Here? With whom?" Not that Harper minded phone sex. She was a member of a sex club. But the club had cleaning policies, and Harper did not.

"Of course here. I missed Paul and he missed me. How else was I supposed to fall asleep?"

"Where did this happen?" Harper looked around her house and prayed that wherever Britany pressed her button was washable.

"The couch."

"Where were we?" Symphony glared at the couch. "Did you clean up after yourself?"

"You were sleeping on the floor, and of course I cleaned up after myself. I'm not a barbarian." Non-alien color had left her skin and Britany's eyes were wide. She didn't look like ten minutes ago she had been about to lose everything she drank last night. "It was right after Emma went into the bedroom."

"You slept in my room?" Harper might have said that a bit harshly, but come on. Everyone else managed to look kind of normal, while Harper could feel the sleep crusted in her eyes and her hair stuck up past her cheek in alarming ways.

"I slept in your room. I'm too old to sleep on a floor." Smart and Amen.

Harper wished she'd had that type of foresight last night. Unfortunately, all the foresight went down her throat with the wine.

Britany jumped up from the stool— *Ah to be in her twen-*

ties— and looped her purse around her hand. "We should go."

Emma slid her bag over her shoulder and leaned into Harper. "If they lied once, they'll do it again. Be careful."

Harper nodded, but she wasn't all that sure she agreed. Alex never lied to her. There might have been some confusion that day in the coffee shop, but he hadn't lied.

"Get our girl to Pahrump in one piece." Symphony patted Alex's shoulder as she passed. He nodded, but obviously had no idea what he was nodding at. The look on his face said he'd be asking soon enough.

"Bye, ladies." Harper walked to the front door and opened it wide.

"Remember." Symphony leaned in. "Enjoy Pahrump and all she has to offer. Get some brunch and some fireworks and do a bit of sharing—then go see what the hell was going on."

"In that order?"

"I'd leave the sharing till the end. He looks like he'd go all night." Symphony winked.

"There are other fish in the sea." Emma slid on a pair of sunglasses before heading out the door into the sunshine.

Yeah, there were other fish, and she wasn't sure if she wanted to deal with another fish at all.

"Have fun." Britany waved as she slid into the passenger side of her car.

Harper closed the door and faced Alex.

His eyebrows were pulled together in an expectant look. "I thought we agreed to wait on the road trip to Hotel Del Coronado."

"Different road trip. To Pahrump."

"Pahrump? What's in Pahrump?"

This was why she'd wanted to wait until the girls left. She'd like to say he looked skeptical, but that was too nice. He looked…confused with a dash of annoyance.

She really didn't want to get into this now. Or ever. "We were all talking last night and Pahrump came up in conjunction with Brad. And so we figured out where he was going, and I thought you might want to go with to check it out."

"Where was he going?"

"I only know it was on Homestead Road." Getting into specifics would only make her look more and more crazy. She not only kept her husband's phone, she still paid for it. Didn't really make her look like the sanest one in the bunch.

"What's on Homestead?"

"I'm not sure."

"Then how do you know he was there?"

She could always say she was psychic. It would probably sound less crazy. But then he'd wonder why she hadn't hit on the lottery. Fine. "I checked Brad's phone."

Alex didn't say anything. He had to know how she was able to check his phone. He had to know that meant she was still paying for the service. "May I see it?"

"Sure." She shuffled to the living room and found the phone on one of the tables. She clicked on the Google app and held it out to him.

Alex scrolled through the screen. "This was a good

idea. It doesn't say exactly where he was, but we have a good target."

"Thanks." She was waiting for the judgment.

She was waiting for the sympathy.

"When did you want to head out?"

"Umm." She looked at her wrinkled clothes covered in last night's wine and imagined how bad her hair was looking. "Can you give me a half hour?"

She wouldn't even ask him for that long, but she didn't want to go on a road trip smelling like a winery. He was being such a good sport about all of this.

"How about I run out and grab you another donut?"

Scratch a "good sport". The man was a god. "Yes, please."

He disappeared out the front door and Harper ran to the bathroom. Thirty minutes. She just needed to de-stink. And maybe blow-dry her hair. Did she have time to shave? Maybe whiten her teeth? Maybe if she did all of them at once she'd have time.

Twenty-nine minutes and counting.

CHAPTER
TWENTY-TWO

AN HOUR LATER, Harper sat in the passenger seat of Alex's car, scratching under her arm and praying the fiery ants, which were undoubtedly what was stinging her body, would go away. Apparently, using a multi-blade razor in the shower without shaving gel was a bad idea. And her gums were irritated, because forgetting that she'd had the tooth whitener on her teeth made her mouth hurt as much as her arms.

Epic fail.

She no longer smelled like a wine barrel though, and her hair wasn't sticking up in Medusa spikes. So not all bad.

"Veer right, and stay straight for fifty miles," Navigation Lady called out from the phone. They didn't have an exact address, but Alex had entered the cross-streets to at least get them to the general area where they needed to go. She watched the little blue dot inch forward—their starting point way behind them and their destination far off the screen.

She leaned her strawberry-scented hair against the headrest. She'd almost taken this drive with Brad, but their schedules had never worked out. It was beautiful, the clear blue of the sky broken up by the sloping russets and khakis of the Spring Mountains.

As they drove along the highway, the mountains faded back and her eyes shut as she imagined this outing was a real date. Brad holding up fireworks at a stand while Harper shook her head no. The old-timer behind the cash register would chuckle and Brad would put the high-powered explosives down with a laugh. The theme from *Full House* ran on a loop.

Then they appeared in her mind at a horse farm. Brad held a bunch of carrots in one hand and offered a horse a single carrot with the other. The horse stretched over the fence, ignoring the single carrot, and snatched the bunch of carrots. The farm owner laughed as Brad crossed his arms in fake disbelief.

Apparently, she liked to dream in Eighties montages. Funny and tragic how all her daydreams included Brad and a life they would never have... a life they might not have ever had.

"We're here." Dream Brad's voice was deeper than she remembered. "Wake up, Harper."

Her eyes flew open. This wasn't a dream. And the voice wasn't Brad's. "We're here?" She was wide awake now and staring at nothing. They were still driving, but the only things in sight were mountains in the distance and dirty tumbleweeds. "Where are we?"

"We're about to turn onto Homestead." Alex drove on, the dot on his phone inching along. And the whole reason they were on this trip hit her like a pop-quiz on a Friday afternoon.

She glanced back and forth, looking for a magical golf course that would have drawn Brad to drive over an hour. But there was no acres of green grass, just a few housing developments, but mostly it was open space and mountains.

"What are we looking for?" Alex looked around. He must have seen the emptiness that Harper saw. It was a valid question.

"I don't know. Brad loved to golf, so maybe he found a new course he liked." She held onto that idea with both hands. Other reasons for him to drive this far were unthinkable.

Alex turned onto a gravel road with a weathered sign saying *omeste d*. Unless *Omested* was some new greeting she hadn't heard of, this was Homestead. Stones spit and ticked along the undercarriage of the car as he pulled off to the side and stopped.

"Are we here?" Harper looked at the phone, but it appeared to be recalculating.

"No." He sat back and ran a hand over the back of his neck. "Are you ready for this?"

Not even a little, but what choice did she have? She needed to find out what happened to Brad and Madeline.

If that meant she had to dig into his past, then so be it. "I'm ready."

Alex stared out the front window. He didn't say anything. And there wasn't anything of note outside the window. Nothing to hold anyone's interest. Yet he wasn't turning away. "Are you sure you're ready? We don't know what we're going to find."

"Golf course? Fireworks stand?" Yep, that was want she was aiming for.

"He drove all the way out here for fireworks?" Alex's lip quirked, but the concern still shadowed his eyes.

"I'm trying to be optimistic."

"I get it. But once we find what drew him to Pahrump, there's no more optimism." He shook his head. "Once you know, you can't take it back."

Every word he said was weighted—like it hurt to even utter. "It sounds like you know from experience."

"I was almost married once and it didn't go well."

"How close did you get?" It might be too personal to answer, but she'd shared her history, it was only fair he share his.

"We made it to the church, not quite to the altar." His stare was still outside the car. Lost somewhere or sometime else.

"What happened?" Whatever it was sounded awful.

"Let's just say she was taking a break from the wedding festivities to do some cardio with the best man."

"Cardio with her dress on?" Why would anyone screw around with someone else on their wedding day? Better yet, after all the money and time needed to get into those elaborate dresses, why risk getting something on it—okay that probably wasn't the first thought on anyone's mind but Harper.

"Yeah." He shook his head but didn't turn from the window. "My mom sent me to the house to grab her shawl. Robin was supposed to be at the church finishing getting ready, so I didn't think to announce I was home."

He ran a hand down the back of his neck and turned to Harper. "I found them in our bed."

"She was with another guy in your bed." Ouch. "Did you burn it?"

He laughed, not quite a belly laugh, but a little better than hysterics. "I thought about it. But by the time I got the idea, they weren't in the bed anymore, so it seemed useless."

"Dark. What did you do?"

"Nothing. I shouldn't have to beg a woman to be faithful. And I shouldn't have to tell my best friend not to sleep with the woman I love. So I packed my shit and left. Sold the house and moved across town."

"That's hard, but weren't you glad you knew?"

"I am. If we hadn't called it off, we'd be divorced or miserable. But you knowing about Brad isn't going to stop anything. It's just going to tarnish your memories."

"Maybe. Or maybe I'll find out he was just who I always thought he was. I'm willing to take that chance to find his killer... to find him."

Alex nodded before shifting the car into drive and pulling a U-turn. They drove a few miles down Homestead and he slowed. Thankfully there was no other traffic.

"Okay, the app says we're about to hit the area. Keep an eye out."

She already had her eyes out. She kept looking for the golf courses. Golf flags. Anything.

"There's a building. Can you see a sign?" Alex pointed to the right.

Neon flashed in the sunlight. Neon was never good. A giant brown dog or something sat on the corner of the sign. Red cursive letters flashed. It was hard to read in the daylight. And it wasn't getting any closer.

Either he'd slowed down or the sign was slowly moving farther and farther away. She turned to Alex. "Hey..." But she couldn't say the words when he was paler than Casper in a dark castle.

She turned to the sign that has somehow inched ever closer. Close enough to see. Close enough she wanted to close those eyes. No. No. No. Not a dog. A beaver.

The Beaver Ranch. This couldn't be it. She pulled out Brad's phone and powered it on. Her husband did not spend time or twenty-five thousand dollars at something called The Beaver Ranch. He just couldn't have.

She scrolled to the app and held up the map of the location. She compared it to the screen on Alex's phone. Son of a...

The location matched—at least it mostly matched. But since there wasn't another building or golf course visible, this had to be it. Unless there was a pop-up food truck that sometimes showed up.

In the middle of nowhere.

Shit. She slid his phone into her purse and shoved it

under the seat. She wasn't bringing her bag inside. If she had to punch someone, she wanted her hands free. Not that she was planning on punching anyone, but it was good to keep your options open.

"How about I go inside and ask a few questions?" The car was off and the keys were in Alex's hand. "You can stay here and relax for a few minutes."

She wasn't sure when he'd parked, but whatever. Today there were probably going to be a lot of things happening around her. She was about to meet the person who dragged her husband out to the desert. Okay, maybe not dragged, but dammit, better to think he was coerced and didn't just come out here of his own accord.

She sighed as she stared at the sprawling single-story rose-colored building with its tattered white shutters. *Beaver Ranch* was scrawled along the front left side in red neon. A metal beaver stuck her leg out of a faded white metal robe, surrounded by short bunches of metal purple sage. Her come-hither look peered from under long black beaver lashes.

The whole scene looked like something out of a demented fairy tale. She was just waiting for an old woman to come outside offering her candy.

"Let's do this." She angled out of the car and shuffled to the white metal fence surrounding the property. She held open the gate as Alex walked through. She slipped the latch closed and lifted it back up. Then down. She thought about leaving it open in case she needed to make a quick getaway, but she left it closed because she was a grown up. She wasn't going to run. Or punch anything.

Probably.

A large wrestler-type at the door said, "Welcome to the Beaver Ranch," in a deep tenor as he opened the large red door.

They walked inside and Harper just...stared. There were no nude women or nude pictures. It wasn't a black leather montage. It looked like her grandmother's living room. Mahogany Victorian furniture with white upholstery. Actual doilies covered side tables.

A woman walked in the room, her high heels clicking on the dark wood floors. Instead of a satin robe and a feather boa, she wore a light blue cardigan over a yellow sundress covered in blue jays.

Her ample hips swayed as she approached Alex. "Hiya all. I'm Camilla. Welcome to the Beaver Ranch. Do you have an appointment?" Camilla shook his hand and then turned to Harper. "I love to see two lovebirds here for a little couple's therapy."

"We don't have an appointment." Alex flashed his badge. "I'm Detective Cabrero with Las Vegas Metro."

"You're a bit outside your jurisdiction here, honey." Camilla's heavily airbrushed face registered annoyance but then she smoothed it out. "What can I do for you?"

"We were wondering if a man came in here."

"Sweetheart, lots of men came in here. They pay extra for it." Camilla smiled, an evil little tip to her lips. She almost seemed disappointed when no one got offended by her frankness.

A picture. They needed a picture. Harper went to the

photos on her phone and pulled up a close-up of Brad. "Have you seen this man?"

Camilla looked at the picture. Harper swore she saw a moment of recognition, but it flashed and was gone.

"Sweetheart, we have rules." Camilla looked from Harper to Alex. "Discretion, darlin'. I can't be telling tales on my clientele. I'd lose them all if I participated in tawdry gossip."

"This isn't gossip." Harper could see the woman knew Brad. Which meant he'd been here. Which blew all of the other reasons for Brad to be in Pahrump out of the water.

"This man was in an accident," Alex told her.

"Oh no, is he okay?" Camilla flattened a hand on her chest and her eyes widened.

"We're trying to trace his movements. Do you know him?" Alex was reeling her in—giving a bit of information, hoping to get her to divulge something. Tit for tat. At least that's what they'd said on *Law and Order*.

"I've seen him." There it was. Camilla had officially seen him at the brothel. "What happened to him?"

"He didn't make it."

"He's dead?" Camilla's eyes rounded as she stared at the phone in Harper's hand.

"Yes."

"Did you see him here?" Harper may have said that, but they weren't getting to the point.

"Why does that matter?" Camilla crossed her arms. She wanted her tat and Harper was willing to tat her right in the face if she didn't start spilling her guts.

"As I said, we're tracking his whereabouts in conjunction with the case." Alex didn't give anything away.

"So, this has nothing to do with the Beaver Ranch?"

"No." And he wasn't lying. So far, there was no connection.

"Fine. But I will deny if anything blows back on the ranch. This is my home, and my girls rely on it for their livelihoods."

"Understood."

Camilla seemed mollified. She nodded. "I recognize him. That fella stopped by a few times to see Mary Contrary."

A few daggers to Harper's chest would have hurt less. Every piece of the brothel puzzle was a serrated knife to the heart and her memory of a marriage she'd mourned for over a year.

"Is Mary here today?" Alex kept asking the questions that needed to be answered. Which was good because Harper couldn't handle it anymore. She didn't want to know.

Well, she did want to know—but was it asking too much to find out all this crap in small increments?

"She quit shortly after he started showing up."

"Did she mention why she quit?"

"She told one of the bartenders she was coming into some money. A few days later she just stopped coming to work. Didn't even give notice."

"So, you never saw her again?" Alex showed his first sign of concern.

"Nope. What kind of person doesn't give notice?"

Camilla shook her head, frowning.

"Wasn't it unusual that she just disappeared?" Alex's voice held an edge. If Mary had disappeared, then this was one more person tied up in this mess. And Harper couldn't deny Mary's connection to her husband.

"Not really. She wasn't here long. Just a few months. She never really got into the job."

"Camilla." Another woman hurried in from the back. "Sorry I'm late. I'm ready to take clients." She wore a black bustier and silk boy shorts. She stopped short when she saw Alex and Harper. Yeah right, Harper was not the one that caused her to stop on a dime. "Sorry, I didn't know we had guests."

"This is Detective Cabrero from Vegas Metro." Camilla turned to the woman, who was as toned as a spin instructor. And everyone knew that because she was wearing teeny tiny clothing that left nothing else to imagine. "This is Sunburst."

"Hi, Detective." Sunburst ran a perfectly manicured finger down Alex's chest.

Harper would be jealous, but Sunburst had already moved the finger of her other hand to Harper's chest. "Hello?"

"Hi, friend of the detective."

"They're not here for couple's therapy. They want to know about Mary." Camilla's eyes sparked with some kind of recognition. "You shared a room with her a couple times, didn't you?"

"Yeah. Is she okay?" Sunburst sounded like a concerned friend, but the quick retreat of her hand and her sudden preoccupation with her nails said something was going on.

Alex stripped his face of any emotion. "She's fine."

We think.

"Do you know of any reason she wouldn't be fine?" Alex asked.

"No. She quit. Haven't seen her since she left." Sunburst was still fascinated with her nails.

"Why did she quit?"

"She said something about her son's deadbeat father finally giving her some money."

Deadbeat father? There was no way Brad was the father. Her stomach twisted into a large tumbleweed, bile rising up her throat. Just no.

"Do you know where I can find Mary?" Alex asked.

"She just got a new place over on Rockafeller Drive."

"Do you have her address on file?" Alex asked Camilla, who shook her head no, and turned back to Sunburst.

"I might have her address in my phone," she admitted.

Alex leaned into her and smiled. "Can you get that for me?"

Sunburst about melted—which wasn't surprising. Alex had that effect. She looked over to Camilla.

Camilla gave a small nod of her head. "Sure. Give him the address."

Sunburst turned and ran back down the long hall presumably to get her phone.

They were going to find out where Mary and the child — that was definitely not Brad's love-child—lived. Fantastic.

CHAPTER
TWENTY-THREE

A HALF HOUR LATER, they had an address and Alex turned onto Rockafeller Drive. If Harper wasn't so focused on what they were about to find, she might see the humor in the fact that the street was named after the Rockefeller's and misspelled. As it stood, she couldn't seem to get her heart to stop pounding in her ears. And she couldn't help wondering what Brad was thinking as he drove these streets.

Pebbles clicked against the side of the car as Alex drove toward one of the few homes lining the street. He cut the engine at a mobile home with cracking blue slats and peeling trim.

A boy with a blond mop of hair sat on a tricycle in the middle of the empty dirt yard. He pedaled furiously, his little legs going up and down, kicking up dust swirls like a cartoon. A teddy bear was tied to the front bars with a belt. "Let's go, Berries."

Harper pushed open the car door.

"Connor, time for breakfast." A woman with dark brown hair stood at the front door, rubbing her hands on the towel in her hands. She was gorgeous—long, wavy hair and sun-soaked skin. She couldn't have been more than twenty-five.

Connor jumped from his bike and yanked at the bear. The belt hung tight to his little tan feet.

"Come on, Con. Let's go."

"I'm trying. Berries is stuck." Connor pulled at the belt and wiggled the bear.

"Hurry up, Nutmeg. I made pancakes."

The conversation stopped. Not just the conversation— hell, that might have kept going. But all Harper heard was *Nutmeg* and the world stopped. She was Nutmeg. Brad called her Nutmeg.

Where did this child get that nickname? Harper was afraid she knew where it came from. What she didn't know was why.

"Harper, are you okay?"

She heard a voice, and she was sure it was directed at her. But all she saw was a blond-haired boy called Nutmeg.

"Harper?" A hand rested on her arm. Alex.

She looked into his eyes, hoping he couldn't see what was going on. Hoping he didn't know she was absolutely losing her shit.

"Harper, we don't know anything yet. Let's go inside and ask her a few questions."

The questions didn't matter. It didn't answer why Brad

was possibly run down. It didn't answer why he would've lied to her.

"Why would someone kill him for having a mistress and secret kid?" She felt the answer in her bones. "Unless it was his wife. I'm going to go inside just to have myself put at the top of the suspect list."

Alex took her hand in his. His hand as warm and soothing. "No matter what we find out, I don't think you're on the list. Definitely not at the top."

"But I should be. That boy looks just like him."

"Did you know about him?"

"What?"

"Did you know about him or her?" He had to know the answer to that question.

"No," she hissed.

"Then you're not the main suspect." He squeezed her hand.

"Who is?"

"We need to go inside and talk to Mary." He hadn't answered her question. And she let him. She could only deal with so many things today.

Connor must have pulled his bear from the handlebars and run inside. The kid and his bear were gone, and the front door was closed.

She could do this.

Alex took the lead and stepped up to the front door of the double wide. He rapped his knuckles on the screen door frame.

The inside door flew open and there she was. Dark hair swam down her back. She had full lips and big blue eyes. She was even better looking up close. "Can I help you?"

"I'm from Las Vegas Metro. Are you Mary Contrary?" Alex held up his badge and Mary stared at the shield.

"I was. What is this about?" Mary looked about ready to snatch up her little lamb and make a run for it.

"You're not in trouble." Alex slid his badge back in his pocket. He must have noticed her panic. "I was hoping I could ask you a few questions."

"About?"

"Brad Specter."

"Sure." Mary opened the door and let them in. The outside of the home might be worn but the inside was warm and bright. Vinyl plank flooring in light oak and the walls painted a soft chocolate brown. A dark blue couch sat in front of a large screen television. A beanbag chair was off to the side.

Connor sat at a tiny table next to the kitchen counter, shoving his plastic children's fork into a stack of pancakes. "Mom?"

"Stay at the table and eat."

"'K." He stabbed a piece of pancake and shoved it at the bear. Bear fur was matted with butter or syrup as he smushed it into its face.

"The bear only gets three pieces. You eat the rest."

"I am." Connor sighed and shoved a piece past his lips and opened his mouth to show his mom.

"Good job, Nutmeg." Mary sat down on the couch and Alex motioned to the seat next to her.

Harper sat a bit further down on the couch, just in case

she felt the need to strangle the woman. She didn't want her to be close enough to touch—just in case. Alex looked at the bean bag chair, shook his head and leaned against the far wall.

"You call your son Nutmeg. Where did you get that nickname?" Harper shouldn't have said anything, but she couldn't stop the words from crawling out of her mouth.

"An old friend." Mary smiled.

"His father?" All the air escaped her lungs as she waited for the answer to that question.

"No." Mary turned to Alex. "What is this about?"

Alex glared at Harper. His eyes said shut up, but the rigidity of his body said he wouldn't feel any remorse if he sent her to the car to bake in the sun. Harper coerced a smile onto her face. "I'll let the detective explain."

That seemed to relax Alex's shoulders. "Do you know Brad Specter?"

"Yeah. He died." Mary angled back and stared at Harper. "Who are you?"

"How did you know him?" Alex tried to get her attention back on his questions, but Mary's unblinking eyes were on Harper.

"I'm his wife." Harper's breath slowed, but she continued. "How did you know my husband?"

"You're Harper?" Mary bounced sideways toward Harper, a huge grin on her face. "Oh my goodness, girl. I'm Mary Sellers. I don't know if he mentioned me. But Brad used to talk about you all the time."

"He did?"

"That man." She wrapped her hand around Harper's

as Mary's face fell. "I was so sad when he passed. I wanted to come to the funeral, but I had to work."

"At the Beaver Ranch?"

"Oh, no, I'd left a few months before." All the hesitation was gone. Her movements were as open as her smile. "Your husband was an angel. After my Connor's father died, I had nothing. I worked at the ranch for four months and it was not for me. I couldn't do it. Not well, anyway. Too much Christian guilt in my heart.

"Then your husband walked in and took me out to the local steakhouse. He checked on me every week and one day he told me he found a local grant for working moms. I was able to quit that job."

"Really?" Harper knew her husband was a great man, but finding random widows…

"Twenty-five thousand dollars." Mary stood and picked up a picture frame from the side table. "I went to beauty school. Full-time. I got my license a few months ago."

…and giving away his entire commission. A local grant for working moms. There had to be a reason. And she had a feeling it had to do with Mary.

"Congratulations." Harper smiled but there was still too much she needed to know. "Do you know why he gave you that money?"

"Oh, it wasn't his money, but he may have recommended me. He found this grant for people who lost their husbands. But I'm assuming he felt bad. He told me how you and him didn't have no children and how it broke his heart. He'd spend hours with Connor."

Harper ignored the knife slicing through her chest. Brad had started talking about kids a few months before he'd died. The "we're never having kids" decision had suddenly morphed into "let's think about it."

That explained why he'd been talking about starting a family. It also explained the pulling away at the end. Spending time with Connor must have changed his mind.

"How did your husband die?" Alex stood on the other side of the room, just watching. Harper had almost forgotten he was there.

"He was working on that new casino, the Peridot, on the far end of town. They were rehabbing the old Cornwall building and a wall fell on him during construction."

"I'm so sorry." No wonder Brad wanted to help. He'd been involved in the purchase of that building. But after they lost seven men to various accidents, they'd closed down the project. "What a terrible accident."

"It wasn't no accident." Mary sat back on the couch. "Nutmeg, are you done eating?"

"Yeah, Mom." Little feet hit the floor and the plastic chair legs scraped. He came into the family room dragging his bear.

"Go put your bear down for a nap. You can watch TV in your room."

"'K." Connor's feet slapped as he ran down a side hall. His door slammed shut.

"Connor's father wasn't killed in no accident. It was negligence. At least that's what Brad said. He was helping me talk to his lawyer friend to sue that big group that owned the Peridot."

He was? The land sale here in Pahrump had been for John's casino expansion. There was no way John wouldn't have helped this woman out. "Didn't the casino give you money for the accident?"

"Oh yeah, but since it was an 'accident,' the money just barely covered Ray's burial and a down payment on this place. The lawyer told us that's all we'd get."

"What lawyer?"

"The lawyer with the casino."

Fucking Paul. See? Still. A. Tool. "If you knew Paul Williams, then why was Brad trying to introduce you?" And why would he introduce the lawyer for John's properties?

"Who's Paul Williams?" Mary asked, frowning slightly.

"He's the lawyer for the casino." He'd been the casinos' legal representative for years. Given they were still working on contracts together—per Britany—Harper didn't think they'd stopped.

"Oh, he might've said his name, but it was all a blur."

"What was the name of the lawyer Brad found for you?"

"I can't recall. But one day Brad came by and handed me a check. He said it was a grant to help out until we could get the lawyer started on the case."

"Brad was probably looking at a local lawyer to handle this." Harper leaned toward Alex, who didn't say anything, probably because he didn't know. There were a lot of things they apparently didn't know. "Did you ever talk to this lawyer Brad found?"

"The guy never called."

"Did you ask Brad about it?" Brad would have kept at it, if he had to contact lawyers on park bench signs.

"He died before I could ask him."

Harper sighed. "Didn't you think that was a little weird, that he died in the middle of something so important?"

"When God says your time is up, your time is up, even if you have irons in the fire. Brad was in a car accident, right?"

Harper nodded, but it wasn't because she didn't have anything to say. She just had no idea how to say it. Brad was trying to find a lawyer to take on John's casino. And then he was in an "accident".

"Did you ever try to find your own lawyer?" Alex didn't look fazed by this information at all. Too bad Harper didn't fall into that category. She was all kinds of fazed. Brad had been onto something. He must have been.

"I tried, but everyone said it was just too big a case."

Too big a case? Was that even a thing in the legal world?

"Can you remember anything else?"

"No." Mary shook her head. "I'm sorry."

Alex stepped away from the wall. "Thank you for your time today."

"No problem. I was so thankful I found Brad. I wouldn't be here without him." Mary grabbed Harper's hand and held on as if she'd float away if she let go. "God bless him and thank you."

"For what?"

"I was pretty low when I met him and I didn't know

what to do. He came down like an angel and he lifted me up. Everything I have, I owe to him. He wanted me to be happy—and I am. I've even started dating again. I never thought that would happen. Thank you for letting him help me."

She wanted to say that she hadn't let him. She hadn't known. But had she known, she couldn't see not helping this woman. She was sweet and kind. And she'd needed that leg up. "You're welcome." Harper smiled and she meant it.

Mary dropped Harper's hand and stood. "Any other questions, or anything I can help with?"

"I think we're done." Alex nodded and started for the front door. Then he stopped and turned back to Mary. "One more thing. How did he find you? Was he a client?"

"Oh goodness, no." Mary laughed. "He's not that kind of man. He didn't fall for the sins of the flesh."

If she only knew. Mary might have been friendly with Brad, but she didn't know the real him. He wasn't big on sin, but sins of the flesh he was all over. But the fact that Mary didn't know him—not like Harper—made Harper's heart dance a happy jig.

"He came to my work one day to ask me about my husband. He said he worked with the casino and he had some questions."

"What type of questions?"

"Whether Ray was an alcoholic or drug addict. If he'd ever been caught drinking on the job. The casino tried to say that my Ray had been drinking, but he wasn't like that. He didn't go around town boozing it up. Not anymore. He'd been a hell-raiser when he was young, but then we had Connor. Ray started focusing on the family. He was a churchgoer."

"Did he ask anything else?" Alex crossed him arms over his chest, staring intently. Something had raised his hackles. And Harper bet she knew what it was.

Brad had sought this woman out. He'd told her that her husband's death was caused by negligence. He'd talked her into finding a lawyer. And now he was dead.

Harper was all kinds of fazed again. There was too much for this to be a coincidence.

ALEX AND HARPER headed back to Las Vegas in silence. This time she couldn't close her eyes. She couldn't sleep. No matter how much she wanted to.

About forty minutes into the return trip, Harper's phone dinged. Britany. *Did you go to Pahrump with detective hottie?*

Yes.

How did it go?

On our way home. Talk later.

CU then.

Harper wasn't sure when "then" was, but apparently they'd see each other. She slid her phone in her pocket and waited for an onslaught of questions. But none came.

Sunlight warmed the front seat as the highway between the Spring Mountains rolled past. Harper glanced over, not surprised to see that same sun had given Alex an almost angel-like halo. He hadn't said a word about Mary and her revelations. He was letting her digest and she could admit she was glad for the time. But something made her want to bridge the silence as they passed into Las Vegas. "Thanks for driving today."

"My pleasure." Alex flashed her a brief smile. "Are you okay?"

"I don't know."

"He wasn't cheating. That's good news."

"Yeah, it is." A sigh gusted from her lungs. "I'm just confused. I don't understand why he couldn't just tell me he was looking into the Peridot casino. Brad had this—this double life he didn't share with me. It's like he didn't trust me."

"Maybe he was afraid you'd get hurt."

She wanted to believe that so much. But he'd started calling Connor Nutmeg. He'd visited him weekly. He wasn't cheating on her, but he was cheating on their life.

"Maybe he was just upset because there were things I couldn't give him." A tear poked at the back of Harper's eye as she watched the landscape fly by. She hated talking about this. But seeing Connor and hearing about how good Brad was with him upset her.

"Kids?"

"Yeah, maybe this was why he kept mentioning kids all of the sudden."

Alex nodded. "I can see that. When one partner wants children and the other doesn't. I had that problem with a woman I was seeing."

"What happened?"

"We broke up when she said she wouldn't marry anyone who didn't want kids."

"And you don't want kids?"

"With my job, I see a lot of things. I don't want my children to have to experience any of it." The shadows in his eyes darkened.

"I can understand that. Deep down I think I was terrified that Brad and I couldn't last." Saying the words out loud wrenched at her heart. They'd had the perfect marriage, except for one thing. But that one thing was everything. "How could we go the distance? We wanted different things. I just always hoped he'd change his mind back, but I think that's why he didn't tell me about Mary and Connor. He'd probably figured out I wasn't going to change my mind." She sighed. "He didn't know I couldn't change my mind—even if I wanted to."

"Maybe, but he also might have been trying to protect you. There's a lot of money at stake, if she was looking to sue. People become expendable when the numbers go up." Those shadows weren't leaving his eyes.

"Could that be what happened to Madeline? Could she have found out that Mary was suing? Maybe tried to help her." Madeline had been a good woman. She wouldn't have let something like this happen without a fight.

"Maybe. Detective Lucas is actually looking into that angle." He merged onto the interstate. "We need more information before we can make that determination. But that's probably a safe assumption."

"What could be so important that someone would kill for it?"

"I don't know, but I'm going to look into that collapsed

casino. I'll see if I can get the file from Pahrump law enforcement."

"What am I supposed to do?" Harper couldn't be frozen out again. She needed to keep busy.

"Relax. It's been a long day."

"But there's so much left to do." She was never going to be able to relax.

"There is and it's my job. I'll keep you posted." Alex pulled down the road from Harper's subdivision.

Regret lodged in her chest. He was leaving and there wasn't really a reason for them to see each other again. He could disappear. She didn't want him to go, but he was right. He had a job to do. She was a teacher with a few days off. "Promise?"

He smiled and reached across the expanse of truck. Electricity zinged up her arm and warmed her chest when his hand wrapped around hers. Just that touch told her everything. He would keep her posted. He would come to see her again.

"Of course." His voice was husky as he turned to her. Their eyes met with a flame of—something that disintegrated all the emotional baggage of the day. He raised their joined hands and his lips slid along her knuckles. The look in his eyes melted her insides into a puddle of want.

She wanted to say she felt nothing. But that would be a lie. And because she didn't feel nothing, she pulled her hand away and sighed. "Thank you." The traffic light had turned green. Was it bad that she hadn't noticed the light or the cars or anything outside of Alex?

"No problem." He cleared his throat and pulled away from the light.

Of course it was bad. She was a married woman. Well, she had been a married woman.

A few minutes later, Alex pulled into her drive and shifted to park. She didn't want the day to be over, but she knew she should just let him go.

"Did you need me to come in?" His words twanged something in her heart. He was worried. About her. It had been a while since she'd felt cared for.

She almost closed her eyes and said yes. She didn't want to be alone today. She didn't want to think about Pahrump or the money or the casino. She didn't want to think about the implications to her friends. But letting him inside her home would be such a mistake. "No. I'll be okay."

"That's probably best." He tapped on the steering wheel. "I really need to get started on this casino thing and touch base with Lucas."

"Of course." She turned her attention outside the window and tried to hide her disappointment. He'd offered to stay, but she wanted him to stay because he wanted to be with her, not because he worried. Not that it wasn't nice of him to worry. She wasn't complaining. Gah! Her mind was racing. And not in a good way.

"I'd really like to see you again."

Her head swiveled right back to him. If she thought *Gah* before. She just moved on to GAH! He couldn't have said the words he'd said. "You would?"

"Absolutely." He turned in his seat and leaned in, his voice gruff.

"I would like that." The words might have come out in breathy bursts.

Closer. His mouth was so close she could almost taste him.

Her lips tingled. Waiting. Wanting. Praying he'd close the distance. His breath tickled along her lips. "Good." His gaze was on her mouth as he licked his own lips.

He hovered there.

She didn't.

Harper leaned forward and brushed his lips with hers. Soft and gentle. His hand found the side of her face as the kiss deepened.

A draft hit her lips as his mouth left hers.

"We can't do this here," Alex whispered with no conviction.

She inched closer, her hand moving to his chest. She didn't want this moment to end. She wanted to hold onto it as long as possible.

"We need to stop." He angled his head back and sucked in a deep breath.

She closed her eyes, willing him to turn, but the willing thing wasn't happening. Alex sat very still. His hands rested on the steering wheel, more of a barrier than an invitation.

"Why?" Harper asked.

"Because we haven't even gone on a date yet."

"We went out for lunch and I made you dinner." And they'd just spent a few hours in the car together. Not exactly a courtship, but technically one of those had to count as a date.

Alex's lip curved into a smile. His eyes sparkled and Harper was sure she was about to be pounced on. Yay, technicality! The look on his face was cute and playful and made her insides throb.

"I want to take you on a real date." He let go of the steering wheel and shifted toward her. "Tomorrow night."

"I'd like that."

"Me too." He intertwined their fingers and slid his thumb up and down on hers. "I like you. I want to do this right."

Her whole body simultaneously crumbled and smiled. Disappointment swam in her veins, but happiness soothed the ache like a balm. He liked her. "I like you, too."

"Good. It's good for you." His smile was bright and genuine.

"It is."

"You should head inside." He smiled and shifted a piece of hair from her face.

That little touch zinged through her treacherous veins at the same time guilt pressed down on her shoulders. "I should go."

Alex pointed out the window. "You might want to talk to your cheering section first."

Harper followed his finer and saw Britany and Symphony holding up their phones with some kind of app open. Britany's phone said 10.0, while Symphony's said 8.4.

10.0? 8.4? "What does that even mean?" Harper yelled

at the closed window, but she was pretty sure they couldn't hear her.

Alex laughed. "Go report back to your tribe. And I'll talk to you tomorrow."

"Tomorrow?"

"I'm sure I'll get something from Pahrump today. I have a contact."

"Of course you do." Not that Harper was complaining. A contact meant information faster. She slipped out of the car. Alex angled from the curb and drove away. The feel of his hands rang through her body. The taste of his mouth hung on Harper's lips. She closed her eyes and bathed in the thought until she heard…

"Ahem." One of the judges cleared her throat.

"8.4?" Harper spun around, her hands on her hips.

Symphony laughed. "I felt there should have been more tongue action on the dismount."

"More tongue action?"

"I told them we should give you privacy," Amelia said, the only one without a phone in her hand. She wore her usual loud colors, green skinny jeans and a red silk shirt that highlighted her darker skin. The woman could pull it off, though. Sometimes Harper was jealous. "I can't believe they pulled out their phones. The good news is, I talked them out of videotaping it."

"Thanks for that." Part of Harper wanted to say that with sarcasm, but she was pretty thankful there wasn't a video of her making out with Alex on the internet. So there was that.

"It would have made a great video for the wedding."

Britany slid her phone in the pocket of her purple jumper. Her blond hair was up in a waterfall ponytail.

"We're barely dating and you're planning our wedding video for the reception." Her voice might have tipped up at the end of that. She could barely wrap her head around a date and they had her married off.

"One can hope." Symphony shifted a fabric bag on her shoulder and pulled out two bottles. She almost dropped one bottle, but caught it on her knee. Her T-shirt, *I do it for tacos*, was torn at the bottom and tied at the waist. "How was your road trip? We brought champagne if we're celebrating, and wine if we're not."

"So, which one are we drinking?" Britany grabbed at the bottles as Symphony yanked them back to her chest.

"Well, he wasn't cheating." Harper was still processing that whole thing. But she was glad she knew him well enough to be sure he hadn't cheated on her.

"We knew he wasn't cheating." Amelia's eyebrows drew together in concern.

"We didn't know. He was going to Pahrump and lying about it." Symphony said it like she was gossip central.

"Have some respect." Britany pushed at Symphony's shoulder. "Do you know why he was going to Pahrump?"

"He wasn't cheating." Harper hadn't realized how much she'd needed to say those words. She'd heard them over and over again—from Alex—in her mind but putting them out there soothed some of the anxiety.

"What was he doing out there?"

Part of her wanted to tell them everything, but Harper wasn't sure how much she should say. She couldn't stop thoughts of Brad. He hadn't told her. And maybe Alex was right. Maybe Brad had been afraid for her safety. "He needed alone time. All I know is he wasn't cheating or visiting brothels."

"He drove all that way to the middle of nowhere for alone time?" Britany asked.

Harper had to say something. "He found a steakhouse he liked." Not exactly the truth, but since he did actually visit the local steakhouse, not really a lie.

The women stared at Harper. There might have been disbelief in those eyes or it could have been shock. Either way, they didn't look like they wanted to let it die. So she had to change the topic. "I propose no more talk of Pahrump or Brad. Better yet, no talk of men at all."

"If we can't talk men, what else is left?" Britany laughed.

Symphony sighed. "I have a vaginal itch."

Britany cringed. "Can we ban vagina talk too?"

"Agreed." Harper walked to the front door, taking out her key.

"I'm thinking we skip the talking and watch some Netflix." Amelia held open the screen door as Harper turned the key.

"I second that." Harper opened the door, motioned them in and followed inside, hoping she could keep her mind off of today and the questions that still lingered.

CHAPTER
TWENTY-FIVE

HARPER'S FRIENDS had left four hours ago, since everyone had jobs to get to in the morning. They'd drank the celebratory champagne with pizza, the perfect end to the night, and had made plans to do it again in a couple of days—when they didn't have work the next morning. They hadn't talked men or murder investigation once.

So why Harper lay in bed staring at the ceiling, she had no idea. She'd tried counting sheep, singing herself a lullaby, and putting the blanket over her head. None of those strategies shut off her mind.

The fifty-pound investigation wouldn't budge from her brain, and she didn't have the muscles to lift it. There were so many questions and she needed to get up early to get some answers.

But instead of resting, she was staring at a sliver of alarm clock light sliced into the ceiling. It looked like a burrito. Which made her laugh. She wanted to share it with someone. Not just someone. Brad.

No. Alex. She wanted Alex to be here, but then again, she didn't. She should really think before she did anything drastic. But she was pretty sure when she went drastic, she wanted it to be with Alex. After the kiss, she wanted more.

His hands on her body. His lips. The look in his eyes as he stared at her like she was the only person who mattered. Her body hummed and her throat dried.

Then there was Brad. Part of her wanted to go back in time and get a second chance. She wanted a chance to tell him what was going on with her body and infertility. How many months she'd dragged that secret around, scared he'd walk away. She'd wanted to tell him all about the obstetrician appointments she'd hidden behind lies of blood draws or dental work. She wanted to tell him about the feeling of emptiness when she thought she'd never be able to give him what he wanted.

She wished she had done so many things before he was taken away—before her heart broke into a million tiny pieces—before…

And none of this was helping her fall asleep.

She threw off the covers and sat on the edge of her bed. It was only ten. Some normal people were up living their lives right now. Why not join their ranks?

Shoving her feet inside slippers with dog faces, she sat on the edge of the bed. What to do? She couldn't go interview bad guys. It was too late for that.

That left out calling her friends or anyone else. She couldn't have another glass of wine without seriously considering AA. She'd already drank alone enough this week. She'd eaten all her donuts. What was left?

There was one thing. The second bedroom.

She ambled into the kitchen and opened the junk drawer. She sifted through takeout menus and rubber bands and twist ties until she found the key.

The cold metal somehow burnt her fingers. She hadn't been in the bedroom since she'd moved in. The moving men dumped the boxes into the spare room and she'd locked the door.

She hit the switch and light rained down on dust-covered boxes and Brad's work desk. If she'd had a spine, she would've gone through it all before she'd paid to move it. But she'd frozen every time she'd tried. It wasn't just the desk. It was what it represented. Her throat dried while her eyes filled with tears.

Three months before he'd died, Brad mysteriously had a change of heart on kids—although given what she'd learned, it wasn't all that mysterious. He'd offered to move his desk so they could set up a second bedroom. She'd questioned it at the time. Why would they need a guest room since they never had guests?

He didn't want guests.

She ripped the moving tape from the desk drawers and balled it into a sticky glob. Setting her water on an unopened moving box, Harper opened the top drawer. She sifted through pens and notepads, tossing anything with no sentimental value into the awaiting trash bag. Next drawer.

Ten minutes later, she'd combed through three drawers of contracts and closing paperwork and found nothing.

She didn't even know what she was looking for, and now she was out of water.

There were still five boxes stacked in the corner. Her eyes weren't ready to close. And she was determined to get to each box. Out to the kitchen, then, to make coffee, before coming back and tackling the first box.

More tape. She pulled it back and tore off the top. Files and files were shoved inside. This was going to take all night. She sucked down a gulp from her mug. Bitter coffee zapped at her taste buds, forcing her eyes open.

Better to see the words, my dear.

Apparently, coffee and exhaustion led to Little Red Riding Hood-adjacent delirium.

She picked the first folder and opened it. Papers with all the answers. Numbers and photos. She knew what was going on. Hallelujah!

Not.

It was a folder with their joint tax return from their first year of marriage. Not that she thought she'd find all the answers in the first folder, but she'd hoped. She slapped the tax folder on top of the desk in the keep pile and moved on.

Five boxes later, Harper had filled multiple trash bags to the top. There were a few legal documents that she wanted to keep, but nothing about the casino sale in Pahrump.

She leaned against the desk and sighed. A weight of discomfort and history was bagged and ready to go. She'd done it, accomplished something. That weight tightening her chest was gone. She felt lighter.

Grabbing the empty cup, she thought about another pot of coffee, but she really needed to sleep—whether she wanted to or not.

Tomorrow, scratch that— it was after midnight—today, in the daylight was a new day. She'd get some sleep and start again.

She could totally do that. She was an accomplisher now. Not a failure or a hider. She could do things. She'd proven it to herself. And she hadn't realized how much she needed that. A win. A win she could control.

She rinsed the cup in the kitchen sink and leaned against the counter. Looked around her home. Even though nothing was removed from the living room or kitchen, the house looked cleaner. Lighter. Until she saw the box from Brad's office sitting next to the couch. She'd forgotten about that one. She might still have room in the last recycle bag.

She sat on the couch, setting the box next to her and tilting open the lid. At least there wasn't tape to deal with this time. Inside was a dress shirt still in the plastic store wrapping. He always kept an extra shirt on hand, just in case.

She put it in the pile to her right—the newly declared donate pile. She pulled out a water bottle from the Bellagio, with a cracked nipple and scratched sides. Garbage. A practically new coffee mug from Strait Construction. It was too nice to toss. That went on the stack to her left. To keep.

Underneath the mug was a sealed envelope. It said "Harper" on the front. She ripped open the envelope and removed the papers inside. The word Pahrump had been scribbled in the bottom corner. Holy shit. This was it.

She laid her hand on the top of the paperwork and ran her fingers along the edges. There weren't a lot papers. It was relatively thin. *Please don't be thin with detail, too.*

Closing her eyes, she straightened out the folded pages. A deep breath, and she opened her eyes.

Spreading them out on the coffee table, she saw a picture of an old building, a thirty-acre plot of land. A piece of paper ripped out of a spiral bound notebook, with Brad's handwriting. The address of the casino. A few drawings. The DeVout logo. And something else. It almost looked like the DeVout logo, but where the DeVout logo was a D formed by a flogger and paddle, this other one was cursive. Doodles. She finally found something and it was doodles.

An article about the accident. Mary was right, the news had painted her husband as an alcoholic. At the top of the page, he'd written a note. *My fault. I'll fix it at any cost.* He'd done that. As much as he could.

She brought the note to her chest and smiled. Helping Mary had been a good thing. He'd affected her life—and her son's—for the better. She gently laid the page on the table and then flipped to the next document. A ledger page. Utilities, equipment rental, and various charges for materials. It looked like normal charges. Nothing out of the ordinary.

The next document, Soil Report from Nye County.

This survey is divided into three parts... blah, blah, blah...*The building on site 311 was built in 1987...hydro-*

collapsible. None of it made sense. *Multiple aquifer collapses… foundation issues… puff dirt.*

In the margin, written in Brad's handwriting. PUFF DIRT.

What the heck was puff dirt? She kept reading. *… powder-like dirt which shifts and sinks when wet. A reinforced foundation must be laid to combat this issue…*

None of this sounded good, but not worth killing over. The next document was a screenshot from a newspaper article.

A 27-year-old Pahrump man, Ray Sellers, who died in a wall collapse last Monday, had an extensive criminal history including drugs and alcohol. The accident occurred at 10 a.m. at the construction site of the Peridot Hotel and Casino. The Peridot was scheduled to open within weeks.

A construction leader with the project has stated, "We are deeply saddened by the tragic accident that occurred today while working on this project. Our prayers are with Ray's family at this terrible time."

The mayor has said that Branson Construction Company is reputable and has had no reported problems prior to this incident, but an investigation is still ongoing.

The building is currently blocked off as the police investigate the circumstances leading to the accident.

. . .

So the building had structural issues. Could that have been reason enough to kill someone? Didn't that happen all the time? They would fix the foundation and move on.

She had to be missing something, but there were no more pages—no more answers. She needed help. She needed Alex. It was after twelve, but maybe, just maybe, he was still up.

She walked to her bedroom and picked up her cell phone. Before she could think about how bad of an idea this was, she opened a text to Alex.

Are you awake?

Silence. No incoming dots. He was probably sleeping, like normal people.

Yes shouldn't you be in bed?

Or not.

Can't sleep. That was a bit obvious, but he did ask. *I'm going thru boxes & found something.*

maybe you can't sleep because you're looking in boxes.

Probably. It really was a chicken or egg question. Was she looking in boxes due to her inability sleep or could she not sleep because she was looking in boxes? Could both be true at once? Or could it just be that she was too damn tired to make any sense? *Can you stop by tomorrow?*

working tomorrow and then I have a hot date. This was part of his work, but she didn't have the heart to question him. Or maybe it was that after going through all that paperwork, her fingers were too damn tired to peck out a whole line of dialogue. Or better yet, it could be the mention of their hot date.

How about I show you before the date.

sounds good. meet at my house? i'll cook

Meeting at his house? She'd never been to a cop's house. Were they like normal houses or were there finger-printing kits and bad coffee? She was going to find out.

Ok. Text me your address. She slid into bed and her eyes wouldn't shut because she was nervous. Or she was confused. The questions were still out there.

What had Brad found? And how was she supposed to find it for herself?

CHAPTER
TWENTY-SIX

MONDAY EVENING and Harper stood in front of Alex's two-story tan stucco house in the middle of Summerlin. Red clay tile roof. Typical suburban home. Nice neighborhood. The house was harmless. So why her feet were basically frozen in place, she had no idea.

She was making progress. She'd sat in her car for a good five minutes and now she was on the path to the front door. See, progress. Why she needed to gauge her progress, another mind buster.

It was a dinner and a book report, nothing else. Yet, knowing Alex was in there alone and she'd be with him—alone—made her nervous. Sweat beaded at her neck as her breathing chopped in her lungs.

For goodness sake, she'd been alone with the man before. They managed to eat and talk and not rip each other's clothes off. So why was it different?

Because it was a date.

But she was an adult. So what if they'd kissed? She

knew how his lips tasted—like honey, for the record. But somehow the guilt swirled and sucked up all the good and she felt... She didn't know how she was feeling.

Inhale. She sucked down a breath and spit it out. Exhale. She could do this. Again. Nothing had changed. She ran a hand over the paisley skirt and peach blouse she'd worn to school that day. Not exactly guy-magnet material. She should've changed. Worn something hotter. She looked like a damn schoolmarm. To be fair, she kind of was a schoolmarm, but who was counting.

Why was she questioning her clothes now? She almost turned around and ran. But that would require running. Not a fan. Pulling her bag higher, she squared her shoulders. She could do this.

As she approached the white door, Alex opened it, wearing black jeans with a dark blue button-down. She jumped, biting back a scream.

"Hi?" His smile was muted. His tone modulated.

"Hi." She held her hand to her heart, hoping to slow the rhythm section against her breastbone. "You scared me."

"I wasn't sure you were going to come inside." He stepped through the doorway. "Are you okay?"

"I'm fine." She wasn't completely lying, just exaggerating the truth. She was kind of fine.

"Do you always stake out houses you're invited to?" Alex smirked, his scar bending, and it looked so damn adorable. Too bad he was smirking at her expense. Jerk.

"Yes, in case they're raided by the cops." Dammit. She should have come up with something better than that.

"I don't think there's any chance of that."

"Are you going to let me in?" She wanted to go in and talk about the papers in her hand and not talk about the awkward that was her life.

"Sure." He stood back to allow her inside.

First impression? The house was nice and it smelled like garlic. In other words, heaven. The entry was small, with a beautiful crystal chandelier. The living area was warm, with light tan carpet, brown furniture, and black side tables. Wood bookcases lined up against the far wall. A few pictures rested on the shelves, but most were covered in books. Books organized by color and height.

"Nice place."

"Thanks. I like it." Alex closed the front door. "Would you like a tour?"

A tour. That would include a bedroom. She was so not ready for any part of that. "Ummm..."

"That's okay." He motioned to the living room, keeping his distance—like she was a skittish bunny. And the way her hand gripped the strap of her bag, that wasn't far from the truth. "The food is almost done, so why don't I just give a quick tour of the main floor?"

Breath filled her lungs. What the hell happened to her? She was a paying member of the DeVout sex club. Yet she was freaking out about seeing a man's bedroom.

"This is the living room." He walked past a set of stairs and pointed to an open door. "There's the bathroom if you need it."

He walked around the corner to a good-sized kitchen. White granite counters and brown cabinets. A breakfast bar separated the kitchen from the dining area. The table was set with plates, silverware and a dozen roses.

"Can I get you something to drink? Wine, soda, water?"

"Soda would be great." If she drank wine, she'd probably do something she'd regret. If she drank soda, she could show Alex all of the paperwork she'd found and run as fast as a skittish bunny could run.

"Dinner should be ready in a few minutes."

"I brought that paperwork." She sat at the breakfast bar, plopping her bag onto the granite.

"Business first." He walked over to the bar and leaned down. "Good idea."

Harper pulled the folder from the depths and set the bag on the floor. "I found a partial soils report." She sifted through the pages and picked out the report.

He took the paperwork and began reading. "Foundation issues?"

"Looks like it. Puff dirt." She then gave him the newspaper article and the report with Brad's notes.

"This means Mary's story checks out," Alex said, reading. "This article mentions Ray's history of drug and alcohol abuse."

"But she said he'd left that behind." Harper took the article back when he held it out, apparently done reading. "Why lie? They were in the middle of building."

"They were almost done. The place was supposed to open in a few weeks, and if the building still had foundation issues..." Alex shrugged.

"Wouldn't they have fixed those?"

"In theory." He rested his hands on the counter and leaned forward. "But if they hadn't fixed the problems and someone died, that would be a problem."

"Then why not cover it up and fix the issues?"

"That might have been what they were trying to do."

"Maybe." Harper handed him the general ledger. "This was in the file too."

He read over the paperwork again. "Something isn't adding up."

"Right." She pointed in the margin. "And then there's this. Puff dirt."

"So they knew it was a problem?"

"I don't know. I just know that's Brad's writing." She sighed. "Have you heard of this Branson Construction?"

"No." Alex pulled out his phone and tapped on the screen. "Branson Construction?"

"Yeah. I looked it up online, but I couldn't find anything. You would think a company big enough to get this type of contract would have some sort of media presence."

He frowned. "Wait. The Sláinte hotel used Branson construction before."

Harper practically ran around the bar to look at the screen. "Not just on the Pahrump project?"

"Looks like it. They won the bid." Alex clicked back and scrolled through the results on his phone.

"We should talk to John." The timer on the oven dinged—which was probably good. Because anytime she mentioned "we," he got a little twitchy.

"Tomorrow. Tonight we have dinner." Alex tossed his

phone on the counter and turned off the oven. "We'll go talk to John tomorrow after school."

She smiled. He actually agreed.

"What?" He looked over at her as he plated noodles and a garlic chicken breast.

Honesty. She had to go with honesty. "You said *we* will go talk to John. It was nice to not have to fight be included."

"It's easier to join 'em if you can't beat 'em." He laughed. "I might have to do some things at the precinct, but we're in this together."

"Good." Her lips curved up and they didn't show any signs of ever stopping. Of course, she had no idea why that pleased her so much. Probably because she was sick of fighting him on all of this. At least, that was her story.

He handed her a plate of steaming noodles. The garlic hijacked the air, making her swoon.

"This smells amazing." Harper sat at the table and unfolded a linen napkin. Fancy and amazing.

"Thanks." Alex leaned in, his face inches from hers. She ran a finger along the smooth scar on the side of his face. "I might have miscalculated."

"Miscalculated?" That came out on a breath, but somehow she'd said the whole word.

"This is my favorite dish, but it's not really date friendly." His finger glided along her chin.

"Garlic?" Why did garlic have to taste so good and wreak such breath havoc? One of life's little tortures.

"Garlic." He agreed and licked his lips. Licked. His Lips.

His hand slowly tilted her face until she was looking into his eyes. "Pre-garlic kiss." He moved slow. One kiss. Two kisses. Small and sweet.

He pulled away. "That's to get us through, because after garlic might be a little uncomfortable."

She smiled and avoided bringing her hand to her lips. They tingled and burned and she wanted him to kiss her again and again. But then the scent of garlic drew her attention and Harper dug in. Her knife slid through the chicken like butter. So moist. And the noodles glistened. She cut at the pasta and created the perfect bite.

Moist chicken and buttery noodles coated her tongue. Delicious.

"Thanks."

Apparently, she'd said that out loud. But in her defense, the food was wonderful, he'd kissed her again and they were going to follow a new lead. This night was turning out to be amazing.

CHAPTER
TWENTY-SEVEN

THE NEXT DAY, Harper was glowing. How a woman could glow while feeling guilt, she had no idea. She hadn't been with anyone but Brad or at the very least Brad had always been present no matter who she'd been with. Either way, he was always there. And now Brad was gone, but it still felt like she was doing something wrong.

After Harper was done with her day job, she and Alex walked through the bright atrium at Sláinte. The entry was all windows, rays of sunlight slicing strips out of the marble flooring. Live green foliage hung from gold wall sconces. Purple dog-eared flowers were planted in groups along the side of the room. Early Dog Violets, if the sign was to be believed. And given the shape of the petals, that name made perfect sense.

She walked with Alex to the front desk and approached a young man in a tan suit. Alex slipped his sunglasses off and stopped a foot before the front counter.

The guy behind the counter wore his hair pulled back

in a ponytail. The suit jacket almost covered the tattoo peeking from the sleeve, but the skewed collar of his dress shirt did nothing to hide the black gauge in his earlobe. His eyes were focused on a computer on the counter, his arms draped at his side.

"Hello?" Alex dipped his head to get the guy's attention.

Without looking up from the computer screen, the guy said, "Sláinte. Welcome to our hotel." He couldn't be more than twenty-one and he had the voice of a sleep app.

Alex presented his badge. "I'm from Vegas Metro and I need to talk to John Byrne."

"He's in his office." The guy crooked his thumb toward a hall next to the elevators. He turned back to the screen and stared. The hotel lobby might be impressive, between the flowers and the sun, but the clerk was not.

Alex sighed. "Where is his office?"

The guy's eyes widened in surprise. "Oh yeah. Sláinte. Welcome to our hotel."

"We did that already." Alex kept eye contact, probably afraid the guy would get lost in a trance before he told them where the office was located. "Where is the office?"

"Ummm…"

Alex ran a hand along the side of his face. "We're looking for John."

"He's still in his office." The clerk looked confused. Which made sense because Harper was pretty darned confused too. The questions weren't that hard.

"Where is John's office?" Alex's fist was flexing at his side. His voice pinched at the end. He was holding the frustration in, but barely, given the vein pulsing in his neck.

"Follow that hallway past the doors to the pool and go right after the butterfly garden entrance."

"Thanks." Alex said at the same time another voice asked, "Harper?"

John, wearing an expensive suit and looking all the professional that the front-desk clerk lacked, walked toward Harper, but stopped when his eyes fell on Alex.

"I'm so glad we found you." Harper was glad. She wasn't completely convinced they'd been given the right directions, although taking a detour to the pool or butterfly garden sounded like heaven. But given Alex's back was flagpole straight and John looked ready to pull out a dueling pistol, she didn't think heaven was in her future.

"I'm glad to be found." John's voice was dipped in sunshine. As always. The guy was always pleasant. He probably peed and rainbows appeared.

Alex moved toward John. "I have a few questions."

"What about?" John waved at a passing guest.

"Maybe we could talk somewhere private," Alex suggested.

John nodded. "I'll need privacy for a few minutes, Brody."

"Sure." Brody went back to staring at the computer. Brody? The kid who sold all his parents' furniture?

John led them down a hallway, cutting off Harper's view of the desk clerk.

"Is that Brody Paskuda?" Harper hadn't seen him since

he'd stormed past her at a dinner party his parents had thrown when he was still in high school. He was all grown up.

"Yes, I'm helping out his parents," John said over his shoulder.

"That's really nice of you. I didn't realize his parents were in his life again."

"It's unfortunate that they don't get along. But now he has a job. I'm hoping that will be enough to keep both sides talking." John stopped near a large window "Have you been here since we installed the butterfly garden?"

"No, I haven't." Harper couldn't help but stop. The scene was magic. Sunlight haloed down over black-eyed Susans, bright pink phlox and white zinnia. Flat rocks and trees were scattered along the space. Butterfly wings fluttered everywhere. A large dark blue butterfly perched on a branch by the window.

Her kids would love this. A few months ago, they'd gone on a field trip to the Bellagio to learn about all the flowers and fauna in their botanical gardens The students had fallen over themselves to see flowers draped over waterfalls and hanging from the ceiling. This had all of that, and butterflies flitting back and forth. It was beautiful.

"If you'd like to take a look inside," John said, "I can get you some free passes. Stop by anytime."

"That would be great." She smiled and stepped away from the window. "We should go."

"Yes, you have questions." John's face glowed in a smile as he said hello to multiple staff members. He led

Harper and Alex further down the hall and around a corner, to where an empty desk sat in front of an open office door.

Once they stepped inside the office, John shut the door. A large desk and a computer occupied one side of the room and a round table with chairs the other. John motioned to the table. "Please have a seat."

Alex pulled out a chair for Harper. "Your company has done some work with Branson Construction." He waited for John to sit down across the table before taking the seat next to her.

"Yes."

"Did you run into any issues with the work they performed?"

John seemed to think about the question, his face morphing into a thoughtful expression. "Not that I'm aware of."

"We're trying to get hold of the owner. Do you have their contact information?"

"Honestly, I wasn't the one who brought them in on the project. That would have been the project manager. I don't keep track of things like that."

"You don't know the companies that work for you?"

John cheeks pinkened as he looked down at the table. "I'm generally only brought in when there's a concern."

"Like the problems at the Peridot."

John shook his head. "Yeah. That was unfortunate."

"What happened?" Alex was asking all the right things. Harper sat back and watched.

"There was some issue with the land that wasn't

divulged prior to the sale. I left it all to my lawyers." John shrugged.

"So you didn't see the soils report?"

"No. I don't know anything about soil or foundations. I usually have too much on my plate to worry about the minutia. That's what my employees are for. The lawyers, the construction manager and the project manager took care of all that."

Someone knocked on the door and it swung open. A woman stuck her head in. "The Nevada Gaming Commissioner is here for your meeting. I've put him in the executive conference room."

"Thank you, Maggie. Can you tell him I'll be right there?" John sighed. "Managing employees takes a lot of work."

"Is everything okay?"

"Just a human resource issue." John smiled. "I'm sorry to have to cut this short. Did you have any other questions?"

"Could we see a list of all the people that worked on the Pahrump project?"

"I can have Maggie send you that information. As always, it was great to see you, Harper. Detective." John stood up, still smiling.

Harper pushed her chair back. Alex stayed where he was.

At the door, John took a folder from Maggie and disappeared. Maggie smiled at Harper and Alex. "Do you know the way out?"

"Can we get that list?" Alex asked her, still firmly planted at the table.

Maggie's smile faltered, but she quickly picked it back up. "Of course. It might take a few hours. Can you leave me an email address so I can send it to you?"

"Sure." Alex stood up and pulled a card out of his pocket. He handed it to Maggie as he passed her. "Thank you."

"You're welcome." Maggie stared at the card like it might grow fangs and suck her blood.

Alex smiled, sliding his sunglasses back down as they left the office and walked down the hall to the atrium. Harper did the same, protecting her eyes from the million points of light piercing the hall windows while she went over the whole interview in her mind.

Alex's knuckles were white as they walked to his truck. He hadn't said a word so far. Which wasn't weird. She hadn't said anything either, but that was more about digesting what John said. He hadn't known anything. If he was to be believed, but John had never lied to her before. But then again, he'd never been asked about a project where a man died.

Alex hit the locks. "Do you think he was telling the truth?"

"I didn't notice anything off about him. So I think he was." She slid into the passenger seat of the car. "What do you think?"

"I'm not sure. How could he not know anything about the soils report? He owns the damn company." Alex shook his head.

"I don't know. Maybe he did leave it to his employees."

"Maybe." Alex started the car and left the parking garage. "I don't know if you have plans tonight, but I was going to do more research if you want to come by my place."

"I'm going out with the girls." Although going over to his place did sound like a good idea—strictly for research purposes—she couldn't bail on her friends.

"That's probably a good idea. Forget about all this for a night."

She'd love to forget, but she couldn't see how that would ever happen. There was too much unanswered. "Who was the project manager and construction manager? And we still don't know anything about Branson Construction."

"Hopefully, Maggie will have something for us soon. They have to have a contact." Alex headed toward Harper's house—at this point, he'd been there so often, he could probably drive it blindfolded. "I'm going to do a little digging at work. See what I can find."

"If Emma's there tonight, I'll see if she knows anything."

Alex reached across the seat and patted her hand. "Try not to think about this tonight. Stay out late and call in sick —I'm just joking."

"Tomorrow is teacher's institute day, so I'm off work."

"Nice. But you should still have fun and relax."

She nodded. Not that she thought she'd relax, but she'd try. After she asked a few questions.

CHAPTER
TWENTY-EIGHT

LATER THAT NIGHT, Harper sat next to Amelia on a bright red paisley couch in the Brambly Hedge Pub, her blue drink making rings on the coffee table. The bar was loud. All over. Bright colored furniture. Floral wallpaper. And that didn't even cover the jukebox asking if she should stay or she should go.

With Vegas being all about the tourism, this place was all about the locals.

Britany stood at the long wooden bar along the left side of the room, wearing another purple outfit, waiting for a pitcher of the blue concoction they were all drinking. Symphony sat on one of the vintage Chesterfields, flirting with a woman that looked barely old enough to drink.

Amelia leaned into Harper and yelled loud enough to be heard over the music. "So, where's your man tonight?"

Before Harper could come up with the appropriate answer, Emma spoke up. "He's not her man." Emma took a sip from her glass.

"Of course he's her man." Amelia took another swig from her drink, Sea Liquori, blue curacao, Sprite and vanilla vodka with a sprig of green something sticking out the top. "You brought him to DeVout. It must be pretty serious to be making out and then go on a road trip with him."

"We aren't..." She almost said they weren't together, but that would be a lie. They might not have been together at the club, but there was definitely something there now.

"I have refills." Britany carried two pitchers filled with blue liquid and all talking stopped as everyone clamored to get a refill.

Harper rose to her feet, avoiding the drop lights hung like vines above the coffee table. She poured a dollop more of blue whatever into her cup. She wasn't drinking, but she didn't want anyone to know that. So, she sat in front of a drink she was barely nursing.

"The pool table is free," Britany said. "Who wants a game?"

"We should all play." Emma stood, drink in hand.

"There is still booze left here." Harper nodded at the pitchers. She still had some questions for Emma. "Emma, want to stay here?"

"Nope." Emma leaned forward, trying— and failing— to get the straw between her lips. "Let's all go play."

"At sixty-four dollars a pitcher, we are not leaving these alone." Brittany slid her finger along the lip of her glass.

Emma snorted. "Sixty-four? Why don't they come with

armed guards?" She might have already drunk down fifty dollars' worth.

Before last week, Harper hadn't seen these women in ages, but if they kept hanging out this way, they were either going to need a new hobby or they'd need to start regular AA meetings.

Amelia giggled. "I'll stay here with you."

Britany leaned toward Emma. "Twenty dollars says I can beat you."

Emma's eyes lit up.

"No!" Amelia and Harper said at the same time.

"What?" Britany's eyes rounded to saucers as everyone in the bar stared at them. That might have been a bit loud, even in this place.

Harper leaned into Britany. "Emma had a gambling problem. She's not allowed to gamble—ever."

"But she owns a casino."

"Yeah, but she doesn't use it."

Emma pouted as she took another drink. "No one will let me gamble anymore, but I showed them. I don't need casinos."

Britany nodded and wrapped her arm around Emma. "Let's go play a friendly game of pool."

"It would be friendlier if we put a five-spot on it," Emma grumbled as she followed Britany.

With Emma and Britany gone, there was quiet. Well, as quiet as it could get with music above and bar patrons yukking it up. Amelia leaned toward the coffee table and took another deep drink. "I've wanted to talk to you."

"Really?"

"The other night you mentioned something about Pahrump and Brad. What was really happening in Pahrump? Did you really think he'd cheat?"

"It's stupid."

"I'm sure it's not." Amelia rested her hand on Harper's —her eyes earnest, probing.

"I thought Brad might be seeing someone in Pahrump." Harper chose to skip over the whole brothel drama. "All the evidence led to it."

"Evidence. What are you, Sherlock Holmes?" Amelia laughed but didn't give Harper time to respond. "Brad could never cheat on you. He adored you."

"Yeah." And thankfully that was how it played out.

"You two were perfect together."

He adored her, but they were far from perfect. And wasn't it sad that it took losing him to find out how far they'd drifted.

"What was he really doing in Pahrump?" Amelia played with the glass in front of her. She looked distracted, but something about the way she tilted her head said that was furthest from the truth.

"He was visiting an old friend." Not exactly true, but since it was an active investigation and Paul was probably involved, Harper didn't want anything getting back to him.

"See." Amelia smiled at Harper and took another drink. "I told you he adored you."

"Yeah."

Amelia slid a finger along the glass, picking up condensation and wiping it on her napkin. Her eyes didn't waver from the glass, and each movement was like her mind hovered elsewhere, lost in thought.

"Are you okay?" Harper asked.

"Mine didn't, you know."

Harper wasn't sure what Amelia was talking about, but she looked so heartbroken. "Yours didn't what?"

"Jasper didn't adore me."

"Of course he does." Harper was pretty sure about that. He seemed to like Amelia well enough at the club the other night. And he hadn't cheated… unless he had. "Did he cheat on you?"

"I thought he had."

"What happened?"

"He was spending time at a job site in Pahrump. He was always gone. That's when I put my foot down. No more construction projects outside of Vegas metro."

"I didn't realize he worked in Pahrump."

"Not anymore." She laughed, short bursts of hollow. "I'd like to think it was my foot that stopped him, but I think it was something else."

"Something or someone?" This conversation was making Harper's heart hurt. If Jasper hurt Amelia like that…

"I asked him." She lifted her glass and waved it at Harper. "I said, 'I'm sick of this crap and I want to know who you've been shacking up with in the desert.' He told me he hadn't been with anyone."

"Then what was he doing in the desert?" Perhaps threatening young widows with a kid named Connor.

"He was dealing with a failed construction project. It was stupid. I was being oversensitive."

"If you were oversensitive, why do you think he doesn't adore you?"

"I guess… I'm just being silly. I don't know. It never felt right." Amelia put down the glass and grabbed Harper's hand in her cold, soggy fingers. "Brad wouldn't have done that to you, though."

"You're right."

Amelia smiled and pulled away. She grabbed a pitcher and poured blue into her glass—well, part in the glass and part on the table. "Oops." She used the sleeve of her yellow sweater to sop up the spill. Her sleeve now had an elbow patch of green.

Harper didn't want to raise suspicions, but given Amelia's current state, Harper wasn't sure that was an issue. "I forgot Jasper was in construction." Not really a lie, she just never thought about it. "He owns the company, right?"

"Yep. All his—well, all ours. We own it."

"What's the company's name?"

"Ozark Contractors."

"Like the mountains?"

"I love the Ozarks. I used to climb them with my sister." Amelia's lips turned down. "I miss her."

"Where is she?"

"She never left. Her husband is a park ranger out there. Got three kids. I always thought our kids would play together. But my kids are getting older and so are hers.

They're not going to be able to play together much longer."

"You could visit her."

"I could." She huffed. "But we're too busy."

"With Ozark Contractors?"

"Yep."

"Do you work there?" Amelia hadn't worked at all when Harper had been part of the club. She'd been a full-time mom who added personalized post-it notes to all four of her kids' lunches. She was a room mom and the head of the PTA.

"I started working part-time when Ashely started first grade. The company ran into some money troubles, but shhhh, don't tell anyone. Jasper wasn't too happy."

"It must have been nice to get out of the house."

"You know it. I don't know how you put up with those kids every day. The attitude and the excuses."

"It helps I send them home at night."

Amelia giggled. "Ain't that the truth. I wish I could send them away at night." Her giggle turned to guffaws. "Can you imagine all the shit I could do at night? I'd be, like, multi-lingual and have my master's degree in, like, basket-weaving."

"Do you need a masters to weave baskets?"

Amelia tilted her head and just stared. "I don't know. But that would be super cool. What do you do? I am the weaver of the baskets."

"Cool." Not really the word Harper would use, but if it made Amelia happy, more power to her. Harper needed to get the conversation back on construction though. "That friend I mentioned, of Brad's, in Pahrump. She's looking to redo her kitchen. Do you know if Jasper would have a recommendation for a company?"

"Oh my god, of course. His company does work out there. We just send one of the other construction managers to handle it."

Not exactly what she was looking for. Redirect. Think fast. "Well, she already talked to a company but I wanted her to talk with you guys first. I don't want some crappy company taking advantage of her."

"Absolutely." Amelia patted her arm. "Some of those construction companies are shady. Nobody wants to encourage that."

"Exactly."

"What's the company? Maybe I've heard of it."

"Branson Construction."

Amelia's eyes lit up. "Oh my god. That's one of our companies. That's the Pahrump branch…"

Harper tried to pay attention to the words still coming out of Amelia's mouth, but it was difficult over the litany of *ohmygod* running through her head.

"…that is so funny…"

Harper touched her phone in her pocket. She needed to call Alex. She needed to tell him that things just got so much more complicated. Not only Paul, but Jasper too.

"Harper? Harper?" Harper looked up to see Symphony standing by the table. "Everything okay?"

"Yeah." Harper nodded. "I have to run to the bathroom." And text Alex.

"The hell you do. It's about to start." Symphony slid

onto the couch and put a service bell in the center of the table. Britany and Emma arrived with a fresh pitcher.

"Are we ready to kick some ass?" Emma yelped, and did a fist pump.

"Kick ass?" Harper pulled out her phone. She just needed to send a quick text without anyone seeing.

"Countryside Trivia Night. The whole purpose of coming here tonight." Britany slapped at Harper's phone. "No phones or they'll think we're cheating."

"All right, blokes and bints. It's time." A man stood at the front of the room. His ratty Slytherin cape hung down to his knees. He waved the wand in his hand and it lit up. "The first question is worth one hundred points."

"Put it away!" Britany hissed, and pushed at the phone until Harper slid it back in her pocket.

"In Harry Potter, who was the second boy the prophecy could have applied to?"

This was an easy one. Harper hit the bell on the table at the same time Symphony's hand slammed on top of Harper's. Ow, ow, ow. Harper winced as stars danced in her eyes.

The man looked at a clipboard and then pointed at Harper. "Slyther-Win, what's the answer?"

"Slyther-Win?" Harper whispered to Symphony.

Symphony glared. Apparently, she was out for blood. "That's our team name. Answer the question, you hit the bell."

"No talking once you hit the bell unless you're giving the answer." The wand was pointed at Harper.

And Harper wasn't moving fast enough. *Who was the*

second boy the prophecy could have applied to. "Neville Longbottom."

"You are correct." The man waved his magic wand. "Slyther-Win, one hundred points."

"Go, girl." Britany shook Harper's knee as they all clapped.

"Another Hogwarts-aphile." Symphony patted her back. "We got this."

Harper couldn't help but smile. She was a true lover of Hogwarts. A Potterhead through and through. This was going to be fun.

CHAPTER
TWENTY-NINE

HARPER LIFTED her head from the bed. Not drunk or hung over. Since she rarely drank—this week notwithstanding—she was pretty happy she hadn't overindulged again. They'd spent the night winning a twenty-dollar gift card for the bar. Thank you, Harry Potter Trivia night. That'd get them a third of a pitcher. She then came home and fell asleep to *Harry Potter and the Prisoner of Azkaban*. Overall, a Potterhead dream.

Seven AM. Teacher's institute day. The day when she should be sitting in training, but she'd forgotten to sign up. She'd sat through two trainings the last few institute days—mostly to avoid her life and being alone— so she didn't feel too bad missing this one.

She sat up and disconnected her phone from the charger on the nightstand so she could text Alex. They'd left the bar so late, she hadn't been able to text him.

I have information

Her phone sat idle in her hand. No response. She tossed it on the nightstand.

The second charger still sat there, Brad's phone at one hundred percent. She picked it up and activated the screen. Her picture was the background. She'd had him as her background for years.

They'd been good years. And she missed him, but she couldn't sugarcoat it any longer. They'd been heading down different paths. She wouldn't ignore it any longer.

She turned on the phone and tapped voicemail.

"This is Brad, you know what to do."

She played it again. She'd loved to hear his voice. So many times she'd sat in her room and listened again and again. She'd held onto the good times. Refusing to see the reality. Because the reality made her feel like a failure—made her feel like she wasn't honoring him.

Because the reality was, they'd loved each other. A lot. But it was over. He was gone and they'd had their issues. She needed to accept the reality and move on. The thought made her chest ache.

She played the message again. The deep timbre of his voice rumbled over the speaker. "This is Brad, you know what to do."

She hadn't. She hadn't known what to do. But she did now. It was time. Time to let go.

This had nothing to do with Alex. It was everything. Brad. Pahrump. Mary. Her friends.

Her friends. How long had she'd gone without having those?

No matter if Brad and she were meant to be or not, he

would hate what she'd become. He'd hate that she was hiding from life. He'd hate she stopped doing the things that made her happy.

She clicked on settings. And stared at the reset button.

It was time to delete this chapter—at least in the phone. She couldn't listen to his voice anymore. She couldn't live in the past.

She clicked reset.

Are you sure? The screen asked the question in her head. Was she sure?

She clicked yes. The screen went to black and turned off. It was done.

She unplugged the charger and looped the cord around her hand. She took them both into the kitchen and slipped them on the counter. She'd take them to school and put them in the electronic donation box.

She couldn't help but stare at the harmless electronics, tears welling in her eyes. Part of her wanted to pick the thing back up and find a way to fix it. She already missed his voice. She already missed having that small piece of him with her. But that small piece had held her back. She needed to deal with this and not look back. Not anymore.

She thought about taking it to the local electronics store. They had an electronic recycle box.

She picked up the phone, but she couldn't do it. It burned in her hand. She brought it to her chest and felt Brad for just a second. He was there.

Baby steps.

She put the phone and charger into the junk drawer. She'd get it to the recycle bin, just not today. She slowly closed the drawer, drinking in the sight of the phone until it was covered.

She clicked on the coffee maker. What was she going to do today? What did people with days off normally do? Even on summer break and weekends, she usually worked at the tutoring center to help her kids get ready for the next year. She wasn't used to this.

She tossed a bagel into the toaster as her phone dinged.

Good morning. I didn't forget about you, but in the middle of something. I'll call later.

I can help. Yeah, that was thirsty, but she had no desire to sit around and do nothing all day.

Give me an hour or so. I'll stop by.

Sounds good.

She had a plan. She took her cup of coffee and pulled the bagel from the toaster, eating it dry. She didn't have time for spread. She needed to get ready for her day as the detective's sidekick. Maybe she'd put on a Deerstalker cap and say "Elementary, my dear Alex."

As she inhaled the dry bread, chasing it with coffee, the front door dinged.

No. No. No. He couldn't be here already. She was still in pajamas. So not ready.

Although the man had seen her hung over and covered in wine, so today had to be better. Right?

Harper kept telling herself that as she stuffed the rest of the bagel into her mouth on the way to the door. She fluffed her hair and looked to make sure she had no stains on her Hermoine pajamas with their bright blue boy shorts.

"That was fast." She opened the door and smiled at the chest of the man standing outside. A man that was definitely not Alex. She looked up into his smiling face. "Jasper?"

"Morning." Jasper's blond hair was pulled back into his man-bun, and his black suit fit him like a second skin. He held up a paper bag from the local donut shop. "Can I come in?"

"Um…" She wasn't sure that letting him the house was the best idea, but since this whole investigation was around car accidents, she should be okay, as long as he didn't bring his car in her living room.

"I brought donuts." He jiggled the bag and smiled. This was Jasper. What was she worried about?

"Of course, come on in." She stood back, and closed the door once he was inside. "Can I get you some coffee?"

"I'd love some." Jasper moved toward the bookshelf as he looked around the living room.

She started the coffee maker and set a mug on the counter. "Cream, sugar?"

"No thanks." Jasper picked up a picture of Brad and stared at it before putting it down. He walked over and sat at the breakfast bar. "Nice place."

"Thanks."

"I'm surprised you left that house in the hills."

"I couldn't really afford it after Brad died."

"Sorry." He shook his head. "I guess I hadn't noticed how much your life has changed since his death."

She tried not to cry that her friends hadn't been around when her life had fallen apart. Not that it was their fault.

She slid the filled mug across the counter. "To be fair, I haven't been around much."

"True." Jasper took a sip from his mug. "Good coffee."

"Thanks." She leaned against the counter. "What brings you out?"

"Straight to the point. I like that." Jasper stared at his coffee. "I heard you have a friend that's redoing her kitchen."

Harper couldn't remember half the stories she'd made up last night to get more information out of Amelia. "I do have a friend." That much was true.

"Amelia said your friend is using Branson Construction in Pahrump."

"Yeah, I think that was the name of the company."

"Do you know her name?"

Mary Sellers. Not that she could say that. What if he knew her name? What if he didn't and she brought attention to that poor single mother and her kid.

"You do know your friend's name, right?" Jasper smirked, but there was something in his eyes. He knew she'd found Mary. He had to. But why would it matter?

"Why do you care about my friend?"

"I thought maybe I could help. Offer free work." He leaned forward. "After all, your friends are my friends."

"She doesn't like handouts." Oh for the love of god, that was terrible. Who didn't like free shit? "She's a private person."

"See." Jasper stood up. "The problem I have is that we don't work out of Pahrump anymore."

"Then she must have gotten the name wrong."

"How did you know that name?" Jasper stalked around the breakfast bar.

"I guessed?" She was such a bad liar. Especially when she was scared. Like now.

Jasper moved closer, not stopping until his breath was at her ear. "I think you're lying, and I think you know why."

Harper shivered. Her body reacted to those words—and not in a good way. Of everything he said, "I think you know why," scared her the most.

"I DON'T UNDERSTAND." Harper shifted her hips into the counter, trying to get away from the hiss of his voice. But there wasn't anywhere to go. "I don't know anything."

Jasper laughed in a creepy, high-pitched way. Or maybe that was just her interpretation. "I don't believe you."

Harper cleared the gulp lodged in her throat. She really needed to work on her lying skills.

"Where did Brad hide it?"

Hide what? The puff dirt, Ray Sellers, and all the rest of it—Brad wasn't trying to hide it. Was he? No, he was trying to bring it all to light. She tipped her chin up. "I don't think he was hiding anything."

Jasper sighed and stepped back. "I'm thinking he didn't tell you."

"Didn't tell me what?" At this point, she could write a book about all the things Brad didn't tell her.

"Look." Jasper leaned against the breakfast bar and ran a hand over his face. "Brad was mixed up with some bad people."

Oh heck no. Not this again. "Brad wasn't mixed up with anything. He was trying to blow the whistle on poor construction practices. He was trying to make things right." Harper's finger dug into his chest. She was close enough to see the shock in his eyes—as well as little gold specks in the brown of his iris. "The foundation report from Nye County said it all."

"Wait. You think this is my fault?" The shock left Jasper's face and now he looked angry. "That foundation report you found, what did it say? Did it say it's puff dirt? Hydro-collapsible, meaning that when it gets wet, it compresses in on itself. And if you build something heavy on the soil, and the original construction was done haphazardly, then the building will start to sink."

"That's basically what it said." But he said it so much more eloquently.

"He hid that report." Jasper shook his head and a tear pooled in the corner of his eye. "I never saw it until it was too late."

"And I'm supposed to believe that."

"Harper, you know me. I would never put my crew into that situation. I wouldn't put their lives at risk. They have families."

Deep down she couldn't understand why anyone would put a person in that situation. "But if you didn't, then who did? It sure the hell wasn't Brad."

"I don't know." Jasper sighed. He looked older. Tired.

"What do you know?" she asked.

"I know that Madeline came to me right before Brad died. She wanted to know if I knew about the soils report."

"Did you?"

"When she showed it to me, that was the first time I'd ever seen it. I swear."

"Then who knew about it? John never saw it."

"I don't know."

"If you already know about this report, why are you looking for Brad's paperwork?"

"I didn't have any proof. Brad was going to give the police what he had before he died. It was for all of us."

"For all of who? This doesn't make sense. If you knew about this and Brad was telling the police..." None of it made sense. And Jasper was trying to make her think he wasn't part of it.

He looked offended when she put space between them. "It's not me," he said. "I needed to get that information to the police. I didn't want what happened to Brad or Madeline to happen to me or Amelia."

"So Brad was killed?"

"Look, I already said too much." Jasper laid a hand on her arm. "If you find anything, bring it to me or Paul. We can help you." He wrapped her in a quick hug before stepping away. "I have your back." He walked toward the door and paused. Looked back. Almost like he wanted to say something. He sighed. "Better yet, leave it alone. I can't bear to lose another friend over this. Just let it go."

And then he was gone. Harper ran to the door and

locked the deadbolt, checking out the peephole to ensure he got into his car and drove away.

He did.

She leaned against the door and closed her eyes. All the oxygen she'd apparently been missing inflated her lungs. She was missing something more than oxygen.

Brad had information on the Peridot—more than what she found in his office, which wasn't enough evidence of anything. But where could it be? Where would he hide something so she could find it but no one would have access?

The house? But she'd gone through that before moving.

His office? The entire office staff had access to everything in his desk.

He had to have a hiding spot. Someplace no one would ever think to look. Somewhere that would be secure. His words came back to her.

It's like Fort Knox. No one is getting anything in or out, even if they wanted to.

DeVout. Brad's locker at DeVout. But DeVout was closed. She couldn't get in the front door. Not without a key. She could call John or Emma.

She pulled out her phone.

u @ home?

Three dots popped up on the screen, and a moment later Emma responded. *Yes.*

need something from the club. meet u in 10?

I'll be there.

In the bedroom, Harper went into her jewelry box and

found Brad's key. Then she dialed the phone and waited. Ringing. More ringing. Voicemail.

"Hey, Alex. I'm heading to DeVout and I'll be back in about thirty minutes. If you get to my house before then, please wait. It'll totally be worth it."

She hung up and ran into her bedroom. She threw on the closest pair of jeans and a Luke's Diner T-shirt, an ode to the *Gilmore Girls*. Not that she'd normally wear it, but she needed to get back here quickly.

And she'd only be out for a few minutes.

TEN MINUTES LATER, Harper knocked on the door of DeVout. Emma answered in full workout gear. The inside of the house was dark, with random streams of light from the windows scattered around the space.

"Thanks for meeting me," Harper said. "Are you heading to the gym?" As they walked deeper into the house, Harper adjusted the shoulder strap of her empty fabric bag. If this went right, it would be full when she left.

"Yeah, meeting John to play a little racquetball before work." Emma smiled.

"I should only be a minute. I need to empty Brad's locker."

"Empty his locker?" Emma ran hand along her chin. "I didn't think he had a locker. You always used the guest locker."

"I did." Harper could barely afford the yearly donation, even when Brad was around. Paying for a locker seemed silly. "But John gave him one a few years ago. Something about winning a bet."

"Sounds about right." Emma leaned in. "Why are you cleaning it out?"

"I want to see what he has in there and… it's time to move on."

Emma stopped all movement as her lips turned down. "That's good. It's time."

"It is." Harper reached out and grabbed Emma's hand for a squeeze. It was time. "I shouldn't be long."

Emma dropped Harper's hand and waved away the words. "No worries. I need to go back to the house and make a smoothie before I leave. Today is mango mint."

"Take your time." Harper slid her hand in her pocket once Emma headed out the back door.

The key nearly burned her skin as she pulled it out and walked through the quiet, empty house. The only sound was the air conditioner kicking on to cool the house from the hot Las Vegas sun.

Walking around the front desk, she turned on the light in the locker room. Locker twelve. Bottom row.

She slid the key into the lock and the door popped open. She inhaled the scent of Brad's cologne, and for the first time, it didn't twist and bend her heart into pieces. She closed her eyes and drew in another breath.

She didn't really have time for this, but she couldn't help but smile. No matter what she found out, the smell brought back memories of the man who was her best friend. She might not have known him the way she'd thought, but in the past week she'd gotten to know him pretty well. He was a good man who fought for a woman and child he didn't even know.

She opened her eyes and pulled a sweatshirt from the peg on the side of the locker. This was how she knew him. A sweatshirt with the image of a Quidditch match on the front and *I'm a Keeper* scrawled underneath. She folded it up and shoved it in the bag at her hip.

She pulled out a red flogging-crop with tassels by the silver handle, a souvenir from their recreation of *Fifty Shades*. She loved the frilly ends and the way they felt swatting against her skin. She almost thought about throwing it out. But she'd missed it so much, she shoved it in the bag, the tassels sticking out the top.

What? A good crop was hard to find.

Next she pulled out a T-shirt, dragging a bunch of objects onto the floor along with it. She picked up a red envelope, her name written in Brad's handwriting on the front. She'd read it later, when she had time. That got shoved into the bag. A travel deodorant and comb went in next.

She ran a hand over the bottom of the locker. Nothing. Dammit. She didn't know why, but she felt like she was missing something. If Brad was hiding anything it would be here. She slid her palm up and down the sides and back of the locker. Still nothing.

Harper checked the top, and sure enough, something was taped there. Kneeling down, she peeled at the tape and pulled out small nub. Not a nub. A tiny jump drive, no bigger than a peanut M&M.

She stuck her head inside and studied the top of the

locker. That was it. She stood up and stared at the little drive in her hand. Did anyone use jump drives anymore? Most normal people used the cloud. Unless they had something to hide.

The front door opened. Emma was back already? Harper figured she had a few more minutes alone. She slid the drive into the bag and shut the locker door. "Thanks for letting me get Brad's things," she called out as she hiked the bag up and walked around the bar and into the front room.

It wasn't Emma. "Brody?"

Brody Paskuda walked towards her, all in black from his hat to shoes. Even the grip of the knife in his hand was black. He didn't say anything, just looked at her. At least she thought that was what he did. All she saw was the knife. Large. With giant teeth.

Harper swallowed the giant ball clogging her throat. "Emma's not here right now, but she should be back soon."

"I don't need Emma. I need to talk to you." His eyes were trained on the bag at her side.

"Of course." Harper swung the bag on her shoulder so it hung behind her hip. Something wasn't right. Not just that there was a knife-toting weirdo in front of her. She tried to keep things normal by smiling. "What can I help you with?"

Brody didn't smile. He didn't seem to emote at all. "I need that bag."

She brought it to her side and giggled. Keep it light. "It's just some of Brad's clothes."

"I need it." He stepped closer into a beam of light from one of the windows. His eyes were dilated. He moved his hand to block the light.

"Why?"

He dove toward her, grabbing her arm. She tried to pull away. To run. But the little shit was strong. Fingers dug into her skin, crushing all blood flow.

"You're hurting me." She yanked at her arm, overbalanced, and fell to the floor. Scrabbling backward, her back hit the bar.

His grip loosened as he stood over her. Glaring. "Give me the bag."

"Why are you doing this?" She looked up at him. He'd changed so much since she'd seen him at the Paskudas' party. He was no longer an angsty teen. He was too skinny and too angry. The only sign of life on his whole body was the logo on his skull cap. She'd know it anywhere. Kimber had drawn the same damn thing on her book report. Something to do with Skyrim.

Brody stepped closer with his hand raised. Fire danced in his eyes. He was mad and about to take it out on her. His mind was obviously ticking, and she didn't want to be around when it finally exploded.

"Skyrim," Harper blurted.

"What?" He lean back and gave her a look.

She needed to keep him talking. Distract him. Just long enough until Emma came back. "Have you gotten all the Daedric Artifacts?"

His expression changed—not quite so angry. That was good, right? Brody straightened up. "I have them all."

Keep him talking. Her mind replayed the report Kimber had written. "Really? Even the Ring of Hircine?"

"Yeah."

"So you like to be a werewolf then, huh?"

"Not really. You can't talk and you can't use any of your powers." The knife in his hand bobbled. It was working.

"So then the ring is totally useless." She was pretty sure that was how it worked. Who the hell knew? She was citing information from a second-grader's report.

"You play?" His whole body relaxed.

"Sure. Doesn't everyone?" Except her.

"What's your character?"

Male. Female. Human. Werewolf. What type of answer was he looking for? What had Kimber said? "I'm Argonian. I like reptiles. How about you?" If this worked, Harper was giving that kid an A.

"Redguard. The adrenaline rush is amazing."

"Yeah, it's fun to play the game."

"I mean the Redguard's ability." Brody's body stiffened and his eyes narrowed. The knife in his hand straightened. "Do you even play the game?"

Fuuuuuuuuuuuuck. Why did she suck at lying so bad?

"All the time." She gulped. Hopefully he didn't notice it. "I just forgot about that."

"Whatever. Give me the bag."

"I don't think…" The sliding glass door at the back of the house rattled open and then shut. Gym shoes scuffed along the tile floor. Emma was back. Thank goodness.

"Why are you still here?" Emma asked. "Shouldn't you be out dealing with that issue?"

Wait. What?

Brody waved the knife. "She won't give me the bag."

"What?" Emma came around the bar and glared at Harper , who was sitting on the floor, freaking out. Because Emma was talking to this guy like they were besties. Which couldn't be, because Harper and Emma were best friends. So this must be a joke. Some sick joke.

Emma didn't laugh and say April Fools. Harper kept waiting.

"Go outside and get the car ready." Emma's anger and attention was angled toward Brody. "Didn't I tell you to get a different car? You already used your mom's car last time. These can't look related."

"I tried, but you didn't want it to be suspicious. Make up your mind." He waved his hands and stomped out the door.

When would someone jump out and say she was being punked?

CHAPTER
THIRTY-TWO

EMMA ACTUALLY LOOKED ANGRY. "What did you find in that locker?"

"Nothing. I was cleaning it out because I want to move on." True. Ish.

Emma went behind the bar and clinked about. Coming back around, she handed a full glass of something pale pink to Harper and grabbed a high-top chair, pulling it closer to Harper. Picking up her own glass, Emma sat down on the chair. "Brody, go to the car and wait."

He nodded and walked out the front door.

Emma crossed her legs and drank deep from her glass. "Why did you have to get involved?"

"What's going on, Emma?" Harper took a drink—ooh, rosé— as she braced her back against the bar so she could stand.

"You stayed away, but then you came back." Emma was talking more to herself than to Harper, but it felt personal. "Then you showed up with a cop—not ideal. But

I figured you'd just want to be friends again. I tried to get you involved. I tried to get your mind off all this bullshit. Why didn't you let Brad and all this shit go?"

"Did you kill him?" In all the scenarios that she'd come up with, all of the bad guys, not one included Emma. "You ran them over?"

"I didn't run over anyone." The implication was there, but the words Emma said a few days ago crossed her mind. Because she didn't get her hands dirty.

"Brody." He must the hands that do her dirty bidding.

"Give me whatever you found."

Harper pushed to her feet, but she didn't try to run. They needed to figure this out. This wasn't like Emma. She wasn't bad; something must have happened. "Why are you doing this? To protect your husband? If he made you do anything, I can help—"

Emma cackled. It was high-pitched and unnerving. "Do you think he knows about any of this? I was doing this for me."

"But why? Why Brad?"

"I'm so sorry about Brad. You have to believe it was an accident. We were fighting and Brody was high, and he didn't mean to hit him. But then Madeline came to me. She must not have known Brad had already talked to me. I got her drunk and Brody took care of the rest."

"You had him run her over? You do realize how fucked up that really is, right?" Harper drank from the glass in her hand. Emma might be trying to get her drunk, but Harper wasn't that big of a lightweight. She could handle one drink without getting so drunk she'd play in traffic.

"Why? Why did you do it? Jasper's crew could've died. I was reading the paperwork. Why didn't you just use the correct footings?"

"The price was too high. I needed to stay within the budget I set." Emma looked like she was on the verge of crying. "I had to take some of the money because John couldn't find out. If he knew… It was one time. It was supposed to be a sure thing."

"You're gambling again," Harper said slowly. Emma had skimmed money from the project. And from the look on her face, it was a lot of money.

"Just a couple times. Online." Emma drank from her glass. Her eyes avoided Harper. Couple times… yeah, right. "Why couldn't you just let this go? I don't want to lose another friend."

"You don't have to lose me. I won't say anything."

"You'll tell that goody-two-shoes cop you're seeing. I looked into him—not even a traffic violation. And you won't be able to lie to him."

"I can. I won't say a thing."

"You said it yourself." Emma spun the wine in her glass. "You can't lie to the one you love."

"I'm not in love with him. I barely like him," Harper protested. "But we can make this right. Tell them it was a mistake. You didn't understand. Something."

"That won't work. They won't see it that way." Emma slumped in the chair.

Harper wanted to make it all go away, but Emma had done things that couldn't be taken back. People were dead. "So what happens now?"

"We're going to finish our wine, and then we're going to go for a walk."

"A walk?" Harper blinked. Her tongue felt fuzzy. Thick. She looked at her glass, head spinning. "What's in this?"

"A little something to make you amenable to what's about to happen."

"That's how you did it. You drugged her and Brody hit Madeline with a car." Harper's legs wobbled like wet spaghetti. Her mouth was dry. She tried to wet her lips and ended up clacking her tongue, over and over. It was a fun sound. "Caarrr. That's a fun word." Harper leaned against the bar. "Fun word. Fun word. Funworddddd." Her shoulder lightened as something disappeared. Her bag was in Emma's hands. "I'm going to float. Float away. Wingardium leviosa. Levee-oh-sah. Levee-oh-sah."

"What did you say?" Emma sifted through the bag and Harper couldn't stop her, not once her feet left the ground.

Harper grabbed onto the bar. "I'm flying." She reached for Emma, pulling on Emma's shirt.

"Stop that." Emma tossed everything back in the bag and hung it on Harper's shoulder.

Harper's shoulder dropped. She was back on the ground.

Emma made an impatient motion toward the door. "Let's go."

Harper moved her feet. So heavy. So slow.

"Come on, Harper."

Harper's arm pulled forward in Emma's grip, her body following along. "Where we going?"

"You're going to go for a walk in the street."

"I'll be a streetwalker." Harper giggled, but deep down something felt off. Why was she walking in the street? She looked at her feet. They were moving but they were in grass. Grass was soft. Harper fell backward and thumped onto the lawn. "Quidditch. Play with me, Harry."

Emma kneeled over Harper, frowning. Harper reached up and moved Emma's lips into a smile. "Don't be sad."

Emma took a deep breath, spit it out, and her skin peeled back, leaving nothing but dark smoke.

Harper wasn't sure if she should be afraid. It would take too much effort. "Dementors."

"What are you talking about?" the glob of smoke growled, showing greasy teeth. "Get up."

Harper rolled to her knees and then to her feet. She was so tired. Emma yanked at Harper's hand, pulling her forward.

"Drive her to the usual place and let her out," Emma said.

"Let her out on her own?" Squiggly Brody sat in the front seat of a blue SUV. "Aren't you coming with?"

"I'm late for racquetball. You know what to do. You don't need me." Emma led Harper around the car. The back passenger door was open.

Harper's feet dragged. Too tired. She couldn't lift her leg to get into the car. Hands shoved against her back. Her face settled against fabric. Her eyes closed and the world went black.

CHAPTER
THIRTY-THREE

"GET UP!"

Harper's face was fused to something. Her head wouldn't move. She wanted to sit up and yell at the voice. *You shut up.* But her mouth was lodged between her face and the something. Nothing was moving.

Air. A breeze cooled her sweaty face as something pulled her up. Her eyes opened to slits. A car? Her head spun and pounded like a cat in a dryer. She felt like she'd been put through the dryer.

"Stand up."

She was sitting in a car. The man wanted her to stand. She wanted the bass drum out of her head. Everyone wanted things they weren't going to get. She leaned her head against the back of the seat. When did it get so heavy?

Maybe when she installed the drum kit.

That had to be it.

Hands wrapped around her arms and she lurched sideways. Her feet hit the ground. Legs jellied side to side as she drooped like an imploded building, sitting on the hard pavement. Uncomfortable. She wanted to stand up. But her body wouldn't listen.

"No!" The owner of the voice must have lifted her because now she was face first on the seat in the car, her legs hanging out the door. There was a loud bang and her body jumped. Well. Her mind jumped. So far, her body wasn't cooperating.

"We waited too long, she's not moving," Brody said. What was Brody doing here? Oh.

"I'm busy." That was Emma's breathy voice. She must be here too.

"I told you I needed you here. She won't stand up." Maybe she wasn't here. Not that Harper cared enough to lift her head and find out.

"Just hold her up." Why was her voice so weird? Like she was on speaker. Right. Brody must have called her.

"How do I hold her up and drive at the same time?" Brody was saying things that just didn't make sense. Why did Harper need to be held up at all? They could just let her sleep. "I'll just lay her in the middle of the road."

"You can't do that. It won't look like an accident. She's such a lightweight." Emma sighed, loud even over the phone. "Drive back to the house. We'll figure something else out."

Harper's legs were bent and shoved into the car. With some swearing, Brody slammed the door shut, leaving her legs bent in an awkward position. Her face rested against the seat. Perfect. Time to nap. Her eyes and ears shut to everything around her.

SILENCE. Harper opened her eyes to darkness and silence. She twisted on the seat, head throbbing. Bad idea. Her knees complained as she straightened them out. She couldn't remember drinking last night, but she must have downed an arsenal of liquor to be feeling this bad. She really needed to stop drinking.

Her eyes focused through the pain. She was in an SUV, not in bed. The car from earlier. She hadn't been out drinking. She'd had wine with Emma. Emma, who used to be her best friend. Emma, who was now the bad guy.

Damn. She sat up and Brad's bag fell to the floor. She leaned her head back against the car seat and thought about picking it up, but right now she didn't care. She felt like she'd been sleeping for days. Maybe it had been. She felt along her hip for her phone. Not there. Not surprising.

No lights were lit on the dashboard, which meant no clock. The only light was coming from windows in the garage door. She squeezed her head, pushing all the pieces back together. A Humpty she was not, because no amount of clenching made her head feel better. But she didn't have time to wait.

She opened the car door. Froze when it creaked. No one was around. She inched to the edge of the seat and let her leg dangle over. She needed to get the hell out of here. Quietly if possible. Quickly most important.

Harper wasn't completely sure what was going on, but she was sure Emma killed Brad and Madeline. And given that she'd drugged Harper, Emma looked to be trying to kill her too. Which just seemed ridiculous. People didn't kill people—unless they were on *Law and Order*.

She dropped her feet the inches to the concrete floor and wobbled. Looking around, she saw the door to the house, which she should probably avoid. She didn't want to walk into Emma or Brody. In front of her was the garage door, but opening that would make a lot of noise.

Which left the smaller door, across the garage. It was her only way to the outside. Good news was her legs stopped wobbling. Bad news, she had a good twenty steps to the side door.

She moved her foot, stumbled and lurched forward. She stopped—just stood there and took a deep breath. She could do this. Another step. Teetered. Another step.

Foot over foot, she stumbled her way across the floor. She gripped the doorknob and turned. Nothing. Locked. She pulled and pushed, but nothing happened.

Looking for some sort of locking mechanism, she rubbed her hand over the knob. Nothing. But it was hard to see. A light would help here. She slid her other hand along the wall, searching for the light switch. There was a lighted button on the side of the door. She pressed it. No light.

Shit. A larger button was next to the lighted one. The garage door. Desperate times. It might make a lot of noise, but she needed to get the hell out of this garage.

Wah-wah-wah came like Charlie Brown's teacher.

Voices. She swore she heard voices coming from outside the building. Alex. She'd know his *wah-wah* anywhere—or maybe she was just really optimistic. But she swore he was outside.

She had to warn him. She pushed the garage door button. Nothing. Again nothing. No opening. No budging. WTF.

Her hand slapped against the button. Open. Open. Open.

She needed to warn Alex and get the hell out. She walked up to the garage door, hooked her fingers on the bottom of one of the windows and jumped. She couldn't see a damn thing.

Harper looked around the garage. She needed… something. A folded step-stool leaned against the wall. That. That was what she needed.

She dragged the step-stool over to the garage door and unfolded it. When she stepped up, the sun blinded her. She rubbed her eyes with the back of her hands.

Everything was blurry. She cupped her hand around her eyes and focused on the shapes outside. She must be in the garage for the guest house where Emma and John lived behind the club because there was DeVout in front of her. A car sat in the driveway and Alex stood out front. He was talking to someone, but she couldn't see who.

She waved her arms and screamed, "Alex! Alex!"

He looked at the garage but didn't move. Not one spark of awareness.

She tapped at the window. More screaming. He didn't move. She hopped, and only realized what a bad idea that was when the stool popped ominously and sagged to one side. There was nothing to grab, and now she was falling backward, arms flailing.

She dropped to the floor like a stone. Her head snapped, smacking the concrete. More dizzy. More blurry.

She counted the birds flying around her head as she cupped her brain. If it made it out of this intact, she'd start taking ginkgo biloba to reward it.

She rolled onto her knees, determined to give Alex a sign. Make him see her. The stool was a big nope, and she looked around for something else to stand on.

The door to the house clicked and flew open. Brody stood there. "What the hell are you doing?" He ran to the big garage door, shoving her out of the way. She might have hit her head again, but who the hell knew. All she knew was that now she needed to get Alex's attention *and* get rid of Brody.

Brody stretched up onto his toes and looked out the window. "The cops."

The windows. Harper could bust up the windows. She just needed something hard and long and preferably pointy. The flogger. Not pointy but the handle was hard.

She slunk to the SUV and slowly opened the rear passenger door.

"I am not going to jail." Brody's face was attached to the glass.

She leaned inside the car, stretching until she could reach the tassels and drag the flogger out of the bag.

"This is so not good." Brody's voice made Harper jump, but a quick look over her shoulder said he was still at the window, like a poodle who needed to be let out.

Faster. She needed to move faster.

Arms circled her body like a vise, pinning her arms in place.

"What do you think you're doing?" Brody's voice was at her temple. His breath hot and smelly.

She dropped the flogger as she squirmed. His grip tightened. Her breath stuttered. This was not how she was going to go. She was not going to be smushed by a druggie with bad breath. She sputtered and gulped as thoughts raced from her mind.

THE VISE around Harper loosened and she could breathe again. She heard Alex. He was still looking around outside, and she was still missing. Probably not a coincidence. How was she going to get out of this? No weapon. She had to think. Use her…

Harper slammed her head back, and heard a crunch. Maybe a nose. Hopefully a nose. Heh. Use her head.

She couldn't catch her breath. But she had to if she was going to get the hell out of here. She picked up the flogger and staggered a step back.

Brody was holding his nose as blood dripped down his arm and smeared his shirt. "What did you do that for?"

"You." *Gasp.* "Were." *Gasp.* "Hurting." *Gasp.* "Me." She held the flogger out like a sword, and if she chose her target just right, it would hurt. But it had to be just right.

"Jeez." Brody's eyes were filled with tears.

She sucked in a breath of air. "Are you going to let me go?"

"No." He wiped his nose with the sleeve of his shirt and held up his fists. "You're not going anywhere."

"Fine." She gripped the silver handle of the flogger and let her arm fall to her side. Limp. Like she was giving up.

Not. Using every bit of strength she could find, she snapped the flogger up and hit him square in the balls. Yep, it was a cheap shot. But so was trying to drug her and run her over.

Brody hunched nearly in half and groaned. Perfect. Harper reversed the flogger and brought the silver handle down on his temple. Once. Twice.

Brody's eyes rolled to the back of his head as he dropped to the floor. His body didn't move. At all. But Harper didn't have time to check on him.

She had to get Alex's attention. Stumbling over to the door, she slammed the metal handle into the closest window. Once. Crack. Twice. Glass exploded and dripped out the door.

"Alex!" she yelled and smashed another window. "I'm in here."

"What the hell?" Alex's voice—and it said words. No more Snoopy-cartoon teacher's random sounds. "Open that garage."

Harper tried, but she couldn't see out the windows. "Alex. They won't let me out."

Emma said, "I don't..."

Alex pulled his gun and pointed it at Emma. "Open it now."

Emma lifted her arms over her head and ran to the garage.

Alex's gun didn't follow her. He kept his gun aimed at someone else. "Move. Follow your wife."

John walked around the front of the club with his hands over his head. He truly looked confused.

Harper could relate.

The garage door slid open. The metal on the door started sliding up, her hand losing purchase. Harper stepped down the stairs before she fell. Again.

Alex barked orders. "On the ground, both of you."

As soon as the door hit half mast, she ducked underneath and ran to Alex, avoiding the gun in his hand. Alex lifted his left hand and pushed her behind him. He pulled out his phone and handed it to her. "Call the first number in contacts and give me the phone."

"What is going on?" John asked. His body lay prone on the ground.

Harper didn't have time to answer. It was a long story. So she dialed the number and placed the phone in Alex's empty hand. She stepped away to give him space, but he reached back and laid his hand on her hip. "Don't go. Please." He didn't look back, his eyes and the gun were focused on John and Emma, but the intensity of the words —the pleading told her those words were coming from his soul. He moved the hand from her hip and lifted the phone to his ear.

"Badge 2771, Detective Cabrero. I have a 418A..." Alex rattled off numbers and words to the person on the other end of the line. Sirens blared before he even had the phone slid back into his pocket.

He dropped his left hand behind him and his hand

rested on her hip. He pulled her close, her front to his back. "Stay here," he said before stepping away.

He moved closer to John, who didn't seem to know what the hell was going on. It was going to be a rude awakening when he found out his wife was pure evil.

Alex stood over John, holstering his gun. He pulled out his cuffs. She wanted to scream out that he wasn't the bad guy, but her attention moved to the garage, where the evil one should be on the ground.

Maybe Harper would accidentally give her a bit of a kick for the whole "gonna kill her" thing. And she definitely wanted to kick her for Brad and Madeline. But Emma wasn't there.

"Where's Emma?" Harper swiveled back and forth until she saw dark brown hair bobbing around the club.

Hell no. Harper ran toward the house—which was more a jog, since she didn't normally run. But desperate times. And there was no way Harper was letting Emma get away.

Her legs pumped. She dug deep. Took one for the team. She called on all the clichés she could think of to just keep going.

Emma stood over John's car and fumbled with the keys. They jingled as they hit the ground. "Dammit."

Emma knelt down and looked over her shoulder. Harper saw the moment Emma noticed she was about to get caught. Emma sparked to life, grabbing the keys and clicking the locks. She flung open the door.

Harper ran the twenty feet in record time and shoved her body between the car and its door.

Emma pushed at Harper's waist as she pushed the keys inside and started the engine. If she drove off, there was no way Harper could stop her. Harper grabbed onto Emma's shirt and pulled her from the front seat.

Harper fell backward, pulling Emma onto the pavement with a groan.

Emma tore at Harper's hands, but Harper just held on. "You are. Not. Going. Anywhere." Harper yanked Emma forward until she lay on the ground, Harper straddling the squiggling body.

Emma kicked and pulled. Her body flailed like a smelly fish as she tore at Harper's arm. Harper was still weakened by the drugs that had no doubt been put into her system.

Harper's grip failed and Emma's feet grappled with the ground. Before Emma could get purchase, Harper lunged for Emma's legs pulling her down. Pinning her arms, Harper straddled Emma. Emma bucked like a bronco, but Harper held firm.

"Stop moving!"

Emma's body went limp. Harper blew her hair from her eyes and turned to see Alex over them with a gun. He held up handcuffs. "Good job. Want to do the honors?"

Harper couldn't help the smile that took over her face. She leaned back and grabbed the cuffs from his hands. "Roll over." Harper helped push Emma on to her front.

Harper grabbed Emma's wrists and clicked her new accessory into place. She went to stand up.

Alex grabbed her hand. "You're pretty good at that."

"Tackling bad guys or putting on handcuffs?"

"Both."

"I might have missed my calling."

"Please no." He shook his head as he holstered his weapon. "I don't think I could handle having you missing again."

She had been in that garage awhile then. The garage. "Brody's in the garage."

"I have someone on it." Alex nodded to detective Lucas escorting John to a police cruiser.

Apparently, while she was fumbling with Emma, the sirens had arrived. Thank goodness. The adrenalin powering her body seeped to the floor as well as her body. She sat on the ground contemplating laying her head on the gravel, but instead leaned against the purring car behind her.

Alex leaned in the car and killed the engine. He watched her with concern on his face. He should be concerned. She'd somehow ended up on a real life episode of *Law and Order*.

The officer that had helped John into the back seat came over to where Emma lay on the ground.

Emma might have been crying. Harper might have felt bad, but then she remembered the woman killed her husband and bad wasn't what she felt anymore. The officer and Alex helped Emma to her feet. Alex stepped back as the other two headed for an approaching squad.

"I don't think he knew what his wife was doing." Harper would like to blame him for not knowing, but she'd been duped too. She'd thought Emma was normal— maybe a little narcissistic. She'd been wrong.

"I don't think he did either." Alex stepped up to her and ran a finger down the side of her face. His hand lingered at her temple where she was sure a bruise was forming. "I couldn't find you."

"I was in the car." She sighed. She didn't want to say the rest out loud. It made it real. But what happened had been real. "She drugged me and then she was going to have Brody run me over 'accidentally'." Harper made sure to add the air-quotes for effect.

"When you noticed I was here, why didn't you lay on the horn of the car?"

Harper mentally slapped herself in the forehead. "I didn't even think of that. I'm going to blame the drugs. It's how she did it before."

"To Madeline and Brad."

A tear poked at her eye as she tried to stand. "Madeline. She said Brad was an accident."

"But why? What was her involvement in the puff dirt cover-up?" Alex reached out and helped her to her feet. His arms slipped around her, holding her in place. Holding her to him.

She liked it. A lot.

Harper's body crumbled into Alex as she smiled. Resting her head on his chest, she felt safe for the first time today.

"Emma was the whole puff dirt thing. She hid the real report. She needed the project to come in under budget because she'd used part of the money. She was gambling again. She needed money. Madeline and Brad found out and they had to be dealt with."

Alex rested his lips on her forehead and sighed. "I'm glad you're okay."

"Me too." She pulled her head back and smiled at him. "Thanks for saving me."

His lips pressed against hers. Strong lips. Warm. Gentle. His lips curved. "I don't think I saved you." He kissed her again. "I saw the way you tackled her. I think I saved her."

"Maybe a little." Another kiss.

TWO MONTHS LATER, Harper tossed paper after paper into garbage cans strewn around the room. It was the kids' favorite day of the year, and she could admit she was pretty excited about it. Last day of school.

"Don't toss that." She grabbed a binder from the trash and held it out to one of her students. "You could use this next year."

"I'll get a new one." Bridgette flounced her bright blond curls as she turned back to her desk and just dumped everything into the garbage. Her father wrote many of the prime-time sitcoms everyone watched on television, so apparently she didn't need to worry about reusing her supplies.

Harper slid the binder into her own box. Her father didn't write sitcoms. She needed to reuse and recycle.

"Five minutes. Let's get everything into boxes before your parents get here."

The kids scrambled to empty their desks as they chatted about summer plans. Normally the kids wouldn't be allowed to talk, but it was the last day—the last day some of them would see each other until the fall.

"Okay, everyone. Grab your bags and line up for the bell."

"Hell, yeah."

"Jeremiah, language."

Her kids giggled as they grabbed backpacks filled to the zipper with folders and binders—pens and calculators. All except Bridgette anyway.

It was organized chaos.

The bell dinged and the kids ran out. She followed behind. It was the last time she'd see some of these kids for a while. Same with the parents, and if she didn't have another one of their kids in her class, she probably wouldn't talk to most of them again.

She could honestly say she'd miss some of these parents—she could also admit there were a few she could live without.

The hallway was just as much chaos. No organization. Children ran. Teachers ushered kids out the door. Parents yelled.

"Did you grab all your school supplies?"

"Where's your sister?"

"Don't make me ground you on the first day of summer, Jeremiah."

It was all coming to an end.

"Harper." John Byrne walked up to her with Henry in

tow. "Henry, did you want to see if your friend, Pete, can come over tonight?"

"Oh yeah." Henry handed his backpack to his father and ran down the hallway.

When he was out of earshot, John turned to her. Dark luggage lined his eyes. "I'm really sorry. I didn't know."

"Alex told me." She smiled to try to ease his mind. The poor guy had been through so much. "It's not your fault."

"Three people died and you could have been a fourth." He shook his head. His mouth curved down at the edges. "I'm just so sorry."

Harper wanted to tell him it was okay, but it wasn't. However, she also wasn't going to kick the poor guy while he was down. "You and Henry lost so much."

"I filed for divorce."

"I'd say I'm sorry to hear that, but I think you made the right call." Being married to a cold-blooded killer was never advisable. "Is there anything I can do?"

"No. Thank you. Henry and I just need to get back to normal."

"Speaking of, I heard you're opening the club tonight."

"Well, I won't be there. Symphony is taking over that part of my business for a while. I'm taking a sabbatical. Henry and I are going to spend some time in Georgia with my parents."

Running from bad decisions and loss. "I can understand that."

"You should stop by the club. I'm sure Symphony would love to see you at her premiere."

"Maybe I will." Harper said goodbye to John and all the parents and made her way back to her classroom. She opened her drawers and put everything into her own box. "Till next year." She wedged the box under her arm and grabbed a bag she'd filled with books.

As she lifted, an envelope dropped from the side of the bag. From Brad. The one she'd found at the club. She'd forgotten about it. Getting drugged and almost killed tended to keep your mind off the little things. Or in this case a voice from the grave.

She put the box and bag down. She stared at the envelope and lifted it to her nose. She took in a breath, hoping to smell Brad but it just smelled like paper. She rubbed the envelope along her cheek. This was in Brad's hands at some point. Although the pain of losing him was starting to ebb, she could admit she still missed talking to him. Some days were better than others.

Sliding her finger under the back flap, she pinched the card till she saw a heart covered Valentine. The inside didn't say the usual schmaltzy things. There was a hand-written note.

Nutmeg - I made some mistakes but know I have always loved you, but things between us aren't right. I need more. We need to talk about the future of our family. And we need to decide if we're in this together. We deserve to be happy.

• • •

Our family. He'd wanted that family, and she wouldn't have stood in his way. Compersion. She'd wanted him to be happy and didn't care who gave him that happiness. And deep down she knew he'd felt the same way. So, she would have let him go.

She closed the card and slid it back in the bag. She knew they were disconnected, but seeing it on paper made it real. He would have gone on to find a woman who would give him kids and she would have gone on to find her own happily ever after. They both deserved that.

"Hey." A familiar voice took her out of her stupor. The man who had been her shadow for the past few weeks. Apparently, you disappear for a couple of hours and you become a flight risk.

"Hey yourself, Detective." Harper slid the note back into the edge of the box.

Alex smiled. "Need some help?"

"Sure."

He picked up the box from the floor and they walked out the door. "We found the man Madeline was meeting in San Diego."

"The Brainiac?" Harper stopped. That must have been a tough conversation. Hey, great to find you, your girl-friend's dead.

"Yeah. He's a UCLA professor and they were in love. She was going to leave Paul and let him be with Britany."

"She knew and was okay with it?" She'd probably noticed their relationship wasn't what it once was. That was a hard lesson to learn. Harper would know.

"Yeah." Alex nodded and a smile spread across his face

as he started walking to the outer door. "Oh, and I ran into John outside."

"He's here to pick up Henry." Like all the other parents. She followed Alex through the quiet hallway. The walls were free of children's artwork. The bulletin boards empty. Very few voices were in the hall. It was a shell of itself without the kids.

"I figured as much."

"I talked to him a bit, too. He said he's going away for a while."

"Well, makes sense. He went through a lot." Alex held open the outer door to teacher parking. "He mentioned Symphony is managing DeVout."

"Yeah, that's a good choice. She'll get to make her changes." Harper laughed. "Although, I have a feeling the house will be used for a lot more porn."

"Especially Star Wars related. The Rise of Skyballer is in their future."

Symphony was going to have a field day with all that power. But she'd do all right. She was smart and knew what people liked.

"So what now?" Harper opened her trunk and placed the bag inside.

Alex slid the box in behind. "Dinner?"

"This early?"

"Well, I thought maybe we could try this new club tonight." His head dropped and Harper swore she saw red crawling up his neck. "It's not a new, new club, but it has a new manager."

DeVout. "So, what are you saying? Do you want to

watch?" Just the thought had butterflies swirling in Harper's stomach.

"I do." He leaned down and kissed her.

Time to make new memories and find her happily ever after.

EXTRAS

Thank you for supporting an independent author. It would be great if you could leave a review or a rating wherever you purchased this book, or on Goodreads.

Would you like to know when my next book is available? You can sign up for my email list at http://www.vanessamknight.com or like my Facebook page at http://facebook.com/vanessamknightauthor.

ABOUT THE AUTHOR

Vanessa M. Knight has always enjoyed writing, and once she found mystery and romance, she was addicted. She props her laptop in the suburbs of Chicago with her family and menagerie of four-pawed claw-babies (AKA cats and dogs.) That laptop has partnered-in-crime to write contemporary romances with a dash of humor and splash of snark.

When she has a few moments to spare, you can find her singing off-key (but she assures everyone it's still considered singing), reading, kickboxing, or killing a few brain cells as she stares at the many sitcoms and dramas available through the Internet and TV.

For more information on Vanessa, including her Internet haunts, contest updates, and details on her upcoming novels, please visit her website at www.vanessamknight.com.

OTHER BOOKS BY THIS AUTHOR

MYSTERY

Christmas Cookies Mysteries

Swing Into Murder

Roxy Horne Novels

Come Die with Me

ROMANTIC SUSPENSE

Chicago's Finest Series

Second Time's the Charm

Stark Raving Mad

Stealing Vegas

Final Strike

Busted Series

Busting In

Busting Out

Busting Through

CONTEMPORARY NEW ADULT

Ritter University Series

Major Renovations

What Happens in College…

Christmas Breakdown

Rushing In

Sophomore Slump

The Make-up Test